BRIAN FL\

THE CREEPING JEN

BRIAN FLYNN was born in 1885 in Leyton, Essex. He won a scholarship to the City Of London School, and from there went into the civil service. In World War I he served as Special Constable on the Home Front, also teaching "Accountancy, Languages, Maths and Elocution to men, women, boys and girls" in the evenings, and acting in his spare time.

It was a seaside family holiday that inspired Brian Flynn to turn his hand to writing in the mid-twenties. Finding most mystery novels of the time "mediocre in the extreme", he decided to compose his own. Edith, the author's wife, encouraged its completion, and after a protracted period finding a publisher, it was eventually released in 1927 by John Hamilton in the UK and Macrae Smith in the U.S. as *The Billiard-Room Mystery*.

The author died in 1958. In all, he wrote and published 57 mysteries, the vast majority featuring the super-sleuth Antony Bathurst.

BRIAN FLYNN

THE CREEPING JENNY MYSTERY

With an introduction by
Steve Barge

DEAN STREET PRESS

INTRODUCTION

"I believe that the primary function of the mystery story is to entertain; to stimulate the imagination and even, at times, to supply humour. But it pleases the connoisseur most when it presents – and reveals – genuine mystery. To reach its full height, it has to offer an intellectual problem for the reader to consider, measure and solve."

THUS WROTE Brian Flynn in the *Crime Book Magazine* in 1948, setting out his ethos on writing detective fiction. At that point in his career, Flynn had published thirty-six mystery novels, beginning with *The Billiard-Room Mystery* in 1927 – he went on, before his death in 1958, to write twenty-one more, three under the pseudonym Charles Wogan. So how is it that the general reading populace – indeed, even some of the most ardent collectors of mystery fiction – were until recently unaware of his existence? The reputation of writers such as John Rhode survived their work being out of print, so what made Flynn and his books vanish so completely?

There are many factors that could have contributed to Flynn's disappearance. For reasons unknown, he was not a member of either The Detection Club or the Crime Writers' Association, two of the best ways for a writer to network with others. As such, his work never appeared in the various collaborations that those groups published. The occasional short story in such a collection can be a way of maintaining awareness of an author's name, but it seems that Brian Flynn wrote no short stories at all, something rare amongst crime writers.

There are a few mentions of him in various studies of the genre over the years. Sutherland Scott, in *Blood in Their Ink* (1953), states that Flynn, who was still writing at the time, "has long been popular". He goes on to praise *The Mystery of the Peacock's Eye* (1928) as containing "one of the ablest pieces of misdirection one could wish to meet". Anyone reading that particular review who feels like picking up the novel – out now from Dean Street Press – should stop reading at that point, as later in the book, Scott proceeds to casually spoil the ending, although as if he assumes that everyone will have read the novel already.

It is a later review, though, that may have done much to end – temporarily, I hope – Flynn's popularity.

"Straight tripe and savorless. It is doubtful, on the evidence, if any of his others would be different."

Thus wrote Jacques Barzun and Wendell Hertig Taylor in their celebrated work, *A Catalog of Crime* (1971). The book was an ambitious attempt to collate and review every crime fiction author, past and present. They presented brief reviews of some titles, a bibliography of some authors and a short biography of others. It is by no means complete – E & M.A. Radford had written thirty-six novels at this point in time but garner no mention – but it might have helped Flynn's reputation if he too had been overlooked. Instead one of the contributors picked up *Conspiracy at Angel* (1947), the thirty-second Anthony Bathurst title. I believe that title has a number of things to enjoy about it, but as a mystery, it doesn't match the quality of the majority of Flynn's output. Dismissing a writer's entire work on the basis of a single volume is questionable, but with the amount of crime writers they were trying to catalogue, one can, just about, understand the decision. But that decision meant that they missed out on a large number of truly entertaining mysteries that fully embrace the spirit of the Golden Age of Detection, and, moreover, many readers using the book as a reference work may have missed out as well.

So who was Brian Flynn? Born in 1885 in Leyton, Essex, Flynn won a scholarship to the City Of London School, and while he went into the civil service (ranking fourth in the whole country on the entrance examination) rather than go to university, the classical education that he received there clearly stayed with him. Protracted bouts of rheumatic fever prevented him fighting in the Great War, but instead he served as a Special Constable on the Home Front – one particular job involved warning the populace about Zeppelin raids armed only with a bicycle, a whistle and a placard reading "TAKE COVER". Flynn worked for the local government while teaching "Accountancy, Languages, Maths and Elocution to men, women, boys and girls" in the evening, and acting as part of the Trevalyan Players in his spare time.

It was a seaside family holiday that inspired him to turn his hand to writing. He asked his librarian to supply him a collection of mystery novels for "deck-chair reading" only to find himself disappointed. In his own words, they were "mediocre in the extreme." There is no record of what those books were, unfortunately, but on arriving home, the following conversation, again in Brian's own words, occurred:

> "ME (unpacking the books): If I couldn't write better stuff than any of these, I'd eat my own hat.
>
> Mrs ME (after the manner of women and particularly after the manner of wives): It's a great pity you don't do a bit more and talk a bit less.
>
> The shaft struck home. I accepted the challenge, laboured like the mountain and produced *The Billiard-Room Mystery*."

"Mrs ME", or Edith as most people referred to her, deserves our gratitude. While there were some delays with that first book, including Edith finding the neglected half-finished manuscript in a drawer where it had been "resting" for six months, and a protracted period finding a publisher, it was eventually released in 1927 by John Hamilton in the UK and Macrae Smith in the U.S. According to Flynn, John Hamilton asked for five more, but in fact they only published five in total, all as part of the Sundial Mystery Library imprint. Starting with *The Five Red Fingers* (1929), Flynn was published by John Long, who would go on to publish all of his remaining novels, bar his single non-series title, *Tragedy At Trinket* (1934). About ten of his early books were reprinted in the US before the war, either by Macrae Smith, Grosset & Dunlap or Mill, and a few titles also appeared in France, Denmark, Germany and Sweden, but the majority of his output only saw print in the United Kingdom. Some titles were reprinted during his lifetime – the John Long Four-Square Thrillers paperback range featured some Flynn titles, for example – but John Long's primary focus was the library market, and some titles had relatively low print runs. Currently, the majority of Flynn's work, in particular that only published in the U.K., is extremely rare – not just expensive, but seemingly non-existent even in the second-hand book market.

In the aforementioned article, Flynn states that the tales of Sherlock Holmes were a primary inspiration for his writing, having read them at a young age. A conversation in *The Billiard-Room Mystery* hints at other influences on his writing style. A character, presumably voicing Flynn's own thoughts, states that he is a fan of "the pre-war Holmes". When pushed further, he states that:

> "Mason's M. Hanaud, Bentley's Trent, Milne's Mr Gillingham and to a lesser extent, Agatha Christie's M. Poirot are all excellent in their way, but oh! – the many dozens that aren't."

He goes on to acknowledge the strengths of Bernard Capes' "Baron" from *The Mystery of The Skeleton Key* and H.C. Bailey's Reggie Fortune, but refuses to accept Chesterton's Father Brown.

> "He's entirely too Chestertonian. He deduces that the dustman was the murderer because of the shape of the piece that had been cut from the apple-pie."

Perhaps this might be the reason that the invitation to join the Detection Club never arrived . . .

Flynn created a sleuth that shared a number of traits with Holmes, but was hardly a carbon-copy. Enter Anthony Bathurst, a polymath and gentleman sleuth, a man of contradictions whose background is never made clear to the reader. He clearly has money, as he has his own rooms in London with a pair of servants on call and went to public school (Uppingham) and university (Oxford). He is a follower of all things that fall under the banner of sport, in particular horse racing and cricket, the latter being a sport that he could, allegedly, have represented England at. He is also a bit of a show-off, littering his speech (at times) with classical quotes, the obscurer the better, provided by the copies of the *Oxford Dictionary of Quotations* and *Brewer's Dictionary of Phrase & Fable* that Flynn kept by his writing desk, although Bathurst generally restrains himself to only doing this with people who would appreciate it or to annoy the local constabulary. He is fond of amateur dramatics (as was Flynn, a well-regarded amateur thespian who appeared in at least one self-penned play, *Blue Murder*), having been a member of OUDS, the Oxford University Dramatic Society. Like Holmes, Bathurst isn't averse to the occasional disguise, and as with Watson and Holmes, sometimes even his close allies don't recognise him. General information about his background is light on the ground. His parents were Irish, but he doesn't have an accent – see *The Spiked Lion* (1933) – and his eyes are grey. We learn in *The Orange Axe* that he doesn't pursue romantic relationships due to a bad experience in his first romance. That doesn't remain the case throughout the series – he falls head over heels in love in *Fear and Trembling*, for example – but in this opening tranche of titles, we don't see Anthony distracted by the fairer sex, not even one who will only entertain gentlemen who can beat her at golf!

Unlike a number of the Holmes' stories, Flynn's Bathurst tales are all fairly clued mysteries, perhaps a nod to his admiration of Christie, but first and foremost, Flynn was out to entertain the reader. The problems posed to Bathurst have a flair about them – the simultaneous murders, miles apart, in *The Case of the Black Twenty-Two* (1928) for example, or the scheme to draw lots to commit masked murder in *The Orange Axe* – and there is a momentum to the narrative. Some mystery writers have trouble with the pace slowing between the reveal of the problem and the reveal of the murderer, but Flynn's books sidestep that, with Bathurst's investigations never seeming to sag. He writes with a wit and intellect that can make even the most prosaic of interviews with suspects enjoyable to read about, and usually provides an action-packed finale before the murderer is finally revealed. Some of those revelations, I think it is fair to say, are surprises that can rank with some of the best in crime fiction.

We are fortunate that we can finally reintroduce Brian Flynn and Anthony Lotherington Bathurst to the many fans of classic crime fiction out there.

The Creeping Jenny Mystery (1930)

"With Creeping Jenny's compliments. She takes but one."

THE IDEA of a gentleman (or gentlewoman) cat burglar is often associated with the Golden Age of crime fiction. Raffles, created by E.W. Hornung, Sir Arthur Conan Doyle's brother-in-law, was probably the most famous, although those tales, from 1898 to 1909, technically predate the Golden Age. In fact, such a character was quite rare, despite such a character appearing in "The Unicorn and The Wasp", the *Doctor Who* episode that featured and paid tribute to Agatha Christie and her work.

One such character, the mysterious Creeping Jenny, takes centre stage in this book, however. The stately homes of England are under threat from the untouchable thief, someone who breaks into the most secure areas and steals a single item, an item that is not necessarily the most valuable item, leaving a vaguely apologetic note.

After a burglary at Cranwick Towers, Inspector Baddeley (from *The Billiard-Room Mystery*) is on the case and his attention falls on "The Crossways", the home of Henry Mordaunt K.C. and his family, as the place where he believes Jenny will strike next. Mordaunt is hosting a party to celebrate the engagement of his youngest daughter, Margaret to one Captain Lorrimer, who intends to hand over the priceless "Lorrimer Sapphire" as an engagement gift. You can see why Baddeley would be concerned, but when murder unexpectedly strikes – and the sapphire is indeed stolen – Peter Daventry (*The Case Of The Black Twenty-Two, Invisible Death*) suggests that Anthony Bathurst might be able to help. But Mordaunt is convinced that Baddeley will be more than enough of a sleuth to get to the bottom of things . . .

Despite returning to the "Country House Party" setting, Flynn seems here to be determined to try something different by keeping Bathurst at arms-length for the majority of the tale, with only the occasional letter from Daventry keeping him informed. Instead we are treated to Daventry stumbling his way through the mystery. Daventry seems to have calmed down a bit since *Invisible Death*, where he was diving through windows and shooting weapons out of villains' hands, but some rationale for this change is shown, as it would seem Bathurst brings out the worst in him. His first letter to Bathurst gives us Flynn's version of how two public schoolboys communicate with each other. While some of it clearly has come from the depths of his imagination, I presume he must have had some experience of such individuals – I cannot believe that the final salutation, "Chin Chin and likewise Tinketty-Tonk", came entirely from the writer's imagination. This does resemble how Daventry behaves in *Invisible Death*, a book where he is almost exclusively with Bathurst, whereas when he's not around, Daventry behaves like a normal human being.

The modern reader needs to set aside one particular episode of sexual politics, concerning how a husband deals with a wife with ideas of independence, which it would take a brave writer to include in modern times, but it's not particularly out of place in a many a book from the Golden Age. *Creeping Jenny* is a hugely enjoyable classic mystery that embraces the country house cliché and presents an entertaining mystery that I'm sure will have most readers looking the wrong way.

The book was reprinted in the US – indeed, the US version is slightly easier to find for the ardent collector – as *The Crime At The Crossways*. It's likely that the cover artist did not actually read the book, as it features a villainous individual clutching a dagger underneath an old crossroads road sign – someone could have told the illustrator that "Crossways" was the name of the house. That was in 1930, nearly ninety years ago. Finally this book is available again to entertain the reader.

Steve Barge

CHAPTER I

IN THE SPACE of six weeks the name of "Creeping Jenny" had become notorious in the southern counties of England and her capabilities immensely respected. A series of daring robberies had taken place from country houses and in each case where the robbery had occurred a card—in shape and size like a visiting-card—had been left behind in the bedroom where the actual theft had been perpetrated bearing the superscription in typewritten characters, "With Creeping Jenny's compliments. She takes but one." In two instances—those of Sir Graeme Grantham's diamond tie-pin and Mrs. Stanley Medlicott's pearl necklace with pendant and tassel of pearls—a ladder had evidently been employed at the front of the house while the company were seated at dinner, and also in each of these affairs very much more valuable articles had been left behind—untouched, quite in accordance as it were with the terms of the visiting-card. Mrs. Medlicott's necklace, for example, which was stolen two nights after Sir Graeme's pin, was worth perhaps a mere matter of one hundred and fifty pounds, while her famous emeralds had been almost at the thief's mercy had a little more care been taken. The view taken by the Superintendent of Police who investigated the affair of the Medlicott robbery was that the marauder had been disturbed and also that the fantastic sobriquet that had been assumed, and the somewhat vainglorious declaration of policy, were entirely misleading, and intended to deceive. The Superintendent, who was looked upon with justification as one of the ablest men in the service, formed the opinion that he was dealing with a man "cat-burglar" of the most advanced and cleverest type who was throwing dust in the eyes of the police and preparing for much bigger "coups." When Sir Graeme Grantham's tie-pin had been stolen, a magnificent pair of amethyst cufflinks had been possibly overlooked and in the Medlicott case it was definitely proved, when the evidence of the various witnesses intimate with the affair came to be examined and sifted, that the thief must have been hiding in the bedroom while Mrs. Medlicott had actually been in there, for it was established beyond doubt that the ladder that had been used in connection with the theft must have been moved from its usual shelter and replaced within a period of no more than nine or ten minutes.

Following upon the two robberies that have been described, very similar occurrences took place in somewhat alarming succession at Mrs. Arthur Midwinter's near Crawley, Mrs. Topham-Garnett's on the outskirts of Rustington and then at the residence of Sir Gilbert and Lady Craddock at Cranwick in Sussex. Mrs. Arthur Midwinter lost a diamond chain with pendant of aquamarine, crystal and diamonds, a guest of Mrs. Topham-Garnett's was relieved of a pair of long drop turquoise earrings and at Cranwick Towers, Lady Craddock herself suffered a loss that caused her a great deal of annoyance. A very valuable opal ring was stolen from her bedroom—a ring for which she held a very strong sentimental regard—entirely apart from its intrinsic value. In this last affair the stains of mud upon a rug in the room, coupled with a broken pane of glass seemed to prove conclusively to the Police-Inspector who was called in by Sir Gilbert Craddock that yet another successful climbing feat had been executed by "Creeping Jenny" before the usual card had been deposited upon Lady Craddock's dressing-table. As a result of his operations several of the better known thieves of this particular type were combed out by the police from the unsavoury seclusion of their respective haunts and their movements, comings and goings, most strictly investigated. But all to no purpose. The inquiry yielded no discovery of any importance and at last it became evident to Scotland Yard that a new star had arisen whose methods displayed a daring ingenuity and audacious originality worthy of a much better cause. For "Creeping Jenny's" unselfishness and altruistic principles still persisted and these traits, more than the qualities previously mentioned, captured the imagination of the public. "She"—if it were truly "she"—still and always "took but one," for Mrs. Arthur Midwinter, Mrs. Topham-Garnett, Mrs. Topham-Garnett's guest and Lady Craddock herself, were enabled out of her Robin Hood-like magnanimity to retain more valuable possessions that might very easily have found their way into this daring robber's pocket. An attempt made by the more sensational and less reliable press to call the thief "La Voleuse" met with immediate failure—"she" had christened herself "Creeping Jenny" and "Creeping Jenny" she remained.

On the morning that the theft of Lady Craddock's opal ring was announced in the newspapers Henry Mordaunt K.C. of "The Crossways" near Cranwick, Sussex, read the account of the affair with somewhat mixed feelings.

"Very good, Mitchell," he exclaimed to his butler who had upon instructions brought him the *Morning Message*, "many thanks. That will do for the present."

Very shortly after the withdrawal of the butler, the famous King's Counsel having exhausted the paragraph in question pressed the bell again.

"I'm sorry, Mitchell," he declared upon the butler's reappearance, "but I shall have to trouble you *again*. Tell Mrs. Mordaunt I want to see her at once—will you?"

Mitchell bowed. "Very good, sir. I will tell Mrs. Mordaunt immediately, sir."

Mordaunt awaited his wife's arrival very patiently, although patience was not his strongest suit. When she entered he greeted her with his customary courtesy.

"Good morning, Olive. I hope I'm not worrying you. But I wanted to show you this. It's er—extremely interesting. You remember what we were talking about last week? Well—have a look here."

He pointed to the column in the paper that described "Creeping Jenny's" latest exploit at the Craddocks'.

Olive Mordaunt took the paper wonderingly. She was her husband's second wife and, of course, considerably his junior. Mordaunt's intimate circle had been extremely surprised at the marriage, for it was openly hinted that the lady chosen for the second union did not quite fill the bill as would have been generally expected. Physically she was decidedly attractive—her dark, somewhat meretricious beauty pleasing most men with whom she came into contact. She read the account that her husband had pointed out to her with an uplifting of the eyebrows. Then the suggestion of a smile played round her lips.

"Getting nearer and nearer," she said. "Is that what you mean, Henry?"

"It is," he replied, "and I am speaking, of course, with direct reference to next week. I wouldn't like anything to go wrong here next week—for Lorrimer's sake. His family I know has always placed a tremendous value on the Lorrimer sapphire as is only natural." He smiled across at his wife. "You will remember, my dear, that I have an excellent reason for saying that. In fact only two other people could have as good a one."

Olive Mordaunt returned her husband's smile and nodded brightly. "I know that, Henry. I remember you telling me when you wrote to me at Cannes, informing me of Margaret's intended engagement. I look forward to meeting Captain Lorrimer." She paused but proceeded almost immediately. "Rather a coincidence—don't you think—that Margaret and he, with Jane and Francis should be at Cranwick Towers at the moment? We shall at any rate get a first-hand account of this last 'Creeping Jenny' affair when they return here. It's an ill-wind, Henry—"

He stroked his firm, clean-shaven mouth. "Yes, I suppose we shall! All the same—I don't like it. I seem to be suffering this morning from a presentiment. I think that's the best word to use to describe how I feel. Our house party and the reason behind it—Margaret's twenty-first birthday and the announcement of her engagement to Lorrimer—have been pretty extensively published—you know—in most circles. The *Morning Message* gave it three paragraphs, Olive, as recently as last Tuesday—very properly so, too. It stated, quite openly, that 'Margaret Mordaunt, third child and younger daughter of Henry Mordaunt, K.C. etc., etc., was to receive from her fiancé—Capt. Cyril Lorrimer, M.P. for the Froam division of Seabourne—the famous "Lorrimer Sapphire" for her engagement ring.' There followed some details—mainly incorrect—concerned with the ring's history." He stopped and pursed his lips in the manner that juries knew so well. "Seems to me, Olive, that that would be just the type of ring—jewel—whatever you choose to call it—to attract this 'Creeping Jenny' person as an incentive. I've got a 'hunch' as our cousins across the Atlantic say—especially as her latest operations were at the 'Towers'—no more than a couple of miles away from us."

"Rubbish, Henry. Now what has that to do with it really? That's only a coincidence—they do happen sometimes. Besides we'll have people staying here that we can form into a Committee of Defence—a Committee of Public Safety we'll call it." She laughed and clapped her hands gaily. "That would be rather fun, wouldn't it?" she cried, supplementing her previous remark.

"How many shall we have?" asked Mordaunt seriously.

"Our own three, back from the scene of the crime, as you might say, Captain Lorrimer and his mother, Adrian Challoner, John Raikes with Mr. and Mrs. Raikes, Mary Considine, Anne Ebbisham, Christine Massingham, Peter Daventry and Russell Streatfeild. You insisted on him—if you remember—although I don't know why—as well as your other old friend Adrian Challoner—another gentleman I am yet to have the pleasure of meeting. One or two of them have kept away a long time since you upset them all by marrying me, Henry." She added the last sentence mischievously, but Mordaunt made no sign that he appreciated its inner meaning. For there was bitterness allied with the mischief and he detected it.

"When are the girls and Francis expected back?" he inquired.

"To-morrow," she answered. "But Captain Lorrimer won't be coming over with them. So Margaret has told me,—at least. She 'phoned yesterday afternoon. He has an appointment in town, I believe—business she says, that in all probability will take him a day or two so that we shan't see him at 'The Crossways' until Monday afternoon some time—the day before the great day."

"H'm," he remarked, as though pondering over some aspect of the matter that had not previously occurred to him, "do any of the others come before Monday?"

"You know there are some coming, Henry, as well as I do. Didn't I tell you so last week? Anne Ebbisham and Christine Massingham are coming over with Francis and the girls from the

Craddocks' place and Peter Daventry will be coming down here for the week-end. Is there anything else that you want to know or have you remembered some of the things I have told you?"

"No—I'm satisfied now, Olive. All the same—I've still that feeling of insecurity. In fact, I've had it for some time. I can't explain it as I told you just now. I've just got it and that is all I can say about it. It is one of those curious, unreasoned anxieties."

No sooner had the words left his mouth than a light knock sounded on the door. Mitchell entered noiselessly at his master's invitation.

"I beg your pardon, sir, but if it is convenient to you Inspector Baddeley would like to speak to you. He says it is very important, sir. What shall I tell him, sir?"

Mordaunt's brow furrowed with annoyance as he considered the butler's statement.

"Inspector Baddeley?" he queried. "What on earth does Inspector Baddeley want with me? Any idea, Mitchell? Did he say?"

Mitchell shook his head gravely. "No, sir—he did not! And I did not inquire. If I had inquired I doubt very much whether the Inspector would have told me. I have noticed things like that before, sir."

Mordaunt looked across at his wife. "Better see him I suppose, Olive—though I can't imagine for a moment what he can want with me." He nodded with decision towards Mitchell, "All right, Mitchell! Tell the Inspector I'll see him at once. Leave him to me, Olive—you clear out—I don't suppose it's anything to cause either of us sleepless nights."

Mrs. Mordaunt acquiesced with unusual readiness for her, and slipped out of the room.

Inspector Baddeley of the Sussex Constabulary looked little changed since his investigation of the "Billiard Room Mystery" at Considine Manor some years previously. His closely cut dark hair still retained its colour, his moustache was as trim as ever and his steady blue eyes had lost none of their brightness. When he spoke it was with the old snap and eminently business-like rapidity.

"Mr. Mordaunt," he opened immediately, "I'm Inspector Baddeley, just put in charge of the Cranwick Towers case. May I claim a few moments of your valuable time?"

The man he addressed looked puzzled but was quick to give his assent. "With pleasure, Inspector. Though I admit I'm completely at a loss to understand why you want me."

Baddeley smiled his quick and pleasant smile. "You don't surprise me when you say that, Mr. Mordaunt. But it's not my way to waste time—anybody's—my own included—and I never beat about the bush. I was called in at the special request of Sir Gilbert Craddock to investigate the latest of these 'Creeping Jenny' escapades. To tell the truth I was rather pleased—you can say if you like that I jumped at the chance." He rubbed his hands to show the extent of the pleasure that the affair had evidently given to him. "I hope, Mr. Mordaunt," he continued, "that by the time I've done with her, 'poor Jenny will be a-weeping'." He smiled to accentuate his sally. "Well, to get along with it—I've made a discovery that I find extremely interesting—but at the same time—shall we say a trifle disconcerting?" He paused to see the effect that his words had had upon Henry Mordaunt.

"Go on, Inspector," said the latter coolly. "I'm listening. I've no doubt I'm going to hear something of interest. Though I don't know what."

"You are that, sir, I can promise you! The point is this. I'm pretty certain and so are the men that have worked on the case with me—including Inspector Bell, who was on it at the first— that the thief who cleared Lady Craddock's opal ring used a motor car. I will qualify that statement by saying either the thief or an accomplice. There were distinct tracks of a car leading from the 'Towers' down a lane very rarely used by motorists in the ordinary way and two villagers who have come forward and given us information state very definitely that a car passed them in this very lane on the night of the burglary just about the time to fit in with this theory of mine regarding the affair."

Mordaunt nodded. "Quite a reasonable theory, too, I should say, Inspector! Motor cars seem inseparable from crime these days. Certainly I can see nothing in your idea that would cause me to—"

Baddeley raised his hand in his eagerness. "Quite so, sir. But that isn't all. That doesn't explain why I'm here to see you. I haven't finished yet—by a long way. The lane to which I refer, Mr. Mordaunt, is that known locally as 'Hangman's Hollow'—the very lane that comes out almost exactly opposite your house here—'The Crossways.' In fact it might be said to be in a direct line of communication between 'The Crossways' and 'Cranwick Towers'." He caressed his neat little moustache with an air of extreme satisfaction and watched carefully the expression on the K.C.'s face.

"Well, Inspector?" said Mordaunt at length, with a certain amount of unconcealed amusement. "I don't deny that what you say is true—but still I find myself—"

Baddeley changed his tone. "Your two daughters and son, Mr. Mordaunt, are I believe guests for the time being of Sir Gilbert Craddock at Cranwick Towers. That is so, isn't it? I am indebted to Lady Craddock herself for the knowledge and—I understand that—"

"That's quite true, Inspector. But what's the point?"

Baddeley was some little time before he answered Mordaunt's last question and when he actually did so, his reply was not entirely direct.

"We have been unable so far, Mir. Mordaunt, to trace the tracks of the car beyond your house. Its tracks as a matter of fact seem to disappear completely as soon as 'The Crossways' is reached. There were the impressions in the lane—plain enough for anybody to see who has the eyes to read and understand such things—but at the end of this lane—'Hangman's Hollow'—they stop quite suddenly. You can't help me, I suppose, Mr. Mordaunt?"

Mordaunt's answer to this bore a tinge of annoyance.

"How do you mean, Inspector? How is it possible for me to help you? In fact I don't follow you at all."

But Baddeley, although he realized the note of asperity, was quite unperturbed. "You can't make any suggestion, Mr. Mordaunt, that would assist me towards an explanation?"

"None whatever, Inspector."

"Then tell me this, sir. Am I right in stating that one of your cars is over in the Cranwick Towers' garage and has been there all the time your people have been staying there?"

Mordaunt looked at him—the surprise on his face unmistakable. "You are, Inspector. But I'm hanged if I know at what you're getting. If you must know, my son drove his sisters over to Sir Gilbert Craddock's ten days or so ago. He's got my six-cylinder Sunbeam over there. But there's nothing unusual in that surely."

Baddeley turned his hat in his hands. "No," he ventured at length, "perhaps not. Perhaps I'm weaving a too fantastic theory about this 'Creeping Jenny' person. Still—" He rose sharply from his chair and prepared to make his exit. "It's my way, you see, sir! I was always one to consider everything, no matter how improbable some of the things may be at first blush. Or seem to be would be a better way of putting it perhaps. However, in this case—I may have strayed a little too far. If I have I'll get back to the main path, never fear. But you never know. A 'Sunbeam' I think you said? Good-day, Mr. Mordaunt, and thank you."

"Good-day, Inspector. Sorry you've had your journey for nothing."

The eyes of the two men met and held each other across the room. Then the door closed behind Inspector Baddeley. Mordaunt took a cigar and lit it, and the hand that held the match was as steady as a rock.

CHAPTER II

"CHRISTINE, my Child," said Anne Ebbisham, as she dexterously swung the car round a sharp curve of the road, "I'm not sorry to be leaving Cranwick Towers. It hasn't exactly been a home of rest these last few days. Take it from my own sweet self, that Inspector gentleman that was so inquisitive about Francis' car and how far 'The Crossways' was away and how long it would take to get there (a) in September travelling light and (b) at Christmas—carol-singing as you went—is no 'bimbo' as they'd say on the 'talkies'. Look out, I'm going to tread on the 'juice' for a bit. The road's as clear as a City church."

As the car gathered speed, Christine Massingham, her companion, looked at her curiously.

"What do you mean, Anne—exactly?" she asked after a moment's hesitation, "about the Inspector?"

"What do I mean?" Anne repeated the question after her very deliberately. "I mean this, my temporarily unintelligent precious. The jovial Baddeley won't have the wool pulled over his eyes quite as easily as some of his predecessors did. If you ask little Annie—and believe me, oh my Christine, you could do a lot worse than that—the sprightly Baddeley has come to the conclusion that the 'Creeping Jenny' affairs have been worked 'on the inside.' I believe that is the correct expression to use in cases of this kind. I invariably buy the midday Wallace. Anyhow, I'll bet a pony to a peanut that he's properly poked the breeze up Papa Mordaunt; do him good too." She jerked her head at Christine. "What was that jolt, dreamy-eyes? Did you notice anything?"

"A hen, dear. Let's hope it was too old for laying."

Anne gurgled delightfully. "You'll be the death of me, Christine."

"If I am, Anne, I shall probably be merely getting my own back. I am noted for my powers of retaliation."

Miss Ebbisham repeated the gurgle. "'With your permission I'm going to stop here for a moment, Cherub. We're quite near 'The Crossways,' another five minutes'll do it. I am going, Miss Massingham, to powder what Francis Mordaunt always describes as my singularly attractive nose." The young lady immediately suited the action to the words. "He is not, I may add, alone in that respect. I always tell him he has catholic tastes. I know no surer way of getting him into a 'snork' than by saying that." She gave her deliciously tip-tilted nose another dab. "All the same, Christine, I was deadly serious just now in what I said and lingering here won't purchase new apparel for the necessitous infant. Inspector Baddeley *suspects some-body*! Somebody *definite*, I mean. That's Anne Ebbisham's one-horse snip. Send five pounds for my unbeatable certainty that's running on Saturday next at Sandown Park—a veritable 'rod in pickle'—and turn the bookmaker's complexion from pale yellow to a deeper saffron. What did I give you for the Lincoln in 1928—when every other sporting—" Anne spoke with the utmost nonchalance, but again Christine threw her a glance of strong curiosity as she interrupted her.

"Suspects somebody! What do you mean, Anne? I believe you know something. Do you mean somebody that you and I know or are you just—"

Miss Ebbisham pushed the self-starter. "I'm not saying any more, Cherry Blossom—my lips are sealed—but keep your ears and saucy eyes open. Old Baddeley looked at Francis as though he were hungry and had been invited to a good meal and when she saw it—as I'm cast iron sure she did—Jane Mordaunt, who had been hanging round, looked about as happy as a canary rubbing beaks with a chinchilla. And she's quite a resolute little person usually. Serve old Lady Craddock right," she added, "shouldn't leave her 'pretties' lying about with 'Creeping Jenny' knocking round. Some people oughtn't to possess anything more valuable than 'bus tickets and tiddley-winks counters, and then somebody should hold their little hands for them when they cross the road." Anne slowed the car down. "There's 'The Crossways,' Christilinda, just ahead of us. That noble pile. So look your dainty best and don't appear too enviously green when Molly Mordaunt first shows you the Lorrimer Sapphire.' In case your virgin verdure should be hopelessly misunderstood and the wrong construction placed upon it. By the way—I've been going to ask you several times—how do you like my godfather—Adrian Challoner?"

Christine smiled at the question and if possible her determined little face grew in attractiveness.

"Very much, Anne. It takes one a little time perhaps to know him thoroughly and to understand him properly—but when you do, I think he's very charming. He's giving me quite a good chance in the new play. You agree with me, I know."

"Oh, yes, Christine. I think he's as white as they make them, but it's a bit different for me to think so, isn't it? I've known him so long, you see. Of course he likes himself a lot but one gets used to that and perhaps in the end it makes him even more attractive."

Christine nodded. "He's terribly fond of the Mordaunt girls, isn't he?"

Anne Ebbisham showed unmistakable agreement. "Too true. Particularly Jane, She told me once when I suppose she felt very confidential that he'd do anything for her. You see he's Henry Mordaunt's closest and oldest friend. Supposed to have been dippy over the first Mrs. M. You know the old stunt, Christine, 'how happy could she have been with either, etc.'— she married the barrister but the actor loved her still—and after her—her children. Since then he's been the stern, silent figure in the background who loved but once and who ever since has been wedded to the what might have been. Dear, dear, very distressing, my precious, very distressing, but it has added to his attraction for the 'first-nighters' and at the same time he's had the exquisite felicity and supreme compensation of being godfather to yours truly. After all, the man can't have every-thing." She laughed and the mischief danced in her blue eyes. "He's a good sort, though, my angel—coming back to serious things again—and nobody could have been kinder to my brother and me than he has—and you'll find he'll help you no end at your job. If you've really got the talent, Christy Minstrel—be perfectly assured that Adrian Challoner will develop it. There's not a man on the London boards to touch him as far as that's concerned. But here we are. Hop out, my chicken. Francis and the girls will be wondering where the dickens we've got to, and we owe it to them to beautify the place as much as possible."

As she spoke her eyes narrowed perceptibly, a fact that her companion noticed immediately.

"What's the matter, Anne?" she asked.

Miss Ebbisham's mouth set in the serious lines of determination. "Look, my angel," she returned. "Gaze lingeringly long upon the gentleman who has just finished his morning call at 'The Crossways' and then give me a reverential pat. Extend to me a gesture of congratulation."

Christine Massingham followed the direction of Miss Ebbisham's eyes with her own, and she saw without difficulty the man whom Anne had indicated. It was Inspector Baddeley. She turned again to Anne and marvelled at the glitter in her eyes. But whether it was of doubt, daring or defiance, she found it impossible to decide. Wherein she was not alone, for others had endeavoured to read Miss Ebbisham and signally failed.

"Wouldn't it be a 'spree,'" murmured that lady, "if 'Creeping Jenny' did a job of gate-crashing at 'The Crossways' and lifted the famous Lorrimer sapphire?"

CHAPTER III

PETER DAVENTRY has been heard to remark many times since, that Molly Mordaunt's "twenty-first and betrothal" dinner was the cause of giving to him the most curious little thrill of his life. He had worked with Anthony Lotherington Bathurst upon one of the latter's strangest investigations, namely "The Black Twenty-two," but the adventure and excitement that had been produced by that case was different from what he was destined to feel ultimately at "The Crossways." Dinner itself had been entirely delightful. Well cooked, well served and garnished by a company of manifold charm. For there were no very obvious passengers in the social boat that put out that evening under the command of Henry Mordaunt K.C. On the left of the host sat Jane his elder daughter, Molly, the "principal" of the evening, flanking him on his right. Next to Jane Mordaunt and in order, came John Raikes, who had been at a preparatory school and afterwards at Winchester with Francis Mordaunt, Christine Massingham, Russell Streatfeild, solicitor of Hyde, Streatfeild and Digby, Anne Ebbisham, Francis Mordaunt, Olive

Mordaunt, Adrian Challoner, the famous actor-manager, Mary Considine, Peter Daventry, Mrs. and Mr. Raikes, parents of the John Raikes previously mentioned, Mrs. Lorrimer, (Captain Lorrimer's mother) and Captain Cyril Lorrimer, M.P., next, of course, to Molly herself. It said something for Adrian Challoner's quality of distinction and power of personal magnetism that they should show so unmistakably in a gathering of this kind. Anne had hoped secretly to have been seated next to her godfather for she found him invariably an intellectual stimulus, but in spite of her disappointment she found Russell Streatfeild, her right-hand neighbour, extremely entertaining.

"You know, Miss Ebbisham," he said, with a twinkling grey eye and in his rather curiously high-pitched voice, "one should never let a host feel that one's first duty is to the cook. The ideal conversationalist should be conscious of three duties—the first to his immediate neighbours—in my own case this evening that particular duty has become a most pleasing one"—he bowed gallantly to Anne and Christine—"the second to his host and hostess—"the third to the company in general."

Anne laughed delightfully. "I believe I'm going to like you, Mr. Streatfeild, and at first I was afraid that I shouldn't. I thought you looked a bit—"

She paused and screwed her nose up as though in doubt of her selection of the word.

Streatfeild smiled. "A bit what? Don't spare me, Miss Ebbisham, if the adjective in question makes a strong appeal to you. I assure you that I of all people—"

"A bit 'legal,'" decided Anne triumphantly.

"Would you have preferred me then to have conveyed the impression of being—'illegal'?" The lines of his mouth rippled humorously.

Before Anne could reply Adrian Challoner's voice came across the table to them. "Don't believe a tenth of what she says to you, Streatfeild. Let me tell you that I never do. I daren't! She's very nearly my worst production. Only my most meticulous care and painstaking assiduity in what I promised for her at her baptism have saved her from being—" He shrugged his shoulders in effective completion of the sentence but there was a smile on his face and laughter in his words.

Anne grinned at Challoner's remark, the imp as usual on duty in her eyes.

Christine answered for Streatfeild who had turned laughingly to Miss Ebbisham herself.

"If Anne's 'very nearly' your worst production, Mr. Challoner, what's your really worst? I'm intrigued."

"Himself," snapped Anne, turning the tables with ready retaliation; "don't ask questions that are so obvious, Christine. That was apparent from the first."

Challoner joined heartily in the general laugh at his expense.

"How's the new show going?" questioned Streatfeild.

"Which one—'Broken Threads'—or the one in rehearsal?"

"The new one—the one that follows 'Broken Threads.'"

"Not too badly—ask Mrs. Massingham. She should be as good a judge as anybody."

"Very well!" said Christine. "Everybody seems quite pleased with it."

"There's only one thing, Streatfeild," put in the actor-manager, "it's a strong play; the big scene in the second act when I'm assassinated is immensely powerful, but, all the same, I'm thinking seriously of altering its title."

"Why? What's it called? I can't remember for the moment."

"'Sin and a Woman.'"

Russell Streatfeild pursed his lips in the consideration of appraisement. "I don't know," he said eventually, "not a bad title as titles go. Why alter it? What's the alternative if you do?"

"*Two* women, surely?" Challoner smiled. Anne's spontaneous explosion was accompanied by the more decorous laughter of the others. Mrs. Raikes laid her hand on her husband's arm with her usual gesture of proprietorship.

"Defend my sex for me, George, against Mr. Challoner's most unjustifiable attack. The next time I sit in the stalls I shall remember it throughout the whole of the performance. It will probably spoil the entire evening for me."

"Do you find us so alluring then, Mr. Challoner?" The question came from Mary Considine and as she spoke Peter thought that the answer would have come very easily if it had been demanded from him. He found himself wishing fervently that it had been.

"Not I only, Miss Considine, I am but one of a battalion," replied Challoner, "and as a champion of your own sex you yourself are irresistible. Besides, look round the table! What do you see? Each one of us is enslaved to one of you, at least. Who would have it otherwise?" He smiled and proceeded to amplify his statement. "Consider my proofs. Lorrimer is hopelessly in love with Molly. You've only got to glance at him to see that. Jane, my own little Jane whom I have ardently and openly worshipped from her cot upwards, has flagrantly entrapped Jack Raikes. Henceforward I walk in the shadows."

"Go on," said Mary, "I find this distinctly daring and decidedly interesting. I had no idea you would be so personal."

"I knew that you would at once be interested if I were. A woman always is. To the average woman these suggestions are like the scent of the earth to the husbandman. What must they be to you therefore? But where was I—how far had I travelled round the table?" He looked round and found his bearings again. "Christine will dangle poor old Streatfeild's scalp from her belt considerably before midnight—Anne will—by Jove—I believe the hussy's listening."

"You bet I am," interposed that lady, "and everything I hear you say about me in that connection will be used as evidence against you. And in the near future at that. If Mr. Mordaunt—"

Challoner waved her remark away lightly. "Anne, Miss Considine, as I have often stated to my most favoured friends, is very probably definitely and unashamedly polyandrous. Make out a list, will you? You can put down Francis, Peter Daventry—"

"You beast," flamed Miss Ebbisham, "of all the—" He dodged something that she threw dexterously at him.

"I'm next, Mr. Challoner—what about me?" It was Olive Mordaunt who spoke.

Challoner's eyes met hers and he spoke a little cynically. "Your husband is your slave, Mrs. Mordaunt, as he should be. *Now*." It is doubtful whether the last word carried to her ears for even Mary Considine and Peter Daventry, who were leaning nearer to the speaker than she was, scarcely caught it.

"I come after Mrs. Mordant," Mary smiled the statement at Challoner.

"You, Miss Considine?"

"Yes."

"Surely it is obvious whom you have enslaved—count me your eternally faithful servant." He inclined towards her with a gesture of irreproachable courtesy and simulated homage. As he did so Lorrimer rose from his seat bending down for a second or so to whisper to his mother.

The likeness between mother and son as their two heads ranged side by side was strikingly apparent to everybody who watched them. They were of equal height. There was the same clean-cut profile, the same raven hair and large, dark eyes, the same laughing charm of countenance. Mrs. Lorrimer, proud of her son and perhaps prouder of his success, patted him encouragingly on the arm as he bent down to her, almost as it were challenging Molly Mordaunt for the prior right of possession. The gesture of the ages!

Lorrimer, as she did so, stroked his thick, almost turbulent hair, and faced the company. Adrian Challoner found himself inwardly complimenting Molly Mordaunt upon the soundness of her matrimonial choice. Lorrimer's forehead was broad and intellectual and his eyes held alertness and steadiness in addition to their other qualities. Challoner discovered in him unusual combinations. There were vigour and some refinement of taste, he thought, and the more usual alliance of intellect and character. But at the same time also a strong hint of sensuality. Looking more closely he considered that he could see besides both knowledge and capacity. Distinctly out of place in the House of Commons, thought the actor-manager.

Lorrimer commenced to speak.

"Mr. and Mrs. Mordaunt," he said, "and friends. You have heard what Mr. Mordaunt has said this evening about Molly—how he has wished her all the luck possible now that she has reached the age of twenty-one and how he has coupled my name with hers and formally announced our engagement. I am both gratified and honoured. I want to thank him both on behalf of Molly and myself. The chief thought uppermost in my mind as I speak to you is that I'm a wonderfully lucky dog. At the moment I wouldn't change places with any man in England—or in any other country of the world—come to that. At the same time I am going to ask you to be witnesses to a little ceremony, a ceremony that has fallen into comparative disuse. I refer to the ceremony of betrothal. Stand up, Molly, please." Molly—radiantly beautiful—obeyed the request of her lover with sunshine in her smile. "The ring I'm giving Molly for her engagement," continued Captain Lorrimer, "is the famous Lorrimer sapphire that is known all over the world, and I'm perfectly certain that you will all agree with me when I say that I couldn't possibly find a more lovely hand upon which to place it." He turned to his fiancée and slipped the ring on her finger. "And thereto I plight thee my troth," he quoted gallantly. "Show them, Molly," he said, "let them see the sapphire—next to you and my mother I would rather lose anything in the world than that."

Molly Mordaunt held up her left hand upon which was the great gleaming sapphire and a burst of clapping from the table immediately greeted her action.

"Thank you, Cyril," she said very prettily and daintily, and then turning to the company. "It's perfectly sweet of you all to have come to wish me luck and it only adds enormously to my happiness to see you here. I am sure Cyril feels the same." She resumed her seat, but her lover remained standing.

"Before I sit down," he proceeded, "I want to tell you something else. Something that is doubtless unknown to most of you. It may seem a strange thing for me to say but in a way the Lorrimer sapphire has come home. Mr. Mordaunt knows full well to what I refer."

The speaker paused for a moment to glance at his host at the head of the table and during that fleeting second of time Adrian Challoner, exercising his usual habit of retrospection, took stock of the faces of the various people upon whom his eyes rested. Olive Mordaunt at her end of the table looked troubled—her eyes were heavy with an undoubted apprehension as they flickered from her husband to Molly and subsequently from Molly to Jane. Molly and her father were listening to and watching Lorrimer with eager rapture and keen interest, respectively—each giving Challoner the suggestion of hanging upon the speaker's words. On Jane's strong and determined face there was the usual air of quiet resolution to be seen even more plainly than normally. Anne Ebbisham's eyes still held the dancing lights of mischief, but Mary and Christine had their features in admirable control. Each was listening intently. He heard Lorrimer's voice again.

"To us, gathered here to-night the history of the Lorrimer sapphire is more than interesting. For the Lorrimer sapphire has a distant connection with the Throne of England and must be at least three hundred and fifty years old. Although it is not known how she came by it, it belonged to Queen Elizabeth and was given by her as a mark of appreciation to Sir Gervaise Mordaunte, the famous ancestor of the gentleman at whose table we are privileged to sit to-night. But Sir Gervaise of the wild and wayward spirit during a carousal one evening diced it away to a certain schemingly avaricious Gregory Lorrimer who happened to be an ancestor of mine. For him, ladies and gentlemen, I make no apology. My father, who told me the story when I was a lad, told me also how the loss of the great sapphire in these circumstances had rankled down the years in the Mordaunt family and how they had attempted many times, by both fair means and foul, to get it back. But they always failed. We Lorrimers, direct descendants of the grasping Gregory, nurture a habit of holding fast to what we have and we kept the great sapphire. Ladies and gentlemen, once again a Lorrimer has taken from a Mordaunt a most valuable possession. But neither by dice nor daring." Captain Lorrimer gestured gracefully towards the girl seated next to him. He went on. "And let me say—I do not think that I can find a better way of expressing what has happened than by saying that the Mordaunts have got the sapphire in exchange. They have got it back at last. By *fair* means! By the fairest means in all the world!" He placed his hand on Molly Mordaunt's shoulder.

As he took his seat to the accompaniment of uncontrolled enthusiasm he passed an arm round his mother and slipped the other into Molly's.

"Lucky young beggar," whispered Adrian Challoner to Bertha Raikes on his left, "two women like that at his feet."

Mrs. Raikes nodded but threw out a defensive prophecy. "My John will prove just as successful as Cyril Lorrimer when the time and chance come, Mr. Challoner, and if they don't come he'll make them. You mark my motherly words."

Challoner laughed and was about to reply to the lady when Henry Mordaunt rose with a curious expression on his face and began to speak. The famous K.C. used the cold, incisive, almost passionless tone that was inseparable from him whenever he spoke to a number of people. It might be described as his *"coram publico"* voice.

"Ladies and gentlemen," he said, "it is now my turn. Captain Lorrimer, my future son-in-law, has told you something of the history of the Lorrimer sapphire. That history it was already my privilege to know. To me and to all loyal members of my family, true descendants of Sir Gervaise—which name by the way I prefer to Gregory—it has always been known not as the Lorrimer sapphire but as the Mordaunt sapphire." He smiled. "We must regard, therefore, Molly's engagement as singularly felicitous. But what I have to say to you now touches more upon the present than the past. There is a fashion, nowadays, to deride the present, sometimes at the expense of the future, more often perhaps at the expense of the past. But its importance to my mind can never be overestimated—because it is real—it is always certain—it is *with us!* So apparently is 'Creeping Jenny.'"

The silence that followed the anti-climax of his last remark was definitely cold in its intensity. Mordaunt, as though keenly appreciative of the fact and of its influence on the situation, lost no time in proceeding with what he had to say. He was always a keen judge of the possibilities of a situation and the talent had contributed largely to his success. Taking a square piece of paper from the inside pocket of his dress coat he startled the company with his next statement even more than he had done with his previous one.

"I make that assertion," he said, "with the utmost confidence, for on this occasion the lady to whom I have just referred has been kind and considerate enough to notify me of her intentions in advance. I received this communication about an hour ago through the usual channel of the post. I will read it to you. 'The announcement in the papers concerning the Lorrimer sapphire fascinates me tremendously. I find myself dwelling on the subject to the exclusion of all other interests. So much so in fact that I have decided to honour your house with a visit in my professional capacity. Expect me some time after eleven o'clock to-night. Creeping Jenny.'"

Mordaunt replaced the paper in his pocket with a grave air and turned to his younger daughter and her fiancé. "My boy," he declared, addressing Lorrimer, "we are warned. And forewarned is forearmed. Shall I take the necessary precautions to guard the ring on behalf of Molly, or are you content that I should leave them to you?"

Captain Lorrimer raised his hand with a gesture of defiance. "I am quite content that you should leave the matter in my hands, sir," he cried. "We Lorrimers have kept the sapphire for three hundred and fifty years. I think I can be trusted to keep it a bit longer, 'Creeping Jenny' or no 'Creeping Jenny.'"

The buzz of conversation prevented him saying any more but suddenly Adrian Challoner's voice could be distinctly heard above the rest.

"Well," he cried, "whoever she is—or perhaps whoever 'he' is—for you never know in these cases—'Creeping Jenny's' a good plucked 'un and a rare sport, say what you like about her. 'Pon my soul I wouldn't be greatly surprised if she successfully carried out her threat."

"Not she," cried Lorrimer, "not she, nor anybody else while I hold the sapphire."

As he looked at the faces of the people facing him Challoner saw Jane, Christine and Francis shake their heads doubtfully and almost in unison in consideration of the opinion that he had expressed.

"You think not?" he cried, with a seemingly sudden impulse. "Well then, I wouldn't mind betting a level hundred that 'Jenny' pulls it off."

Anne Ebbisham leaned across the table with outstretched hand, her eyes aflame with excitement.

"Done," she exclaimed, "done! That's a bet. Book it with me. I'll call on you for the hundred in the morning."

Peter Daventry couldn't help noticing the expression on Russell Streatfeild's face as he watched her fascinatedly.

CHAPTER IV

WHEN JANE Mordaunt opened her eyes on the following morning, it was with a dim and vague sense of foreboding. The morning in question held the first touches of autumn that the year had so far given, but although Jane noticed the fact, the impression that it made upon her mind was but an ephemeral one. She would have found it utterly impossible to explain how she felt had she been interrogated, but the feeling had first come to her perhaps at the dinner-table on the previous evening when, following upon her father's sensational statement and Captain Lorrimer's subsequent challenge, Anne Ebbisham had made that somewhat fantastic wager concerning the Lorrimer sapphire with her father's old friend Adrian Challoner. She herself had known Challoner since the earliest days of her childhood-remembrance and something had told her when he gaily flung out the suggestion of the bet in his usual cavalier manner that he would be successful and not Anne Ebbisham. It was a mystic, shadowy and indefinable something, perhaps, but nevertheless she had had it and had known that it was there and

John Raikes, at her side with his hand on her arm and his eyes looking into hers, was equally conscious that she was engulfed temporarily by a wave of emotion. When he had first noticed it he had pressed her, half-seriously and half-laughingly, for an explanation but she had shaken her pretty and determined little head and successfully evaded the issue of a direct answer. As she propped herself up in bed upon her right elbow the events of the previous evening came racing back to her one by one— at first nebulously—and, after that, with a distinct measure of clarity. What had Russell Streatfeild meant when he had whispered to her a few minutes after Anne had held out her hand across the table to—The flowing current of her thoughts was checked suddenly, almost precipitately. There was a knocking upon the door of the room next to hers and when she heard it Jane Mordaunt sat straight up in her bed. The knocking was repeated—once, twice, thrice, and grew in the nature of its attack. Then she heard her father's voice in the corridor and its tone held for her an unusual petulance.

"What is it, Rayner?" she heard him say. "What is it? If you knock any louder you'll disturb everybody. Show a little common sense; do! What is it?"

Rayner's voice came in immediate reply and the maid's voice contained a note of agitation that Jane even from the recesses of her bedroom detected at once.

"I'm sorry, sir, but I can't wake the mistress. This is the third time I've tried, sir, and I can't get any answer from her at all. I don't mean the third time I've knocked, sir; I mean the third time I've come upstairs, sir. I must 'ave knocked a dozen times all told. I don't like it, sir, truth, I don't. It seems to me that something must be wrong."

"What on earth do you mean, Rayner? How can anything be wrong? Your mistress is asleep; she was very tired last night. I know that because she told me so before we came to bed. The time was only a quarter to twelve." Mordaunt was contemptuous towards the maid's pessimism. But Rayner stuck obstinately to her point.

"I've never known the mistress not to be awake a good hour before this time, sir! Besides, there's another thing that's not quite usual."

"What's that?" Jane heard her father ask sharply.

"Her bedroom's closed, sir. I can't get in. The door's locked, and that's not an ordinary thing for the mistress. I always take her tea straight in to her, sir, long before this time."

If it failed to impress Henry Mordaunt, Jane realized the truth of the remark and slipped on her dressing-gown.

"I will go into your mistress's room to satisfy you, Rayner," said Mordaunt, with the air of a man who is settling a vexed question for all time. He returned to his own apartment which evidently he had recently left somewhat hastily to interrogate the maid and passing quickly through the door that connected the two bedrooms entered the one ordinarily occupied by his wife. A moment's glance around it was enough to assure him that the room was empty. The door leading out on to the corridor had no key in the lock on the inside as he had half-ejected to find. He tried it; it was locked. Then his eyes travelled instinctively to the bed. Here again he was puzzled, and it must be confessed somewhat shocked—the bed had not been slept in. It was—to all intents and purposes—untouched. He walked right up to it and save for a slight depression on one side as though some object had lain there for some little time it was as tidy and trim as though newly made. Where in the name of goodness, he asked himself, could Olive be? He turned to find his daughter Jane behind him.

"I heard Rayner knocking, Father. I heard what she said to you. I came out of my room at once. Where's Olive? What does it mean?" She was breathless as she asked the two questions.

Mordaunt shook his head blankly and the puzzled expression on his face became even more pronounced.

"I can't make it out at all, Jane. I can't understand it. I last saw Olive about a quarter to twelve last night. She came up about twenty minutes or so before I did—she was tired and had a bit of a head, she told me. She also intimated that she wouldn't require her maid. As to this position this morning and her absence from this room, I can't make the slightest—" He stopped and shook his head as though to emphasize his complete inability to understand the situation with which he found himself confronted.

"What do you propose we do?" queried the practical Jane.

"Suppose we must have a look all round; she may have been taken queer in some way. Perhaps she's downstairs somewhere. Tell Francis—but try to keep it from the others—including Molly. For goodness sake don't let us disturb the guests if we can possibly help it. Don't tell Francis *all* we know either when you go to him—just let him see that I want him for something that's pretty important. Don't particularize."

Jane disappeared immediately upon her errand. It was quickly executed and very soon Mordaunt had his son and elder daughter at his side in Mrs. Mordaunt's bedroom.

"I had to tell Rayner," he announced, "that Olive wasn't here. I had to—it was imperative—there was no alternative. I've also told her to keep her mouth shut." He spoke to Jane and looked from her to his son at the same time with a suggestion of inquiry.

"I just told him that you wanted him, Father, and that it was urgent—no more," explained his daughter, dutifully anticipating the remark that Henry Mordaunt was about to make.

"We can't find Olive," Mordaunt informed his son, coming to the point at once, "and what is much more significant as I see it, is the alarming fact that her bed has not been slept in. I tell you frankly, Francis, I am at a complete loss what to make of it. I thought I had better send for you."

Francis frowned as he digested the information. "Are her clothes gone?" he asked.

His father stared at him for a second or two.

"There are no clothes to be seen in the room—if that's what you mean. You can see that for yourself, surely?" He gestured impatiently round the room to point his remarks.

"I mean outdoor clothes, Father, in case she's had to go out somewhere. Have you looked in her wardrobe?"

Mordaunt favoured him with another stare. "What could she have wanted to go out for, Francis—and where? Be sensible, my boy, please! I'm, afraid I'm in no mood at the moment to listen to moonshine and exaggerated theories like—"

Francis quietly intervened. "I'm sorry, Father—but you'll pardon me pointing it out to you, I'm sure, but you never know, do you? It's a pretty clear thing she has gone *somewhere*, isn't it? For instance, I've an idea! Goodness knows why, but it's just come to me. Supposing she got on the track of 'Creeping Jenny'—and followed her—or 'him' as Challoner said—for all we know. Eh? How about that for a possibility? Supposing too—"

Mordaunt's face paled, and his hand shook a little as he grasped his son's theory and all that it might mean.

"Don't suggest that, my boy, whatever you do. The position as we know it is quite bad enough. For Heaven's sake don't make it any worse. Don't put ideas like that into my head."

"Let's get to work then," exclaimed Francis. "Standing here arguing amongst ourselves won't find her—there's nothing more certain than that. What about the grounds?"

Mordaunt reluctantly concurred. "Yes, I suppose we'd better have a look round. You're quite right, Francis. Get Bennett at once; tell him we think that Olive may have been taken ill somewhere. Don't tell him any more than that. I'll be down and join you in a few moments. Get back to your room, Jane, and don't let Molly get wind of anything being wrong."

He turned quickly away and his son and daughter did as he had directed them. Within the space of a few moments Mordaunt joined Francis and Bennett, the gardener, at the door of the garage and heard his son tell the latter that Mrs. Mordaunt was not in her bedroom. Beyond the mere statement of that fact he said nothing.

"My father and I think we ought to have a squint round outside, Bennett, in case anything's wrong. So come along with us, will you?"

The gardener, who was a quiet, undemonstrative and uncommunicative man, lifted his cap to the elder Mordaunt and gestured an assent.

"Have you been all round the garden this morning, Bennett?"

"No, Mr. Mordaunt. I haven't been a step farther than the hothouse. There's been several jobs to see to in there for some time now and I never moved out of there till Mr. Francis here come along just now and told me as how you wanted me. So I've not been anything like round, sir—not yet, not by any manner of means."

The tour of the garden of "The Crossways" yielded nothing of any importance, and the suggestion to return was already being considered when Francis Mordaunt had another idea.

"What about the old well?" he exclaimed. "We haven't thought about that? Could Olive have—?"

His father interrupted him sharply. "What are you talking about, Francis? Do you realize what you are saying? How could she possibly have gone down there? It will be a terrible thing if she has—"

Francis saw immediately what his father was thinking. "Of course I don't mean anything like that, Father. It was only the idea of searching everywhere that came to me and made me say what I did. I'm sorry if I upset you."

The gardener looked at the elder man and shook his head as though in remonstrance. "After all, sir, look at it how you will, Mr. Francis is quite right. The old well's a right-down dangerous place, there's no gainsayin' that fact. Many a time I've said to folk round here that it ought to be covered up. In fact, I as good as said so to Mitchell only the other afternoon. Perhaps the mistress has had a fall or something. If so we ought to go and see."

"I suppose you're right, Bennett. Anyhow, you and Mr. Francis between you have persuaded me that we ought to go to have a look. So don't let's waste any more time but get along there as quickly as possible."

The well to which reference had been made was situated beyond the orchard at the extreme eastern edge of the grounds belonging to "The Crossways." It was old and disused as Bennett had stated, and was a good ten minutes' walk from the house itself. As the three men made their way towards it over the grass, heavy with the autumnal dew, passing the apple trees with their windfalls at their feet each felt, although in a different way, that something had happened at "The Crossways" during the last few hours that would have the inevitable effect of changing it for evermore. None of the three by some strange sense of anticipation as they more nearly approached the old well, entertained any doubt whatever that it was going to afford them some explanation of Olive Mordaunt's extraordinary absence. Each felt the strange certainty that this last errand would not turn out to be fruitless. As they turned the last twist in the path that eventually brought the well into actual view there appeared to be nothing visible that could be termed in any way out of the ordinary. The grass all round sparkled with the sheen of the sun on the dew as it slowly triumphed over the curling wisps of mist that heralded chill October and the quick coming of autumn. Francis Mordaunt, unable to restrain his impatience, broke into a run for the last hundred yards or so and came first to the destination. If there were anything dreadful lying ahead he desired to face it first and be able on that account as it were to assume the greater part of its responsibility. When he came to the edge of the well and looked down into its depth, he was grateful for the few seconds' grace that his speed had given to him. The body of his stepmother lay there at the bottom of the well in a huddled heap of horror, and Francis Mordaunt knew beyond any powers of contradiction that she was dead. But he kept his head and in a second his common sense asserted itself. He waved his father and the gardener back a few paces and cried to them sharply.

"She's here. She's fallen down in some way. Perhaps she's only injured. We must get back to the house for help. We must have ropes and a hurdle."

But Henry Mordaunt faced the shock that he knew the sight would give him before he turned with them upon the journey back to the house. Like his son before him he knew too that his wife was dead. He fell to worrying and wondering in the transient moments of his sorrow as to how her death had been encompassed, for it was grotesque and not in the order of things; she was years younger than he. When after considerable labour and difficulty the body was raised and brought back to the house and his son entered the library where he himself had retreated during the carrying out of the unhappy task, he put the question to him that had agitated his mind from the first moments of the discovery.

"How did she die, Francis? From the fall only?"

Francis Mordaunt shook his head gravely. "I'm afraid not, sir—although, of course, I can't say definitely till a doctor has seen her. I've sent Bennett along for one—also for the police. But to all appearances she has been murdered—stabbed—through the heart."

"Good God!" cried Mordaunt, "what does it all mean? What can it mean?" He paused and turned over in his mind another aspect of the matter that had occasioned him some anxiety. "Tell me, Francis," he said eventually, "how was she dressed—was it her evening cloak that I saw as I—"

"Yes, Father. She had her ermine cloak over her evening dress. She must have put it on on purpose to go out. Apparently she took her handbag as well, for we have found that also." He looked at his father and then quickly went on once more. "Have you thought of what I said, Father, when you first called me into the bedroom this morning? I can't help referring to it again. About 'Creeping Jenny,' I mean—don't you think this affair all points that way? Supposing Olive did hear something? And then—"

Mordaunt bit his lip before shrugging his shoulders. "It hardly seems to me likely or even possible that Olive would—still—"

A tap sounded on the door and there was also to be heard the buzz of voices.

"Come in," he called. The door opened.

"Good morning, Mr. Mordaunt," said the man who entered, "you sent for me, I believe?"

It was Inspector Baddeley.

CHAPTER V

"I DID, Inspector, or rather my son here did. We are in serious trouble. My wife, I fear, has been murdered." Mordaunt's voice broke as he made the announcement. "Did you bring a doctor with you, Inspector?"

"Doctor Elliott will be here in a few moments, Mr. Mordaunt. I telephoned to him directly I received the message that your man brought. But tell me all you can, please, as quickly as possible. What are the circumstances of Mrs. Mordaunt's death?"

Mordaunt told the story in detail as he knew it—from the moment that Rayner had first sounded the alarm, to the finding of the body in the well. He also mentioned when he had last seen his wife.

Baddeley listened with the keenest attention. "Stabbed through the heart you think, sir," he said, addressing Francis. "Have you found the weapon that was used, by any chance?"

Francis Mordaunt shook his head. "No. Haven't looked for it, Inspector. Haven't had time to look for it. It isn't half-an-hour since we got the body out of the well. My father and I have just waited for you to come. We haven't really had any time to do anything else."

"I see." Baddeley rubbed his chin with his thumb and forefinger. "Any trouble that you know of during the night? Any alarms, for instance, that might have disturbed Mrs. Mordaunt and caused her to dress herself, lock her bedroom door, and go out of the house?"

Father and son shook their heads in simultaneous denial of the Inspector's suggestion.

"Neither of us heard anything, Inspector. I have asked my son about it," answered the elder man, "and my bedroom is, of course, connected with my wife's. If it were so, why should she take the key with her? Anything that might have happened to upset or disturb her should most certainly have affected me in precisely the same way. And as it happened I was particularly on the *qui vive* last night."

Baddeley noted the last remark but for the time being tried another tack. "Had Mrs. Mordaunt any personal trouble that you are aware of, sir?"

"No, Baddeley, none whatever as far as I know. Certainly nothing that she has confided to me or that—provided that were not the case—I have ever observed."

"Been in good spirits lately?"

"Yes, I think so, Inspector. Much as usual I should say. Certainly there was nothing noticeable the other way. Of course we've been pretty busy for the last few days over the arrangements in respect of my younger daughter's engagement. But I should say that—making allowances for excitement and pressure of household responsibility—my wife's spirits had been quite normal."

"No!" The interruption came from Francis. His tone was sharp and short. His father turned to him with surprise.

"No? What do you mean, Francis? That Olive was not in good spirits? If what you hint at is true it's news to me."

Baddeley turned to the young man. "Tell me what you want to tell me—I shall be pleased to hear it. Perhaps it will assist me a great deal."

Henry Mordaunt looked curiously at his son. "Surely, Francis, you aren't referring to that 'Creeping Jenny' business that I mentioned last night at dinner? Because if you are, I can tell you candidly—"

"No, Father, I'm not. I made up my mind to leave that to you to tell the Inspector later on. What I am about to say has nothing whatever to do with that. It is something quite different. But Olive was not herself all day yesterday. I am able to make that statement without fear of contradiction and with no reservations whatever. I noticed the fact on several occasions and I'm perfectly certain that if you taxed them about it and told them what I have said that my sisters would confirm it—especially Molly. Because they noticed it, too."

"How was the lady then, Mr. Mordaunt, prior to yesterday—all right?"

Francis considered the question for a minute. "As far as I can judge, yes. That is to say that I didn't notice anything untoward or abnormal about her then like I did yesterday. But at the same time, Inspector, I should like to warn you that that evidence of mine isn't worth very much. For I was out in the car nearly all Saturday and Sunday, so that I didn't see very much of her on those two days."

"H'm, I see." Baddeley turned to the elder man. "And you noticed nothing of what your son has mentioned, Mr. Mordaunt?"

"Nothing, Inspector. But what he says has rather disturbed me. It has made me even more worried than I was."

Before Baddeley could develop the question, however, a knock on the door heralded the entrance of Doctor Elliott. He intimated to the Inspector that he desired to see the body of the dead woman immediately.

"Where is it, Baddeley?"

"In the garage, Doctor. Young Mr. Mordaunt here gave orders for it to be taken in there. I quite see his point that the body had to be taken from the well to make sure that she was past help, but all the same I wish I had been on the spot when they did it. You had better come with us, Mr. Mordaunt," he added, addressing the K.C. "I'll have a chat with you later on about what you were on the point of telling me." As Mordaunt raised his eyebrows at the remark, Baddeley continued in explanation, "About 'Creeping Jenny,' I mean."

The four men entered the garage where the body of Olive Mordaunt lay. Doctor Elliott's inspection was quickly made.

"A clear case of murder, in my opinion," he said after a comparatively brief examination of the body. "And death, I should say, must have been almost instantaneous."

"Stabbed through the heart, Doctor?" inquired Baddeley.

"There is a deepish wound above the heart," replied the doctor. "The dagger or knife that has been used has been driven in with a good deal of force by the assailant. It has entered close to the breast-bone between the second and third ribs. The left lung has been punctured and the aortic arch almost divided. So great was the force of the blow, the pulmonary artery has also suffered severely. It would have been impossible for the victim to have lived more than a few seconds."

Henry Mordaunt's face was colourless. He looked like a man who had seen a ghost.

"One question, Doctor Elliott. Is it possible from what you have seen for my poor wife to have laid violent hands on herself?"

The doctor rubbed his forehead. "Yes, just possible I think, perhaps—but highly improbable. Very, very highly improbable. So much so that you can rule out the bare possibility. It is quite true that the wound might, judging solely from its position, have been self-inflicted—but all my medical knowledge and experience prompt me to say that in my opinion it was not. For instance death would come to the victim so quickly—almost as I said just now—instantaneously, that I think the weapon that had been used would be found, of a certainty, either clasped in the hand or at least lying close beside the body. There would be no time to rid oneself of it after it had been used."

Baddeley uttered an explanation. "We can't say yet that it *isn't* close to the body, Doctor. It strikes me very forcibly that the weapon that was employed to murder Mrs. Mordaunt may be still down the well. What do you say, Mr. Francis?"

"I think not, Inspector. There is just the possibility of it, I grant you, but I think we should have spotted anything in the nature of a dagger or knife when we recovered the body, had it been there. However, you can make certain on the point, Inspector, when you have a look yourself."

Baddeley nodded with some suggestion of emphasis. "I shall have to, there's no question about that." He turned again to the doctor. "Another point, Doctor Elliott, before I forget it. How long would you say that this lady has been dead?"

"About twelve hours, Baddeley," replied the doctor, "perhaps more." He looked at his watch. "I should put the crime down to have taken place somewhere about midnight, say at a stretch between twelve and three."

"Thank you, Doctor. What about the body generally? Are there any signs of a struggle having taken place before the blow was struck?"

Doctor Elliott went back and looked at the dead woman's wrists and hands. "In my opinion, no, Inspector. The body is bruised very considerably, but the bruises are quite consistent with the fall, I should say, and entirely what I should have expected having regard to the circumstances of how, I imagine, she met her death. I think it came to her suddenly and was too surprising for her to struggle. There is a severe bruise on the left elbow, three scratches on the right wrist, an abrasion at the back of the skull and several bruises in the lumbar region of the back. I should assert without hesitation that directly the blow was struck, Mrs. Mordaunt fell backwards into the well and death came to her almost at once."

"H'm, I see," said Baddeley, as they left the building. "Now, Mr. Mordaunt, before I walk over to the scene of the crime, tell me, what was this 'Creeping Jenny' business about which you were talking? You can guess why I'm interested; apart from the murder of your wife."

Mordaunt put his hand to his breast pocket and took out his wallet. From the wallet he extracted the letter he had received the day before and handed it to Baddeley.

"There you are, Inspector," he said. "This is the matter to which my son referred. Read what the letter says."

Baddeley read it with grim intentness. "Got the envelope, Mr. Mordaunt?" he asked somewhat curtly.

"Here it is, Inspector." Mordaunt handed it over.

"H'm. Address typed like the contents. Cranwick postmark. The sender was on the spot in advance then, in all probability." Baddeley rubbed the ridge of his jaw as he spoke. "*Very* interesting, sir. Very interesting indeed. And makes me wonder quite a hat-full, too. I should be very pleased to hear what you think of it yourself, Mr. Mordaunt."

"Well, that's a bit of a poser for me to answer, Baddeley. I may surprise you when I tell you, but I incline to the opinion that this letter that I received was authentic, something in the nature of a real warning. I think that this criminal—'Creeping Jenny'—was undoubtedly attracted by the Lorrimer sapphire and intended, if possible, to get hold of it. As to the sending of the letter—well, history holds many instances of criminal giving warning of crimes that they intended to commit, and usually it was the victim, you will find, who received this advance information."

"Yes, I'll concede its possibility. Did anybody besides you and your son know that you had received this letter? Did Mrs. Mordaunt know it herself?"

"Yes, she did, and every one of my guests, everybody, Inspector. I told them all at dinner last evening."

"I see! So that the 'Creeping Jenny' threat may be said to have been public property, eh?"

"Absolutely, Inspector. I think that if 'Creeping Jenny' had put in an appearance at 'The Crossways' last night a warm reception would have been in store."

"There was no alarm of any kind you say in the night?"

Mordaunt shook his head firmly. "None whatever."

"And you know of nothing being missing this morning?"

"Of course not. I presume I should have heard of it by now."

"H'm, makes me think strange thoughts. Takes me back to my interview with you the other day, Mr. Mordaunt. I'm thinking that somebody's going to get a surprise; somebody not very far from here, too: something in my bones tells me so. Take me over to the well, Mr. Mordaunt, will you please? I think that my next step will have to be a look round in that vicinity." Baddeley's voice was curt and his actions brisk.

As they reached the last stretch of grass that lay in front of their intended destination the Inspector pointed to the green surface.

"Not much to be learned here," he said with a kind of rueful resignation—"These are your prints of this morning, I suppose, gentlemen? Couldn't have happened better for the criminals?"

Francis nodded. "I expect they are, Inspector. But you mustn't blame us because we came along this way. It's so easy, you know, to be wise after the event. My father, the gardener and I together certainly walked across here early this morning and I've no doubt obliterated anything that might have been here for you to read. But I can truthfully say that had we known when we came what we know now—what was awaiting us—we should have been more careful."

The Inspector nodded. "Quite right, sir, I grant you that. But perhaps it's not so bad and all the damage hasn't been done after all. I shall have to make a thorough investigation. But here we are, I fancy; let me have a look at the well-bottom." Baddeley walked to the side and looked over. "Describe as accurately as you can if you please, sir, how your stepmother was lying and the *exact place where* her body was when you first looked down and saw her."

Francis indicated the position. "Just there where I'm pointing. She was lying slightly on her left shoulder."

"H'm—h'm—and her evening cloak was on?"

"Yes."

Baddeley took out his note-book and made an entry. "It means me going down there if I want to be sure of one or two points. All the same it's not a single-handed job, that's very plain." He turned away, his eyes fixed once again on the green expanse of grass that surrounded the old well. Suddenly they saw him stoop.

"Hallo—hallo, Mr. Mordaunt! What's this, eh? What's the meaning of this?" He picked something very carefully from the top edges of the grass.

Francis Mordaunt saw that the Inspector held four or five pieces of charred paper in his hand. Baddeley held them out to the others for inspection. They were quite black and any writing that might once have been on them was now indecipherable.

"Fragments of a letter it seems to me, gentlemen, from the sizes of the pieces. May be nothing in it, of course, affecting our case. Still, you never know and I'm not disposed to take any risks." He placed the fragments with careful deliberation between the leaves of his official note-book. "Have a glance round, do you mind, gentlemen," he ordered. "See if you can see any sign of a weapon anywhere about. It isn't likely, I grant, but there's no knowing. A murderer very often loses his head after he's committed his crime and throws a knife or a revolver away. Work round in all directions, will you, gentlemen?"

Mordaunt and his son did as directed but to no purpose.

"No luck, gentlemen," Baddeley made the announcement eventually as a matter of course. "I think, Mr. Mordaunt," he added, "that I'll go back to the house for the time being and come out here again later. I should like to look into one or two matters inside the house, sir, before they get too cold, if it's all the same to you."

Mordaunt acquiesced immediately. "Certainly. Anything you like, Inspector. What do you desire to do exactly, Baddeley?" he said when they had regained the house—"and where particular do you wish to go?"

Before the Inspector could frame his reply to the two questions there came an interruption. Several of the members of the house party, among whom, of course, by this time the dreadful news had spread, were grouped together in the hall. As the Inspector entered the house with the two Mordaunts one of the group stepped forward and accosted the K.C. It was Captain Lorrimer.

"Mr. Mordaunt," he said, "forgive me interrupting you but I have just heard the bad news. My sincerest sympathy to you in your trouble." He then looked round for a second, dropped his voice and said something else.

Mordaunt looked up at him with an unmistakable start. "Certainly, Lorrimer, certainly," the others heard him say. "I am in entire agreement with you. By all means inform the Inspector at once." He turned to Baddeley. "Baddeley! This is Captain Cyril Lorrimer, my prospective son-in-law. He has something to tell you that he considers of the greatest and gravest importance. He would like to speak to you privately, that is to say with nobody present beyond myself and my son."

"Bring him into the library, Mr. Mordant," said Inspector Baddeley. "I have an idea that I know what it is that he wishes to tell me."

CHAPTER VI

As the door closed behind Captain Lorrimer the three men who had accompanied him into the room formed the opinion that he had excellent grounds very probably for the statement that he had just previously made to Henry Mordaunt. It was evident to all three of them that Lorrimer's agitation was real and sustained. There was no doubt that he had had a shock of some kind.

Inspector Baddeley motioned him to a seat and then took one himself at the head of the table. "What is it that you have to tell me, Captain Lorrimer? Let me see if it's in accordance with my anticipations. I'll play fair, and tell you if I'm wrong. No, I won't. I'll tell you."

Lorrimer looked at him rather curiously. "I don't know quite what you mean by those remarks, Inspector. Anyhow, when I've told you what I'm going to you'll be in a position to judge for yourself if you're right or not."

Baddeley raised his hand. "Just a minute, sir. One will be ample, I think. Before you put me wise as to this story of yours I'll tell you what you have come to tell me. Then there'll be *no* doubt about it. I'll tell you beforehand in order that you'll be able to see that everything's all square and above-board. You've come to tell me, Captain Lorrimer, that you've been robbed in the night of the famous Lorrimer sapphire, now haven't you?" The Inspector looked round the room with a glance of undisguised triumph as he asked the question. He prepared himself for the thunders of applause. But his satisfied complacency was ill-founded, and his supreme confidence misplaced for he was destined to receive a denial. Captain Lorrimer in fact shook his head and the movement, trifling as it was, brought Baddeley's mental gymnastics to a somewhat summary conclusion. The House of Theory that he had built came toppling down ignominiously.

"No, Inspector," said the Captain, "that is not so. Whatever gave you that idea? You're wrong there. I'm the wrong man for 'Creeping Jenny' to try her tricks on. The Lorrimer sapphire is still in my possession." He looked round and then seemingly satisfied, lowered his voice to almost a whisper. "But all the same," he continued, "it's a remarkable thing that what I have come to tell you does concern the Lorrimer sapphire. But in a somewhat different way." He paused and turned to his future father-in-law with an inquiry. "Does the Inspector know the circumstances properly? Why I am here, and other things? If not, it would assist him somewhat, I think, if—"

Mordaunt nodded. "I see what you mean, Lorrimer. I'll inform Baddeley now. Captain Lorrimer, Inspector, is engaged to my younger daughter, Molly—er—Margaret—and he intends to give her the Lorrimer sapphire as an engagement ring. But I expect you knew that."

At this point Lorrimer himself took up the running again. "You see the position, then, Inspector. Now, I should have let Miss Mordaunt keep the sapphire last night—it was my original intention that she should but for that letter Mr. Mordaunt here received by post from 'Creeping Jenny.' I take it that you have already been informed of that?"

Inspector Baddeley immediately nodded an affirmative. "Yes. Go on," he added.

"That letter, Inspector, made me alter my mind and also come to a decision. I resolved not to risk either the sapphire or perhaps the safety of Molly herself, by letting her wear it during the night. It wouldn't have been fair to her—and besides that I've had plans in operation for some time now directed towards the safety of my sapphire. Now, gentlemen, I've had to inform you of these matters so that you can understand the position better. What I next have to tell you is this." He leaned over the table towards the Inspector and spoke very quietly and impressively. "Mrs. Mordaunt was murdered by somebody for possession of the Lorrimer sapphire, I'm certain of it!"

The husband of the murdered woman sat bolt upright in his chair at Lorrimer's surprising declaration. "What?" he exclaimed incredulously. "What on earth prompts you to say that? What do you mean?"

Before Lorrimer could reply Henry Mordaunt went on, mastered temporarily by his excitement and emotion. "You will have a very difficult task to convince me of that," he said with definite challenge in his tone.

Lorrimer's quiet response was intensely sympathetic.

"I can understand you saying that, sir," he rejoined, "and I feel for you tremendously. But I know what I'm talking about. Listen carefully, please. After I left you last night, sir—you remember my last words, by the way, in all probability—Mrs. Mordaunt sought me; she begged me to let her watch the sapphire during the night. Her explanation was that she felt absolutely certain that the attempt *would* be made to steal it from me that night and that if she had it, it would be quite safe. Well, Inspector—not to put too fine a point upon it—I was puzzled. I may as well admit that at once. But I laughed at her fears, I told her that in my opinion the sapphire was in no danger whatever—that I had been successful in keeping it so long that I wasn't going to lose it now—and moreover when I had been warned—in the bargain. But try as I would, gentlemen, and argue as I might, I couldn't shake Mrs. Mordaunt's belief in what she was sure was going to happen. She was obsessed by the idea."

"Just a minute, Captain Lorrimer," put in Inspector Baddeley, "did she seem certain that *'Creeping Jenny'* was going to do the stealing? Emphasizing my point. Did she mention 'Creeping Jenny' by *name*, can you remember?"

"Oh yes, Inspector, every time. That undoubtedly was the trouble. 'Creeping Jenny's' letter had done the trick as far as Mrs. Mordaunt was concerned, there's no doubt about that."

"Thank you. Go on, sir, if you don't mind." Baddeley was getting more and more interested. Perhaps, after all, his theory wasn't going to prove so very wide of the actual mark. Things seemed to be shaping towards that direction.

"Well, I stuck to my guns, Inspector, and poor Mrs. Mordaunt stuck to hers. I think that each of us had been born with more than an average supply of obstinacy. But in the end, I compromised—although, of course, Mrs. Mordaunt wasn't aware of that fact."

"Compromised, Lorrimer?" asked Henry Mordaunt, with a frown on his brow. "I don't follow you. How did you manage to do that?"

"In this way, sir! For a long time now I have possessed a paste imitation of the Lorrimer sapphire. It has formed the basis of my plan for keeping the original and is—I may tell you—an exact facsimile. I know the difference between the two, but it would take an expert to detect it when shown the two rings for the first time. Consider this fact alone. Geldarstein himself was seven seconds distinguishing the real one. When I realized last night that Mrs. Mordaunt was in such deadly earnest an idea came to me suddenly, and at length I satisfied her by giving her the paste stone to mind, letting her imagine, of course, that she had the real Lorrimer sapphire in her possession." Lorrimer rose and paced the room in extreme agitation. "Mr. Mordaunt, I shall never be able to forgive myself for what I did for I fear that by doing so, I unwittingly sent her to her deaths. For as I said just now I am afraid that Mrs. Mordaunt was murdered for possession of that sapphire. Doesn't it seem so to you, gentlemen? What else can I—in my position—think?"

There was silence for the matter of a few seconds as each man contemplated the possibilities of what they had just heard. Then the elder Mordaunt broke it.

"What I can't understand, Lorrimer, is this. Why on earth did my poor wife *want* to mind the wretched thing? Even if 'Creeping Jenny' had taken it, how would it worry her—beyond the fact of ordinary loss? In what way did it concern her more than me, for example? Why should *she* have been so perturbed about the prospect of it being stolen? That I find incapable of adequate answer."

"And I agree with you, Mr. Mordaunt. Just what I think myself." Baddeley spoke crispy and curtly. "In fact," he continued, "it seems to me that there's only one possible explanation. What I've just listened to is corroborative. The key to the 'Creeping Jenny' puzzle will be found to be in this district somewhere, I'm pretty sure of it. And I'm sure of this too, *Mrs. Mordaunt knew something!*" He brought his hand down on to the table in sharp emphasis, and drummed with his fingers on its surface. "And by Moses I'll find out what it was before I'm finished. What time did this interview take place?"

"About a quarter past twelve," replied Lorrimer.

Baddeley turned to Francis. "Here we begin to progress, sir. This may account for her being somewhat unsettled on the Monday as you suggested, sir? Don't you think so?" Before Francis could reply, Baddeley fired a second question at him. "I suppose she didn't confide in you at all, eh?"

But Francis answered the question with the utmost coolness. "She did not, Inspector. I should have told you if she had when I first mentioned the matter. Also I can't see myself that my step-mother's anxiety or worry or whatever you choose to call it could have had anything to do with this 'Creeping Jenny' business. At the time of which I speak my father hadn't received 'Creeping Jenny's' letter."

"Very likely you can't, which doesn't concern me." Baddeley turned his attention to Captain Lorrimer. "Where were you, Captain Lorrimer, when you handed this imitation sapphire of yours over to Mrs. Mordaunt? I'm interested to know that."

"I gave it to her in the corridor outside her bedroom door."

"Directly after your interview with her?"

"Immediately, Inspector. It was the natural conclusion to the interview. I finished by saying that I would do as she wished and give way to her in the matter and go and get her the stone. I did so at once."

"Nobody could have seen you in the corridor, I suppose?"

"I hardly think so, Inspector. There was certainly nobody about that I saw. I think several of the house party had gone to bed."

Baddeley changed his tactics again. He came back to Mordaunt the elder. "Something you said when I first arrived this morning has come back to me. You stated, if I remember your words correctly, that you were specially alert during the night. 'On the *qui vive*' was the expression which I think you used. Am I to understand that that was so out of compliment, shall we say, to the threat from 'Creeping Jenny,' or had you any other reasons for being so?"

It was a moment or two before the K.C. essayed an answer. It seemed to those that awaited his reply that he was making up his mind about something. When he at length commenced to speak his words came very slowly.

"Your question and the way in which you have put it, Inspector, bring me to something rather curious that happened last night at dinner. Perhaps that was in my mind when I spoke to you before."

"Curious? Please explain, sir."

"I will," rejoined Mordaunt. "I don't know whether I told you the details before, but I read the letter that I had received from 'Creeping Jenny' to my company as they sat at the dinner-table. Naturally the reading of it created a good deal of interest and excitement. Captain Lorrimer expressed his opinion that 'Creeping Jenny' would be unsuccessful in her attempt; that he would hold his sapphire against her. The atmosphere was not only tense and dramatic—but also I think a little theatrical—which is different. Then the incident happened that I just described as curious. It was born no doubt of this touch of the theatre. One of my guests is a very old and dear friend of mine—Adrian Challoner, the celebrated actor-manager of the Ramillies Theatre, London. You can imagine how he, of all people, reacted to this atmosphere that I have just described. He offered to bet a hundred pounds that 'Creeping Jenny' would get away with the Lorrimer sapphire. I think he stated that he was making the bet because her pluck—and—er—grit appealed to him. The challenge was a general one." Mordaunt stopped and wiped his forehead with his handkerchief—the three conditions of suspense, anxiety and grief through which he had travelled and through the last of which he was still journeying were proving a little too much for him.

"Go on, Mr. Mordaunt," said Baddeley. "This is very interesting indeed. I should also like to know whether that bet was taken by anybody."

"Challoner's bet was taken," replied Mordaunt. "It was taken by a very charming girl who is staying here and who happens strangely enough to be Challoner's goddaughter. Her name is Ebbisham—Anne Ebbisham. Her people were close friends of my first wife."

Baddeley furrowed his brows thoughtfully. "Anne Ebbisham?" He repeated the name slowly after Henry Mordaunt and the tone in which he said it held not only a definite question but also, it seemed, a doubt. "The name is familiar. I rather fancy I've had the pleasure of meeting that young lady before. Am I right in stating that she has recently been staying at Cranwick Towers, the residence of Lady Craddock?"

"That is so, Inspector; my two girls were staying there with her."

"I thought so," added Baddeley. "I remember that particular young lady very well indeed. I don't think she'd want anybody to hold her hand crossing the road. I shouldn't say that she was afraid to go home in the dark either. And she took this Mr. Challoner's bet—eh? Bet him a hundred pounds that 'Creeping Jenny' wouldn't bring the job off—eh? And that the Captain here wouldn't lose his sapphire? Well now, I quite agree with you, Mr. Mordaunt, that *is* curious." He rubbed the ridge of his jaw again. "You will observe, gentlemen," he continued pleasantly, "that this young lady has apparently won her bet. Mr. Challoner has forfeited his hundred pounds. Just now I was wondering what Mrs. Mordaunt knew. Now I'm wondering what Miss Ebbisham knew." Baddeley stood at his chair by the head of the table for a few moments deep in thought. Then he turned to Captain Lorrimer. "Thank you, sir," he said warmly, "for your information. As you stated, it is of the utmost importance, especially at this stage of the case. It may serve to put me on the right track when I get the threads of the affair into my hands. You have probably saved me a great deal of time. At any rate it has made me alter my arrangement. Please excuse me, gentlemen, for the time being."

The Inspector made a hurried exit from the library and made his way to the telephone in the hall. From there he quickly established communication with the men he wanted and outlined to them all what he desired them to do for him. In less than an hour's time he met them at the old well and further operations were at once commenced there. Roper, the Inspector's first assistant, carried them out very painstakingly and thoroughly. Despite the most assiduous search there was no weapon to be found within the well, but away in one corner lay two burnt match-ends which Roper brought to the top and handed with triumph to his Chief.

Baddeley's eyes brightened perceptibly at the find and after examination he carefully placed the two ends in his pocket. "No sign of any weapon down there, Inspector," said Roper, "you can bank on that."

"Quite sure, Roper?"

"Absolutely, sir. I've been over every inch of the ground."

"Well then, I'll say this, Roper, I think it's very strange. I should have expected a weapon of that kind to have been flung away by the murderer directly after the crime had been committed, wouldn't you? Seems to me to have been that kind of murderer."

"Yes, I think I should, Inspector. But you can't say! Which way did he go?" Roper looked round as though expecting to find the answer to his question plainly written somewhere or other for all to see.

"My dear Roper," replied Baddeley, "a herd of elephants couldn't have left more traces behind of their movements than the people here have done this morning. Anything of last night's origin has been beautifully obliterated. It's only in books that these wonderful footprint clues are found. I'd hug myself to be a detective in a book."

Ten minutes later he pushed open the door of the library. As he did so his face registered surprise. Henry Mordaunt and his son were seated almost exactly and in the same places as they had been when the Inspector had left. But Captain Lorrimer stood on the rug in front of the fireplace and faced them. Real as had been his agitation before, it had now increased tenfold, for the distress in his voice was evident to everybody present.

"Inspector," he cried as Baddeley entered the room, "I'm very glad you've returned. I am sorry to say that my confidence has been misplaced. I have just discovered that the Lorrimer sapphire has been stolen during the night—stolen from my bedroom. 'Creeping Jenny' must have been in 'The Crossways' after all." He turned and sank into a chair.

CHAPTER VII

BADDELEY's eyes danced with excitement and his fingers went instinctively to caress the trim, military moustache of which he was secretly rather proud. It was a gesture of his that always followed a feeling of satisfaction.

"Things are moving, Captain Lorrimer! What did I say when I spoke to you before?" He looked across at Lorrimer who seemed extremely cut up at the realization of his loss. "Come, sir," continued Baddeley, "we must unite our best forces to get it back to you. And if we work together that will be a very good reason why we should be successful. For there's one thing, gentlemen, that I'm pretty well certain about." He paused and looked at the company of men as though challenging any one of them to ask his meaning.

Henry Mordaunt sensed this and came to the question. "What's that, Inspector?"

"That the Lorrimer sapphire isn't very far away—yet. I don't think it's had time to be." Baddeley brought his fist down on to the table with one of his emphatic thumps. Following up the action almost immediately he swung round on to Captain Lorrimer. "By the way, Captain Lorrimer," he asked, "it's just occurred to me, any sign of the usual 'Creeping Jenny' visiting-card in your bedroom? You know what I mean, don't you?"

Lorrimer jerked up his head with signs of sudden and almost startled interest, his eyes wide open. "By Jove, I never thought of that. I didn't notice any, Inspector, now you come to mention it, but I don't know that I can be said to have looked very carefully. I was so amazed when I discovered the loss that I just came straight down here to find you and tell you."

Baddeley rubbed his cheek with the knuckles of his left hand. "Quite so, sir. I can understand that. Well, there's nothing like making sure. We'll have a look ourselves. And now—at that. Lead the way to your bedroom, sir—do you mind?"

Although it was to Lorrimer that Baddeley had addressed his last remark, Henry Mordaunt acted upon the instruction and piloted the three men up the stairs to the bedroom in question. As they ascended Baddeley spoke quietly to the man just in front of him. Mordaunt listened and nodded. "I will see that that is attended to, Inspector, in fact, I thought about issuing orders myself to that effect. Everybody shall be here when you want any of them."

Entering the bedroom Francis gave a cry of quick discovery. His eyes alert and keen had picked up something that Lorrimer's in the first agitation of the loss had missed. Propped up against a photo frame that stood on the dressing-table was a visiting-card, or, to be exact, a card that looked like one. Baddeley swooped on to it, like an eagle descending triumphantly upon its prey. What he read upon the card appeared to convey to him a certain measure of satisfaction for he turned to the others and acclaimed his acquisition.

"The usual typed message, gentlemen, and the usual name at the bottom. I say 'usual,' although I don't suppose anybody here has seen it before. But no doubt you've heard of it. It's the greeting that 'Creeping Jenny' always leaves behind her." The three men looked over the Inspector's shoulder. The message they read was short, sharp and to the point. "With 'Creeping Jenny's' compliments. She takes but one."

"As per invoice," remarked Baddeley. "The mixture as before. Now, Captain Lorrimer, tell me at once: you discovered the theft about half-an-hour ago, I presume?"

Lorrimer became thoughtful. "Yes, it would be about that, Inspector. Not much more than that, certainly. But I think I had better explain one or two things to you before we go any farther. I shall save time in the end."

"Just my idea, sir. For instance—you previously mentioned to me that you had made certain plans or arrangements—anything you like to call them—with regard to safeguarding your sapphire. May I ask what those particular plans were? That question, you see, arises now very pointedly."

"Exactly what I was about to explain, Inspector Baddeley. Candidly I feel an awful ass about it now—speaking to you as I did." He looked at Mordaunt as he spoke and embarked at once upon a venture that was almost in the nature of an apology. "I'm tremendously sorry, sir," he exclaimed sympathetically, "it must seem to you very much as though I'm putting my own slight loss before your loss—you know what I mean, sir. Please don't think that of me, it's just the fact that the loss of the sapphire has come along at this moment and taken 'centre stage' as it were for the time being."

Mordaunt recognized the appeal in his voice and paid due deference to it. "I understand perfectly, Lorrimer, so don't worry about it. I can guess exactly how you feel about everything. There is no need for you to reproach yourself over anything that you have said."

Lorrimer wiped his forehead with his handkerchief. "Thank you, sir. What you say makes me feel a lot easier. It's very generous of you to put it like that. Now I'll out with what I was going to tell you, Inspector. My plans for keeping the sapphire were excessively simple. You see those two sticks of shaving-soap?" He pointed to two sticks of shaving-soap of the ordinary variety, shape and size, that stood on the side of the table.

Baddeley's and the eyes of the others followed his indicating finger.

"Yes," snapped the first-named brusquely. "What about them?"

"The first one—this one nearer to me—is a stick of soap that you could purchase in any shop that stocked it so we can pass over it. But look at the second—you'll see that it's somewhat different. Pick it up." The Inspector obeyed the bidding, took the second stick and examined it. "Notice anything about it?" inquired Lorrimer eagerly.

"It's a bit light," confessed Baddeley. "In weight I mean—certainly lighter than the other one." He tested one against the other in his hands.

"Right," said Lorrimer. "Turn the second one upside down and look at the bottom of the stick." Baddeley did as ordered and what he saw surprised him. The soap had been hollowed out at the bottom something after the manner of a certain type of wine-bottle and there was a cavity into which the Inspector had no difficulty in inserting his finger.

"That cavity there, Inspector, was my hiding-place for the sapphire," said Lorrimer sadly, "and it's always turned up trumps up till now for I have reason to believe that more than one attempt has been made in the past to steal it. I'd have laid a thousand to one against anybody getting away with it—'Creeping Jenny' included. But there you are—the impossible has come off this time."

Baddeley looked up and fingered his chin reflectively. "I am going to ask you a very pertinent question, sir," he said, "and I want you to give me a very frank answer. Who else besides yourself knew of this secret of the shaving-stick? Don't except anybody—no matter how intimate that particular person may be." As he spoke Baddeley watched Lorrimer's face. Was it fancy on his part or did a shade of anxiety cross it? However, there was no hesitation in Lorrimer's voice when he answered:

"The only other person in the world who knew of the hiding-place of the Lorrimer sapphire was my mother—which is equivalent to my saying—'nobody else.' That is to say from your point of view, Inspector."

"Not quite, sir—speaking as an Inspector of Police," returned Baddeley, "although I appreciate your meaning. Is Mrs. Lorrimer—I presume that is the lady's name—staying here now?"

"She is," replied Lorrimer with some show of surprise, "but I don't quite follow why you should—"

"That's all right, sir. But if you'll allow me to say so again, my standpoint in the matter must be dissimilar to yours. I'm sure you won't mind me pointing that out to you."

It seemed that Mordaunt was about to speak as Baddeley finished his sentence, but the latter, proceeding again almost immediately, was too quick for him.

"For instance, Captain Lorrimer,"—Baddeley seemed now to be speaking with a sense of great responsibility—"have I your word of honour that your fiancée, Miss Margaret Mordaunt, was unaware of your method of hiding the sapphire? The sapphire, mark you, which you were going to present to her."

Lorrimer flushed at the Inspector's question. "You have my word of honour, Inspector Baddeley! That should have been clear to you from my first answer. Only my mother knew! I have never discussed the matter with Molly in any way at all. The question of my losing the sapphire while staying down here was never definitely considered between us prior to Mr. Mordaunt here getting the letter from 'Creeping Jenny.'" He turned impulsively to the man to whom he had just referred. "You can corroborate that for me, sir—or at any rate you can—"

Mordaunt nodded. His face was now showing very obvious signs of the trouble that had come to him. To Francis it seemed that he had aged years in the short space of twelve hours.

"I can't contradict you, Lorrimer," said the K.C. to the man that had appealed to him, "and I'm certain that the Inspector is quite satisfied on the point. Aren't you, Baddeley? But that brings me to something that I was about to say a moment or two ago. Something that came to me a little while back which I think Baddeley should know, although I must admit that I don't know why I think so," he continued wearily, "except for the fact that the more you tell a man in a case of this kind, the more chance you give him of obtaining results."

Baddeley expressed his agreement with a quick movement of the head. "I'm all for that, Mr. Mordaunt. And I must say that I wish everybody thought in the same way as you do. It's the tight-lipped variety of people that so often ties a man's hands almost as soon as he's started. Makes you put up a couple of stone over-weight right from the beginning. I'm listening to what you've got to say."

The K.C.'s drawn face grew a shade more troubled. But he turned to Lorrimer as though eager to revive a memory in the latter's mind. "I'm going to take you back a stretch, old man—

to a semi-private sort of conversation you had with me after I'd read 'Creeping Jenny's' warning to you all at the dinner-table."

Lorrimer wrinkled his forehead in consideration of Mordaunt's statement and Francis looked anxiously at his father—evidently in great wonderment at what was coming next.

"Do you mean directly after or some considerable time after? Because I'm not altogether sure that I—"

Mordaunt cut in. "Not directly after—I don't mean then at all. I mean towards the end of the evening when I spoke to you about Challoner's wager with Anne Ebbisham. Can you remember the terms of your reply to me?"

"By Jove, sir,"—Lorrimer brought his two hands together under the stress of his excitement—"now you mention it I should just think I do. And I think I begin to see where you're heading! You're referring to the terms of my projected wager—if 'wager' it could be called."

Mordaunt held up his hand to check any further explanation upon which he might venture. "You said to me that if 'Creeping Jenny' were successful in the threat that she had made, you wouldn't shave again while you were here. Tell me now, Lorrimer—so that Baddeley here may entertain no doubt upon the point—when you spoke in that facetious way—were you thinking of the sapphire's hiding-place? What was uppermost in your mind at the moment?"

Lorrimer broke in, his impetuosity mastering his patience. "Oh yes, sir. Of course I was. I'm perfectly willing to admit it. The place where I was going to put the sapphire that night was undoubtedly uppermost in my mind as I was speaking. All the same I don't see for the life of me how anybody could freeze on to an oblique reference like that. Even if anybody had been near enough to us to hear what I said. Which I'm pretty certain did *not* happen." He spoke with most decided emphasis.

"What have you to say with regard to that, Mr. Mordaunt?" The question came from Baddeley.

"I shouldn't like to say, Inspector. Because for me to confirm what Captain Lorrimer has just said to you will conflict with the theory with which I've been toying now for some little time."

Baddeley regarded him curiously. "What theory is that, Mr. Mordaunt?" he asked very softly. "That somebody did hear Lorrimer's remark concerning his shave?"

"And not only heard it but was smart enough to put two and two together. Although I agree with him that I saw nobody near us."

Francis Mordaunt intervened here unable to restrain himself. "But, Father," he said, "don't you see what that means? It means that 'Creeping Jenny's' somebody inside this house, which is ridiculous." He lowered his voice as he spoke again. "Such a thing can't be."

At this last expression of opinion Baddeley looked up and threw out a disagreement. "Oh, why not? Tell me, please, why not? It's my turn now to make a confession. As a matter of fact that's a little idea that has commended itself to me for a matter of some days now. Surprised?"

But Henry Mordaunt did not answer the question put to him. A tap sounded on the door and instead of replying he looked across the room in that direction. Baddeley motioned to Francis Mordaunt to open the door.

CHAPTER VIII

ADRIAN CHALLONER stood on the threshold. Although as well groomed as ever and just as faultlessly attired his face nevertheless was not entirely unperturbed, for his striking features bore unmistakable signs of worry and trouble.

"May I come in, Mordaunt?" he asked, as Francis opened the door to his knock. "Believe me, I wouldn't trouble you had I not a very grave reason for so doing." The likeness of the words he used to those that Lorrimer Had employed struck Henry Mordaunt immediately. As Challoner spoke he held out his hand for the hand of the man to whom the words were directly addressed. Mordaunt understood the meaning of the gesture and extended his hand in obedience to it. Challoner pressed it in silent sympathy. His eyes then travelled towards Inspector

Baddeley, who, if appearances went for anything, was far from being pleased at what he evidently considered an unfortunate interruption. But Adrian Challoner excelled at the handling of difficult, delicate and even embarrassing situations; it must be remembered that he frequently numbered two "Star" actresses in his casts and the female of that species is certainly more deadly than the male.

At this moment—realizing the meaning of the look on the Inspector's face—he brought the battery of his personal charm to bear upon Baddeley. "I ask your pardon, Inspector," he said, with delightful and disarming candour, "for what must appear in the nature of an interruption. I fear that I have disturbed what was perhaps a most important conference. You must forgive me. But, as I hinted to Mr. Mordaunt here a moment ago, my reason for so doing is neither whimsical nor fantastic. When you hear what I have to tell you I am sure that you will instantly acquit me of anything like unjustifiable interference—a quality nobody hates more fervently than I do."

Baddeley bowed somewhat stiffly. "At the present moment, sir, I should like to point out that you have the advantage of me. I do not even know your name. If Mr. Mordaunt will remedy the omission—well then perhaps—" The Inspector stopped and looked inquiringly at the man whose name he had mentioned.

Mordaunt repaired the breach. "I am sorry," he apologized, "I forgot. This is Inspector Baddeley of the Sussex Constabulary; he has come over from Lewes to investigate matters. Mr. Adrian Challoner, of the Ramillies Theatre, London."

Baddeley was impressed and bowed rather jerkily. "Pleased to meet you, sir, although I'm sorry the circumstances are such as they are. Needless to say I've very often heard of you, although I've never had the pleasure of seeing you on the boards. I'm afraid I don't get as far as London very often. Not, of course, that it's too late for me to pop in to see you one night. What was it that you were desirous of telling me, sir?" He indicated a chair at the side of the table which Adrian Challoner promptly accepted. The actor surveyed his audience carefully before he commenced to speak. By now he was entirely at home and his atmosphere established. When he spoke his tones were measured and quiet.

"The news of Mrs. Mordaunt's death is, of course, known now all over the house. These things are exceedingly difficult to keep secret. Rumours fly quickly, I'm afraid. And already there is an ugly word being whispered in connection with it—murder. The gardener—Bennett—has found it difficult to keep silent about what he knows. It is in relation to that rumour that I have intervened in your conference. I will begin, Inspector, by asking you a question. How was Mrs. Mordaunt killed? Or if you prefer it at this stage—how did she meet her death?"

"How have *you* heard that it happened?" Baddeley countered question with question.

"Very well, Inspector, have it your way." Adrian Challoner was the personification of urbanity. "I have been informed that Mrs. Mordaunt was stabbed to death. Is that correct?"

"Near enough," replied Baddeley, "go on."

"In that case, Inspector, may I ask you if the weapon with which the lady was killed has been found, or what you imagine may be the weapon? I will come to the point. Has any weapon been found?"

Baddeley rubbed his lip with his fingers. "We have not made a thoroughly exhaustive search yet, Mr. Challoner. That has been impossible. The grounds of 'The Crossways' are extensive, and there have been several other things to do. But the weapon is not anywhere near where the unfortunate lady's body was found. I have been over the approximate ground thoroughly and have been able to establish that fact. I presume though that you have some special reason for asking the question that you have done?" He caressed his moustache, inviting Challoner's reply. The latter pulled the chair upon which he was sitting a trifle nearer to the table and lowered his voice.

"You are right, Inspector, I have. A very special reason as you call it." He turned to the others who were listening intently. "You, my dear Mordaunt, are aware, I know, that I have a new production in rehearsal at the present time. But I will assume that Inspector Baddeley has no knowledge of the fact. This, then, for his information. I am putting on 'Broken Threads' at the moment but six weeks' time will see the *première* at the 'Ramillies' of my next play. It is called 'Sin and a Woman.' I tell you these seemingly irrelevant facts in order that you may grasp the true significance of my next piece of information. 'Sin and a Woman' is a political drama and I play the part of a great states-man who becomes virtually the uncrowned King of England—a sort of British Mussolini, if that will help you to understand the idea better. The climax of the play arrives at the third act curtain when I am assassinated and the scene of the assassina-tion is staged outside the Houses of Parliament. The author has followed as far as possible the assassination of Julius Caesar by the conspirators before the Capitol. There are modern counter-parts in the play of Brutus, Cassius, the envious Casca, Marcus Antonius and the others. Now I come to the significant part of my story. In the script the playwright has given directions that the daggers used should be as nearly as possible like those used by the conspirators—on the basis of history inevitably being forced to repeat itself. I refer, naturally, to such matters as appearance, shape and size—actually they will be 'props,' of course. But I have made it my business to obtain a dagger of the old Roman pattern, and it was my intention to have the 'prop' daggers manufactured to resemble this particular weapon in every detail. When I came down here, I brought it with me as I had very recently called upon the particular firm that I am employing to make the others and whom I also intended to see again immediately upon my return. *That dagger, gentlemen, was taken from my room sometime last night and for all I know it may have been used to kill Mrs. Mordaunt. That's why I'm here now.*" Adrian Challoner paused to watch the effect of his ominous words upon the man to whom he had primarily addressed them.

"Where did you keep this dagger?" Baddeley put his first question promptly.

"Do you mean habitually, Inspector, or where did I keep it down here?"

Baddeley frowned. "What I mean is—where had you put it in your room—in your bedroom, I presume you mean. The room from where you say it has been taken?"

"There, Inspector, I must plead guilty to a certain amount of carelessness. When I unpacked my suit-case upon my arrival, I took the dagger out—among other things—and left it on the dressing-table. I intended to show it to Miss Massingham—one of my cast who is staying here. It was my intention to replace it in the suit-case later. But I forgot my intention and went down to dinner without it. When I went to bed later on all thoughts of the wretched thing slipped from my mind. It was not until this morning that I missed it."

The Inspector knitted his brows again. "So that—strictly speaking—you couldn't swear whether it was there on your dressing-table when you went to bed or not?"

Challoner tossed his head impatiently. "I suppose I couldn't, Inspector, and I know it's confoundedly careless of me. All the same I'm certain in my own mind that it could not have been there, and I'll tell you why. If it had been, I should have been bound to have seen it and I should have put it away in accordance with my original intention. I'm convinced that the fact of it *not* being there was the real cause of my temporary forgetfulness. It's like everything else of that kind, if the—"

Baddeley interrupted him. "Perhaps, perhaps not. But you can't prove that and it's waste of time trying to. Let's get on with the job, leave conjecture out of it and confine our attention to definite facts. Now one point about your story strikes me very forcibly. Did anybody know you had this dagger with you? You say that you didn't show it to this lady you mention."

Adrian Challoner drummed with his fingers upon the table in front of him. "I was afraid that you would ask me that question, Inspector, and I realize that I cannot blame you for doing so. Must I answer?"

Baddeley's face was set as he made his reply. "It is not in my power to bring any compulsion against you, Mr. Challoner, at this stage of the case, and I've no doubt that you know that very well. You must please yourself what you do. I imagine you will find it no new experience. But if your duty isn't plain enough for you to see in front of you—ignoring the fact of your friendship with Mr. Mordaunt here, which should make the call of duty even more imperative to you—well then all I can say—" The Inspector broke off abruptly and shrugged his square shoulders with a wealth of meaning.

Adrian Challoner, however, was not the man to be rattled by remarks of that sort. He was always the complete master of himself and Baddeley's insinuation was launched in vain against his unruffled imperturbability. When he next spoke he did so with as much dignity as ever before.

"Very well, Inspector Baddeley. I accept the position as you point it out to me. I will give you the information for which you have asked. There were three people in 'The Crossways' who knew that the dagger was in my bedroom. They knew because I told them. I use the past tense deliberately—you will understand why when you hear their names. It came about like this. We had made up a bridge four and the subject of my new play cropped up in conversation just as it had done at dinner an hour previously."

"Their names, if you please, Mr. Challoner," rapped Baddeley, all excitement.

"Mrs. Mordaunt, the lady who we believe has been murdered, Mr. Russell Streatfeild and Mrs. Lorrimer—this gentleman's mother."

"Nobody else?"

"Not to my knowledge, Inspector, unless of course my remarks were overheard which I don't think could have been the case," Challoner stated firmly.

Baddeley's next question was startling in the extreme. "Who is the author of your new play, Mr. Challoner? This murder play that you mentioned just now?"

Challoner eyed him with studied composure. "Why do you ask? What's the point?"

Baddeley scratched his cheek. "Just an idea, Mr. Challoner, that's all. You can never tell where you'll get by following up everything."

"I'm sorry then, Inspector, but I can't tell you. That's why it struck me that it was strange you should have asked. The play came to me from an agent—Surtees White, a well-known man—after having been previously tried out by the Thespian Society. The author's name as shown on the typescript is Essex Kent—but it is an open secret to all of the people who are concerned with it, that this is a *nom-de-plume*. There is a rumour, I may inform you, however, that the pseudonym covers the identity of a woman who is well-known on the Turf, but I do not know if reliance can be placed upon it."

"H'm, that doesn't get me very far, I'm afraid. Can you give me the address of this agent chap?"

"Quite easily. Nine, Portsmouth Walk, Covent Garden."

"Thank you." Baddeley produced his note-book and jotted down the information that Challoner had given him. After doing this he appeared to study something which had already found a place within his notes. Suddenly he looked up.

"Mr. Russell Streatfeild?" He pronounced the name as an inquiry and looked in the direction of Henry Mordaunt.

"A friend of mine, Inspector." Mordaunt's reply to the glance came at once. "He is staying here at my especial request."

"What is the gentleman by—er—profession, Mr. Mordaunt?"

"A solicitor, Baddeley, senior partner of Streatfeild, Hyde and Digby."

The words came fluently and smoothly enough but Baddeley's sharp ears detected something in Mordaunt's voice that was not quite normal. Was it his imagination or was Mordaunt for some reason chary with regard to passing on the required information? He determined to leave the matter fallow for the time being without, however, dismissing it from his mind altogether. There might come opportunities in the future for a successful re-opening. He referred again to his list and evidently found what he wanted.

"There is a Miss Christine Massingham staying at 'The Crossways' I believe, Mr. Mordaunt. The lady, I take it, is the one Challoner mentioned just now?"

"That is so, Baddeley. She is a friend of the Miss Ebbisham who is Mr. Challoner's god-daughter."

"Yes! I am aware of that fact. I've met the latter young lady very recently. Am I right in imagining from what Mr. Challoner said that these two young ladies are actresses—that is to say professional actresses?"

"Not altogether. Miss Massingham is an actress certainly, as Mr. Challoner informed you. Miss Ebbisham is not."

Challoner proceeded to amplify Mordaunt's answer. "Christine Massingham is resting at the present time, Inspector Baddeley. But she goes into the cast of my next play 'Sin and a Woman.'"

Baddeley's eyes opened wide. "That's very interesting, Mr. Challoner. Did this Miss Massingham know by any chance of the existence of this dagger of yours?"

"Miss Massingham certainly knew of the dagger's existence—she could hardly rehearse without knowing of it—but she equally certainly did not know that I had the dagger in my possession down here."

"Might *she* not have overheard what you say that you told the others? The slightest hint in her case would have urged her to connect matters."

"Christine Massingham was not in the room when I was playing bridge so there was no possibility of what you suggest." Challoner was decisive.

"I can vouch for that," put in Francis. "I saw her with Jane and Anne Ebbisham. They were going to have some music or something while your four were playing bridge."

"Very well, then, gentlemen," declared Baddeley, "I won't detain you any longer. Thank you, Mr. Challoner, for your information and you too, Captain Lorrimer. The problem that I have to solve is by no means a pretty or an easy one and it will take a lot of looking into. There are still several matters I want to attend to here so I'll arrange to call back in an hour or two's time. If convenient to you, that is, Mr. Mordaunt."

As Mordaunt nodded acquiescence, Baddeley made his exit and closed the door behind him. The uppermost thought in his mind as he made his way out was this: Not only had Mrs. Lorrimer known the secret of the shaving-soap but she was also one of three people who knew the facts of the dagger that Adrian Challoner had brought with him to "The Crossways." In other words, she fitted into both sides of an equation. Baddeley decided that the case as a whole was looking a little brighter.

CHAPTER IX

PETER DAVENTRY received the news of the murder of Mrs. Mordaunt with a sense of acute shock. Upon previous occasions when he had been concerned in the company of Anthony Bathurst with cases of a similar nature his association had been somewhat more indirect. He had, as it were, approached the matter from the outer circle. But in this instance he found himself actually within the circle when the crime had been committed, and this consciousness aroused certain feelings within him that he had previously not experienced and which he now found somewhat difficult to analyse satisfactorily. His first thoughts after the full realization of what had occurred had come home to him were naturally of Anthony Bathurst. This surely would be a case after old Bathurst's own heart! Francis Mordaunt, in the temporary absence of his father who was in consultation with Russell Streatfeild (and partly relieved no doubt from the oppression of horror and suspense by the opportunity of recital) had confided to most of the men of the house party at "The Crossways" the cardinal facts of the case as they had so far been elicited and would have proceeded to add more of the details had it not been for the advent upon the scene of Anne and Christine and his own two sisters. Peter Daventry scanned the faces of the four girls in order that he should be able to judge, if possible, of the effect which the sudden tragedy had produced upon each of them. Jane Mordaunt was pale and "nervy," but still retained that suggestion of quiet self-reliance that distinguished her almost invariably. Her sister Molly, the younger of the two of them was of the type that does not react to conditions of grief and horror with any strong degree of emotion unless the tragedy involved concerned her very intimately and absolutely directly. As the present sensation at "The Crossways" did not, she surveyed the situation with what can be perhaps best described as a kind of plaintive wonderment. She was intensely sorry that Cyril Lorrimer had lost his ring, and to do her justice, not so much because it would have been her ring but more on account of the fact that it was through her, in a way, that her lover had lost it. This gave her a feeling of part responsibility. She was well aware of the tremendous value he placed upon it and apart from this of the fervour with which he had always cherished it. It was much more difficult for her to understand completely that her stepmother was dead and that—according to popular belief—she had been murdered. As she considered all that had happened since last night Molly Mordaunt desired to be detached from the affair as much as possible, but, failing that, to be as close to her sister Jane as she could achieve. Anne Ebbisham, Peter decided, was not, upon this eventful morning, altogether free from worry. She always looked eminently delicious with her laughing vivacity and almost audacious charm, and this last-mentioned quality of her appearance had not deserted her now. The challenge still lurked in the dark-blue depths of her eyes and her delightful little nose had not lost its *soupçon* of aggressiveness but Mistress Anne was certainly not quite so "care-free" this morning as was her wont. It seemed to Peter Daventry as he watched her face that she was endeavouring to explain something to herself; that something was troubling her for which she was making continued and abortive attempts to discover a satisfying solution. But she was on guard and obviously had strict hold upon herself and also upon her feelings. All the same this look that Peter Daventry noticed made fugitive appearances upon her face and in Peter's secret opinion, only served to enhance her adorableness. Christine Massingham, more used than her companion to public ordeal and conditions of "nerve-strain," was perhaps the least affected of the four girls; that is to say outwardly. But inwardly she felt the dreadfulness of the situation as keenly as any. She loved

Beauty and beautiful things and her whole nature frowned with uncompromising finality upon wanton wickedness whenever it disturbed her enjoyment of this power of loving. As Peter's glance left the roguish charm of Miss Ebbisham—it must be conceded with some reluctance—and came to rest upon the more dignified loveliness of the inimitable Miss Massingham, he formed yet another opinion. If there were something that was puzzling the former lady—then most certainly this latter lady had noticed the fact just as he himself had done, for several times Christine had cast a swiftly penetrating look in the direction of her friend. Anne Ebbisham, unconscious of this, and as unconventional and daring as always, approached Adrian Challoner with the directness of habit and somewhat startled Peter Daventry with her opening remark. She had gone right up to her godfather.

"Mr. Challoner," he heard her say impetuously, "I don't want to seem or sound too utterly dreadful for anything, but there's something that I feel I must say to you. Let's try for the moment to forget about Mrs. Mordaunt. After all we shan't do her any harm if we do—shall we?" Her fingers worked nervously for a moment or two as she faced Challoner, and then she went on in a sudden burst of candour. "I'm not a callous cat—really I'm not—though I expert I sound like it and all of you are dotting me on the list as one. What I wanted to mention was my bet with you. It's perfectly awful, I know, that things should have turned out as they have—it seems like a judgment on some of us—but that isn't to say that we're very much to blame—is it? I said last night I'd call on you for the hundred in the morning— didn't I?" She surveyed him with vivid eagerness, commanding the attention of the whole group of onlookers as she did so. For a moment or so there was an intense silence. Challoner replied to her gravely.

"You did, Anne."

"Tell me," she said, as eagerly and as tensely as before, "I just heard Francis say that you've seen the Inspector—I haven't. Is 'Creeping Jenny' suspected? Does Inspector Baddeley think that—"

"Half a minute, Anne, half a minute!" Challoner curbed her impetuously with an uplifted hand. "Don't anticipate things too much. Before you go on any farther, let's understand where we are and what your question exactly means. You ask me if Baddeley suspects 'Creeping Jenny'—suspects her of what?"

Anne's reply came promptly and decisively. "Of the theft and the murder?"

Challoner's reply seemed to hold a tinge of coldness or at least so it sounded to Peter Daventry's ear.

"To 'suspect' 'Creeping Jenny' of the theft is surely some-what—er—tautological. It would be supremely ridiculous to entertain any other possibility. The Inspector has definite evidence to that effect. I am told 'Creeping Jenny,' with that lady's habitual courtesy and forethought, left her usual card behind in Captain Lorrimer's bedroom. The card, I may say, bore upon it the correspondingly usual message. Baddeley therefore does not need to be a super-sleuth to suspect the lady whom we have been discussing. With regard to the second half of your question, Anne—that relative to the murder of Mrs. Mordaunt, I'm afraid that I'm not in a position to tell you anything. I know nothing of Baddeley's suspicions. For all I know he may suspect any one of us." Challoner made the statement with an almost exaggerated nonchalance. But Anne Ebbisham to whom he had spoken seemed to pay no regard to its actual meaning or significance.

"I wasn't thinking about the murder so much," she said quietly. "I was concerned more with the robbery."

She stood there for a little while biting her lip and the look of puzzledom that Peter Daventry had detected on her face before returned for just a brief instant. Suddenly, however, she jerked up her head and looked at Challoner again.

"I'm not paying the bet that I seem to have lost—*yet a while*. I'm not being unsporting. I've an idea that's almost a—I'm going to claim—what is it you call it in banking—three days grace? For I'm not sure that 'Creeping Jenny' *did* steal the sapphire. Despite what Inspector Baddeley knows or even thinks he knows. Come, Christine, my cherub, for I feel that I'm wanting your companionship. It's not going to be good for me to be alone." She linked her arm in Christine Massingham's and the two of them walked off slowly.

Challoner commenced to quote. "One like the Rose when June and July kiss," but Peter let go a low whistle, as he watched them saunter away and the actor broke off to watch them likewise. But when the two girls were out of ear-shot Peter gave way to a sudden inclination.

Lorrimer, Adrian Challoner, Francis Mordaunt, John Raikes and his father were standing together in a group. Peter Daventry went up to them and addressed the first named.

"Lorrimer," he opened a trifle nervously, "Heaven knows I'm far from wanting to butt in on this business and when I do shove my oar in it's only from a strong desire to lend a helping hand, so to speak. I hope you realize that's so and all that. But are you open to receive suggestions, old man?"

Lorrimer showed signs of surprise but nodded in semi-acquiescence. "That's quite all right, Daventry. I understand what you mean. But what is it you want to say to me?"

"I was wondering if an idea of mine would find favour with you—that was all. I take it nothing would please you better than to get to the bottom of this affair. Apart from the loss of your sapphire, you see there's the other—"

Lorrimer broke in eagerly upon Peter's expression of opinion. "I shall leave no stone unturned to get to the bottom of it, Daventry—if it takes me all my time and best part of my money. You can rest assured on that. I feel—" He clenched his hands in emotion. "I can't tell you how I feel," he concluded.

"Good man—likewise good egg," returned Peter. "That's the kind of stuff I like to hear, because it clears the way so beautifully for what I'm going to say. Ever heard of Anthony Bathurst?"

"Bathurst?" Lorrimer wrinkled his brows interrogatively. "Bathurst? You're referring to the—"

"Crime-investigator—that's the chap. He's cleared up at least half-a-dozen cases that had Scotland Yard guessing properly and running round with their noses down to *terra firma*. I happen to know for an absolute fact that Sir Austin Kemble, the Commissioner of Police, simply swears by him and has called him in off his own bat for very awkward cases. One was the affair of the 'Peacock's Eye' at Seabourne. Remember it?"

Lorrimer nodded and the men round him moved their heads in support. Francis observed that his father and Russell Streatfeild had by now joined the company and were evidently listening attentively to what Peter Daventry was saying. The tall clean-shaven solicitor seemed keenly interested and spoke in an undertone to Henry Mordaunt. Peter Daventry, unobservant of his two additional hearers who stood some distance behind him, proceeded to supplement his suggestion.

"Well, it's like this—cutting a long story short—I'm a close, personal friend of Anthony Bathurst and I'm pretty certain that a word from me would induce him to take up this case for you, Lorrimer. I can assure you that you couldn't put it in better hands."

"This is tremendously good of you, Daventry. There's nothing that would please me better. As I told you just now I'll move heaven and earth to probe this mystery to the bottom. When do you think you could fix things? Is Bathurst in a position to—"

Before he could complete the question Henry Mordaunt took a step forward towards him. To the onlookers it seemed that he was not too well pleased with something. When he spoke, this impression was confirmed.

"I quite appreciate Daventry's offer, my dear Lorrimer, and also the spirit that prompted it. But if I may be allowed to say so, my own interest in this terrible affair is the paramount one. What I have lost can never be replaced. That I think would be conceded by anybody. I know that it would be by *you*, for it never occurs to me to doubt your generosity. That fact established, I must ask you then to consider my wishes before anybody's. I say emphatically, that I do not wish that a private investigator should take up the case. Certainly not at this juncture. Later on, if nothing transpires and the cloud still remains I might perhaps reconsider my attitude. I could not, however, even promise that, unconditionally." Mordaunt's voice was hard and his face a model of impassivity. "For the moment," he added very clearly and decisively, "I am very well content to leave the case in the hands of Inspector Baddeley. What do you say, Streatfeild?"

CHAPTER X

LORRIMER thrust his hands into his pockets and stared at the retreating figures. Eventually he shook his head and turned to Peter Daventry.

"Well, I'm afraid that's that, Daventry. When Mr. Mordaunt gets an idea of that kind into his head, he takes some moving. Take my word and there's not very much chance of shifting it. I could give you a ten-fold assurance on the point."

George Rakes nodded entire agreement. "Just what I was telling my son here. Henry Mordaunt in that mood is the last word in obstinacy. I've known him years and have seen him in this mood too often not to realize what it means. I can't understand his attitude. Though I should imagine, from what I've heard of the case, that Inspector Baddeley could do with all the help he can get. Particularly so—if it's in the nature of such skilled assistance as Mr. Daventry indicates." He gestured towards the man whom he named.

Peter grinned appreciatively. Mordaunt's abrupt reception of his proposal had at first annoyed him, but his natural resilience and buoyancy had very soon dismissed the sensation of annoyance and were bringing him back to himself again.

"I couldn't have put it better myself, Mr. Raikes, and although you said it unknowingly, I fancy, you're quite right about this Baddeley Johnny. He'd skip like a regiment of rams and young sheep combined if he thought Bathurst and he were going to work in double harness. The mountains and the little hills wouldn't have an earthly with him—and for the best of all reasons, too." Peter Daventry emitted a reminiscent chuckle as Raikes regarded him inquiringly. "Because I happen to know that the very first case old Bathurst handled was down in Sussex here and this self-same Baddeley was the Police Inspector in charge. He was eating out of Bathurst's hand by the time the final curtain came down. Don't think old Bathurst told me so—he's not that sort—I've had it from others who know what they're talking about." Peter shrugged his shoulders sagaciously. "Still—there you are—if Mr. Mordaunt won't budge in the matter—there's an end to it—it's no use talking about it any more. After all, as he pointed out to us just now, it's his pigeon and that being so he's entitled to handle it in his own way. I'm sorry, Lorrimer."

The man addressed shook his head slowly. "No need for you to apologize, Daventry. But I can't very well close with your offer in face of what was said, can I? Mr. Mordaunt may change his mind later on. If he does I hope your offer will still hold good. I certainly shan't forget it."

Later, in the privacy of his bedroom, Peter began to examine the various facts as Francis Mordaunt had presented them to him. He started at the beginning and marshalled them in some order. Mrs. Mordaunt had been found at the bottom of the old well wearing her evening cloak and with her handbag near to her; according to medical evidence stabbed through the heart, killed almost instantaneously. She had also, the evening before, been sufficiently interested in the safety of the famous Lorrimer sapphire to beg Captain Lorrimer to allow her to mind it for him during the night. Why? That was a poser. Disturbance on account of the threat from "Creeping Jenny"? If so—what kind of disturbance—ordinary, such as might be reasonably expected from anyone—or specially particular, arising from the possession of definite knowledge? Peter silently debated the two possibilities for a moment or two. Then Anthony Bathurst's oft-repeated maxim came home to him—"never commence to theorize in the absence of data." Its truth and effectiveness were more apparent to him now than they had ever been before, if only for the fact that on this occasion it was he himself who was in control of the thinking-machine. He determined to abandon the theoretical therefore and content himself for the present with a review of the facts and of the facts only. Surely, if Bathurst were here himself, he would concentrate for the time being upon the two "main" features of the case—"main," that is to say as far as investigations had by this time reached. These, Peter concluded, were the stealing of the "pukka" sapphire from Lorrimer and the theft of the dagger from the bedroom occupied by Adrian Challoner. Who among all the people at "The Crossways" had the necessary knowledge to be able to obtain either? That question appeared to him as the crux of the whole affair. Peter embarked upon a process of elimination affecting the two categories. Whom could he eliminate from (a) Knowledge of the authentic sapphire's hiding-place and (b) Knowledge of the existence even of Challoner's dagger? Not having been placed by Francis in possession of the whole of the evidence given by Captain Lorrimer and Adrian Challoner to Inspector Baddeley his adventure of embarkation finished very soon after it began. As far as he could see from the knowledge that he had at his command the only people whom he could fairly confidently place in his first category were Mrs. Lorrimer and Molly Mordaunt. Concerning the second, the only suggestion that his brain could harbour was that *possibly*—only *possibly*, mind—Christine Massingham had known that Challoner had brought down the dagger from the Ramillies Theatre to "The Crossways." It soon became clear to him that he could insert no one person into each of the two divisions. Out of which conclusion there certainly came no help! It seemed to him that he was very much as he had started. He was about to indulge in a further survey of the incidents of the case when there came a knock upon his bedroom door. To his invitation of "Come in" there appeared Henry Mordaunt and Inspector Baddeley. The latter appeared to be exceedingly preoccupied, but the host of "The Crossways" seemed eagerly alive to the exigencies that the case was going to demand from him. He had recovered somewhat from the shock of the first stroke that had been dealt him and was living now in a state of mental emotion—his mind, it might be said, under the potent influence of the drug of excitement.

"Daventry," he opened quickly, "Inspector Baddeley wants to have a word with you. He has seen all the others and desires to complete his round of inquiries as soon as possible. I am sorry to intrude upon you, but of course, you quite realize that in affairs of this—" Mordaunt stopped as though at a loss to continue.

Peter helped him out. "I understand, Mr. Mordaunt. Don't worry about that sort of thing. I've been expecting something of the kind. I shall be pleased to hear what the Inspector has to say. Chair, Mr. Mordaunt? Chair, Inspector?" Peter motioned the double invitation and each of the men accepted.

The Inspector's eyes sought those of Mordaunt. "Where is Mr. Streatfeild got to? He was very anxious to be present at the other interviews, why isn't he with us now? Is he one of those people that soon get tired?" There was a spice of resentful sarcasm in his tone. "Or does he exempt Mr. Daventry from the necessity of being interviewed?"

Mordaunt shook his head with a suggestion of cold annoyance. "I am sure I don't know and can't tell you. He has gone downstairs again, Baddeley. He informed me that he wished to have a look at something down there. I don't think that Mr. Daventry or your proposed interview with Mr. Daventry had anything to do with it for a moment. And I fail to follow you when you refer to such a thing as Mr. Daventry's exemption. I'll leave you to it."

Baddeley opened his mouth as though to reply to Mordaunt's statement but evidently thought better of his intention for he desisted as Mordaunt walked from the room. Instead he turned to Peter Daventry. "Just a few questions, Mr. Daventry—and the usual ones that fall to the lot of us police in matters of this kind. They're more or less a matter of routine, you know. Can you throw any light upon the murder of Mrs. Mordaunt?"

Peter shook his head slowly but very certainty. "I can't, Inspector, and that's a fact. Haven't the foggiest! As a matter of fact when you came in here just now I was trying to piece things up a bit without being at all successful, I can tell you. I've missed the turning properly. It seems to me you know—"

"Tell me this, Mr. Daventry. Were you with the deceased to any extent, during the last day or two? I mean, did you have much opportunity to observe if she were pretty normal, as it were? In her usual spirits and so on? Nothing happened, for example, to upset her in any way?"

Peter twisted his mouth to one side. "No, Inspector," he declared after due consideration. "No, I don't think so! Although perhaps—mind you, I only say 'perhaps'—"

"Perhaps what?" snapped Baddeley. "Please be as explicit as you can, Mr. Daventry."

The latter gentleman raised his hand in deprecation. "Hold hard, Inspector, don't rush me, and don't imagine things. I never was a five-furlong sprinter. Staying's my *forte*. The remark I was about to make has, I am afraid, a very minor significance. I was merely on the point of saying that on Monday last, I don't think that Mrs. Mordaunt was in quite such good spirits as had revealed themselves in her—shall we say—over the actual weekend. That was all. I think the fact may be said to have been *just noticeable* as you might say. Nothing more, I assure you."

Baddeley regarded him very seriously. "Can you cite a definite example of that?"

Peter pursed his lips. "Afraid I can't, Inspector. I thought you would have gathered that from what I told you. It was simply an impression that I got from Mrs. Mordaunt—nothing more. Perhaps I shouldn't have mentioned it, Inspector, only you asked me to—"

"Not at all, Mr. Daventry. You did quite right to mention it. It's the sort of thing I was after. I may inform you that it coincides to a certain extent with evidence that I have already received from another quarter. You have confirmed a statement that had already been made to me. If only for that, I regard it as valuable. There is nothing else, sir, that you feel you would like to tell me?"

"Nothing, Inspector. I'm a one-story wallah. I wish I could help you more." As Peter turned away from Baddeley the two men in the bedroom heard a medley of voices outside. One was undoubtedly Lorrimer's, the other Peter Daventry was unable immediately to recognize.

But evidently Inspector Baddeley did for he crossed the room with rapidity and pulled open the door. "What is it, Roper?" he queried. "Do you want me?"

The man addressed laboured under the stress of an excitement. His cheeks were flushed and his eyes alive with interest.

"Yes, Inspector. I asked this gentleman here to find you for me. Shall I come in?"

Baddeley nodded. Roper entered followed by Captain Lorrimer. Before Roper spoke he looked askance in the direction of the last-named.

"That's all right. You can speak before these gentlemen, Roper," explained Baddeley in answer to the look. "What is it you have to tell me? Out with it, man."

"Right, sir. In accordance with the orders you gave me and the others, a thorough search has been made at the bottom of the old well. There is no weapon to be found down there, Inspector—I'll go bail on that! Every inch of the ground has been turned over and been combed absolutely thoroughly. There's no weapon down there such as we've been seeking. But while we were looking for it we've found this, Inspector." He opened his hand and displayed a ring that held a huge blue stone. "This was down the well, Inspector, right away in one of the corners."

Lorrimer's eyes blazed with excitement as he stretched out his hand to take it. Baddeley nodded again to Roper and the man passed the sapphire over to Captain Lorrimer. They watched him eagerly as he took it and examined it. Then they saw him shake his head in disappointed discomfiture, and hold the ring for Baddeley to take.

"No luck, gentlemen," he announced with a touch of melancholy, "this is not the Lorrimer sapphire as I hoped that it might be. This is the imitation stone that I gave to Mrs. Mordaunt to look after last night. She must have taken it out with her when she went to meet her death. I fear, Inspector, that my theory's going to prove to be the right one after all."

CHAPTER XI

WHATEVER talents Mr. Russell Streatfeild may have possessed in the direction of strict veracity, they were certainly not overwhelmingly in evidence when he excused himself to Henry Mordaunt a short time previously. For the errand of importance which he had mentioned to Mordaunt and Mordaunt to Baddeley as requiring his immediate presence downstairs was entirely non-existent. That is to say one must suppose so, judging by his subsequent actions. For having quitted the company of Mordaunt and the inspector and having carefully watched them from a coign of vantage enter Peter Daventry's bedroom, Mr. Streatfeild quietly made his way *upstairs* again and slipped into another bedroom altogether. It happened to be the bedroom of his host. Passing quickly through the connecting door that has been described before, he next entered the bedroom lately occupied by the woman that had been murdered. Once inside he made straight for the dressing-table. Prominent in the front thereof were several articles of cosmetic significance and inseparable these days from a lady's *toilette*. There were lip-stick (chanel-red), hare's-foot, powder-bowl, rose-ochre, Rachel soleil, eyebrow pencil and tiny lash-brush. As they had been left, an investigator would have been pardoned had he formed the opinion that Mrs. Mordaunt had paid great pains towards the adornment of her complexion very shortly before she met her death. Russell Streatfeild nodded as though with a certain amount of satisfaction. He took from his pocket the torn corner of an envelope that had obviously passed through the hands of the Postal Authorities. It bore upon it three stamps—three halfpenny stamps over-marked with the usual date, time and place. Looking carefully round the room and at the same time listening intently he walked across to the grate and went down upon his knees in front of it. But to no purpose. The grate was innocent of everything that he hoped he might have found there. He thought carefully over what Henry Mordaunt had told him. He dared not stay long in the room in case Baddeley finished with Peter Daventry over-quickly and then chanced to take a stroll in this direction. That was the last thing he desired to happen. He ran his eye over the bed, gave the dressing-table another quick glance and slipped out of the room as adroitly and noiselessly as he had entered. His next operation was one that required the greatest possible care. Mr. Streatfeild descended one flight of stairs and came to the turn that led to the next. Here stood a superb statuette of Polyhymnia which Henry Mordaunt had had installed there many years previously out of compliment to the profession that had made him famous. As is usual with statues of the Muse of Eloquence she was shown holding her dainty forefinger to her equally dainty lip. The other hand, fingers upwards, was extended to the onlooker with an expressive gesture. Mr. Streatfeild approached the statuette and bent down to read the inscription upon its base. He thought he knew it but resolved to refresh his memory. "Apt Silence sets off Language to the best Advantage," he read. Once again he nodded, seemingly in enjoyable and even fastidious agreement, and then looked round about him almost stealthily. The coast was clear, he concluded. As far as he could judge there was no one whatever to be seen or heard anywhere near to him. He stood and listened for a moment. All was quiet. Mr. Streatfeild inserted the finger-tips of his left-hand into the corresponding pocket of his waistcoat and took out a key—in size, shape and general appearance an ordinary key of an ordinary door. This key he hung carefully upon the raised fingers of Polyhymnia and in the same second glided away silently and retraced his steps upstairs. "The Golden Silence is the Silence which is the Fruit of Patience," he murmured to himself. Outside Peter Daventry's door he paused and listened—for danger lurked for him inside. He could hear the voices of Peter himself, Henry Mordaunt, Inspector Baddeley and Captain Lorrimer. There was also another voice in occasional action which for the moment he failed to recognize. But when he heard the Inspector address it in reply as "Roper" he realized and understood that it must belong to the man who seemed to be Baddeley's chief assistant. Mr. Streatfeild smiled in satisfaction. The conference from what he could gather seemed to him to be almost in its initial stages. The eyes of the listening Mr. Streatfeild gleamed with adventurous excitement as he decided there and then to take another chance. A matter of a few seconds more saw him inside

Captain Lorrimer's bedroom, the door of which however he carefully left ajar.

"I'm on more certain ground in here, at least," he said to himself upon entry. "Mrs. Mordaunt's bedroom may shed little light upon her murder—its actual relationship to it may very possibly be insignificant—but *here was the sapphire*—the Lorrimer sapphire—from here it was taken—why on earth wasn't I more careful last night—" His meditations ceased abruptly as he glanced quickly round the room. Facing the bed was the dressing-table. On the left of the dressing-table was a large basket-chair. The only other article of furniture of any size was the great carved wardrobe on the left of the entrance door, standing almost flush with the wall. An idea struck Mr. Russell Streatfeild as he stood there and as a result thereof he took another rapid glance at the land outside and then he tiptoed across the room to the wardrobe. He opened the doors as though about to venture upon an experiment but shook his head decisively and quickly shut them again. Walking round to the side of the big wardrobe he peered behind it. Then he tried to squeeze his body between the wardrobe and the wall. It was impossible. All the same, he considered, that wasn't to say necessarily that a feat impossible physically for him was impossible for everybody. He was a tall man and well-made, in addition to his height. A smaller man might find the attempt well within his power—much more so a slimmish girl or woman. He put his shoulder to the piece of furniture and with a steady heave shifted it slightly from its previous position. Was he mistaken or did the dullish line of almost invisible dust that the wall behind bore as a result of the wardrobe's proximity show signs of a recent slight disturbance? He looked carefully at what he fancied he saw and even as he did so something at the back of the heavy wardrobe caught his eye. On a small projecting splinter of dark wood such as constantly adorns these articles of furniture there was caught a tiny wisp of flimsy something. Russell Streatfeild bent down with extreme care and with thumb and forefinger gently removed it. It was a minute piece of filmy biscuit-coloured lace. He knew now what he had very much desired to know. Captain Lorrimer's bedroom ceased to interest him. He replaced the wardrobe and as he pulled the door of the room quietly behind him his thoughts turned to Inspector Baddeley. Should he inform the Inspector of what he had discovered behind the wardrobe? Or not? Perhaps it would be safer from his own point of view if he kept his own counsel. It might prove awkward if Baddeley got to know certain other things as he very well might if he were informed of this. Streatfeild pictured the unsuspecting Lorrimer watched from behind the wardrobe as he had put away his precious sapphire in its cunning hiding-place! Watched by whom? If he could answer that question it would solve perhaps more problems than one. Mr. Streatfeild rubbed his cheek with his finger. He cast his mind back to the evening before the murder. His reflections were sartorial. Could he remember the dresses of the various ladies? He had always prided himself upon the accuracy of the power of his visualization. Anne Ebbisham had worn a dainty frock of pale pink georgette with a deepish cascade at the waist line. Jane Mordaunt's frock had been a very attractive sleeveless pearl grey crêpe-de-chine embroidered with linked circles of a light canary yellow. "Not bad for a mere man," said Russell Streatfeild to himself. "I don't know whether my descriptions would pass muster in a Society weekly but that's how they appeared to me at any rate. 'Twill serve my purpose at the moment." Who else of the ladies was there? Five more he counted. Mary Considine, Molly Mordaunt, Christine Massingham, Mrs. Lorrimer and Olive Mordaunt herself. Even she could not be eliminated in this connection. Miss Considine had worn a frilly sort of skirt with rows of pleated tulle (he thought the stuff was) and Molly Mordaunt a sort of beige taffeta, with a pronounced "dip" at the back and—! Lace to intensify the dip! Yes—that was undoubtedly so! He must remember that. Now for the others that remained. Mrs. Lorrimer had been attired as became her years, in black velvet, Christine Massingham with an eye no doubt to her dark hair and creamy skin had worn very pale green—realizing that pale neutral tints and clear cold colours heightened her very definite allurement—while Mrs. Mordaunt herself had worn the frock in which she had been found dead. Streatfeild had seen it. It was entirely innocent of lace of any kind. Only Molly then could be definitely placed in the lace category. And Molly was Lorrimer's fiancée! As far as he could see she, least of all, had occasion to covet possession of the Lorrimer sapphire for it had been given to her. What reason could she have to steal it? He made his way from the bedroom stealthily, pondering over the situation as it now presented itself to him. On the whole it had changed somewhat, for his clandestine investigations had yielded a good deal. He had seen what he wanted to see in Olive Mordaunt's bedroom—he had discovered something highly important in the bedroom from where the sapphire had been stolen, and best of all he had very cunningly disposed of that tell-tale key! For he had felt very uncomfortable all the time that he had retained it in his possession. If Baddeley had discovered the fact—Mr. Streatfeild smiled grimly to himself. He had been exceedingly foolish, he told himself, to have retained it for so long as he had—and shook his head gently. As he did so he nearly collided with the gentleman whom he had just been considering. Evidently the conference in Peter's bedroom had terminated, for the Inspector was walking fast, obviously bound at once for another destination.

CHAPTER XII

"CHRISTINE, my very beautiful one—sharer of my chintz-curtained bedroom and fellow-artiste," murmured Anne Ebbisham, following upon her interview with Adrian Challoner that has been described, "I am tempted to doff my bonnet." She patted her hair.

"Doff your bonnet?" queried Miss Massingham with uplifted eyebrows. "Explain, darling, do."

"In recognition of true and undoubted worth, my sweet! 'You're a better man than I am—"Creeping Jinn."'" Miss Ebbisham quoted her atrocious parody with delicious nonchalance. But for all that—and despite her consummate ease—a discerning observer would have detected something other than

nonchalance in her tone. Anne's puzzle was not yet solved satisfactorily.

"What do you mean, Anne, really and truly?" Christine knitted her brows and her eyes were full of her question.

"I mean just this, my pet of the Harem. You heard what
Cyril Lorrimer said last night at dinner, didn't you? You heard
of his precautions for keeping his sapphire—and you heard me
make my bet that Jane the Serpentine would be an also ran if
she entered for that particular Handicap. I thought I was on a
good thing, Christine; for frankly I was very sceptical indeed of
'Jenny' pulling the deal off in a house like this and under those
conditions. *Yet it appears that she has done it!* Therefore I
elevate my toque. *Comprends-tu?*"

Christine's answer was not what Miss Ebbisham had
expected.

"Anne," she said quietly, but very directly, "you're rattled.
I've never seen you quite like this. 'Creeping Jenny's' getting on
your nerves, my girl! You're worried over it."

Anne Ebbisham knocked the ash from the end of her cigarette
and extended the hand that held it. The gesture was almost regal.
"Look at that hand, my child. And mark it well. Does it shake or
is it tremulous? No? Where then are those nerves of which our
Christine speaks? I am still Anne, one hundred per cent."

She was coolness personified. But Christine Massingham
refused to be shaken off by her attitude. She reiterated her statement. "I don't care about that. I'm positive I'm right and I'm
positive something's worrying you. I've noticed it for hours now.
You may be able to bluff old Baddeley, Anne, but you certainly
won't bluff Christine."

Miss Ebbisham's eyes flashed as she shot a glance at her
companion. "Over-confident, aren't you, O Beauty of the Chorus?
To call you a super-optimist would be hopelessly inadequate.
The bright young friend of mine who makes it his practice to
find 'the first three' in a big race with a fork, having graduated
from the first stage of winner-finding with the common household pin, pales into insignificance beside you, my world-beater."
Miss Ebbisham dropped her banter suddenly and found a new

seriousness. "Apropos of what you're saying though, Christine, has it occurred to you that murder's been done here while we slept; that our hostess of all people has come to a most horrible death? It isn't exactly a stupefying surprise therefore that I should be a bit jumpy, is it? I'm not used to having my friends stabbed or thrown down wells." Christine opened her lips as though about to reply, but then changed her mind and closed them again. Anne noticed the hesitation and according to her habit came at once to the challenging point. Miss Ebbisham usually saw her objective and went straight to it regardless of ordinary obstacles. "Well, what were you going to say, Christine?" Miss Massingham ran her forefinger along the lace square that did duty as her handkerchief. Then she shook her head dubiously. "I don't think I'll say it, Anne. After all I'm only judging by—"

Miss Ebbisham's interruption was very definite. "You certainly *will* say it, Christine, whatever it was! You aren't going to arouse my curiosity like that and then coldly ring off. Not in these cami-knickers! What was it, my angel?"

Christine Massingham looked straight in her companion's eyes. But she could read nothing in them to cause her to alter the opinion that she had formed. "As you please, then, Anne. Have it your own way. It may as well come out now as later. What I was about to say was this. It isn't Mrs. Mordaunt's murder that has made you 'nervous,' it's something else."

"Really, Christina! Aren't you perfectly marvellous?" Miss Ebbisham's *sang froid* was by now a little too overwhelming to be sincere. She helped herself to another cigarette, but this time the hand that took it wavered a trifle. "And upon what particularly dazzling exercise of the science of deduction do you base that statement?"

"Don't be sarcastic, Anne," replied Christine. "It doesn't suit you. Remember you asked for my statement and you got it. So don't be unsporting about it. And it wasn't anything brilliant on my part either—come to that. For you were 'nervy' and 'rattled' first thing this morning; some time before you knew about Mrs.

Mordaunt's murder. I noticed it when you were dressing. Well, how now—my child?"

Anne grimaced to hide her discomfiture. The twin devils of mischief danced in her eyes, for she never knew defeat till the whistle. She made a last attempt to defend the position that she had taken up.

"Oh," she declared lightly, "so it's Christine of the Ever-Open Optics, is it? And such beautiful ones at that. What a gorgeous stroke of luck for all the boys in the world. How I wish the fairies would change my sex for me. But how does our Christine of the Secret Service know when I first heard of Mrs. Mordaunt's murder? I await her statement thereon."

Christine kept steadfastly to her course. "I presume that you heard of it at the same time that we all did. When Francis brought in the news! You were with me then; we were standing together in the morning-room. How is it possible for you to have known of it before? To have done so could only mean one thing, that you—"

Anne Ebbisham laughed. "Of course, of course. I'd forgotten that. I'll be good and confess nicely. I can see now it's the only thing for me to do. It wasn't the murder of Mrs. Mordaunt that put me on edge. It's something else. I say '*it is*' because I'm still like it." She lowered her voice considerably as she approached the kernel of her confession. "Have you noticed, Christine, that this 'Creeping Jenny' person—whoever she or he is—seems to be following us about? Or *me* to be more exact and truthful."

Christine nodded gravely but with evident composure. "I have noticed it lately, Anne, I admit. But I can't remember all the early cases in which 'Creeping Jenny'—"

"Listen, cherub," cut in Anne using her fingertips in emphasis, "I was at old Grantham's when 'Creeping Jenny' bumped off his diamond tie-pin, and I was at Flora Medlicott's when the pearl necklace vanished. Played two—won two! Don't you remember I wrote to you about each of the cases?"

"Perfectly, Anne, and I've thought of it many times since. I was resting at the time those two happened. What came after them? Can you remember?"

Miss Ebbisham wrinkled her dainty forehead, before proceeding to her next finger. "Then came the affair at the Midwinters' when the diamond pendant was stolen; then the Topham-Garnett robbery—earrings, wasn't it; and after that the business at Cranwick Towers last week. Now I'm in the thick of it again."

"So am I," said Christine, "come to that! I've been with you on the last four occasions, remember! So that I can claim almost equally with you to have been—"

"Don't be feeble, Christine," returned Miss Ebbisham aggressively. "Pull yourself together. I'm on the bill every time. Jolly old Roast Beef and Yorkshire! The gladsome Baddeley can go right through the card with me; 'never absent, never late.' It's like taking money from a blind man. That's what's been whanging the grey matter about this morning, if you must know. You can't get away from it; I must be Balm in Gilead to a really bright detective—money for chocolate—a sitting pheasant—a miner's dream of home—a—"

Suddenly her tone changed as though a new idea had taken hold of her. "Christilinda, my Queen of the Eastern Sea, has anything struck you about what I have just been saying?"

"Don't know that it has, Anne. What's the idea now?"

"I can see a ray of hope. The blue sky is peeping through. I've just thought of something very strange, my chee-ild, and also very peculiar."

"Let's hear it, then."

"Well, it's just occurred to me that I am not the *only* pebble on the foreshore! I am *not* the *only* soap-sud down the sink. I am not—"

"My dear Anne," expostulated Miss Massingham, "don't be so frightfully cryptic. Explain yourself—do."

"That's exactly what I am doing, my sweet. Can't you see what I'm getting at? I am not the *only* Chili in the jar of Piccalilli—there are three others who have been present on every occasion when the ubiquitous 'Jenny' has crept abroad. The honours are divided. Dost realize that, my Pride of the Circus?"

Christine frowned. "Three others?" she questioned.

"Three! The Mordaunt Trinity—Francis, Molly and Jane. Yet not one Mordaunt, but three Mordaunts! I'd forgotten all about them! So after all I may only be Baddeley's alternative selection—'if absent—Anne Ebbisham' just an each-way proposition—he may only have a 'to place' bet on me."

She rocked herself to and fro. "That's a comforting thought, Christine, that is. A very comforting thought, my pet. I feel a wee bit better and brighter. Things may not be so bad as I was imagining they might be."

"Anne," asserted Miss Massingham with a distinct touch of severity, "you're talking a lot of 'punk.' You're just babbling. Think—think—think! There were mud-stains in Lady Craddock's room. Don't you remember what the detective said—the rugs showed them unmistakably—and besides the glass of the bedroom window had been broken. Those burglaries were all done by a professional thief working on the outside. I'll bet that with my trifling knowledge of the cases. When the truth comes eventually to be discovered—if, of course, it ever is—you'll find that 'Creeping Jenny' is a well-known cat-burglar or something working these 'coups' under another name. And no doubt it's all a matter of putting the police off the scent. You see if I'm not right. I don't know much about this sort of thing, but I'm confident I'm correct here." Christine grew quite heated in the development of her suggestion.

"Perhaps, lovely; perhaps not. I wouldn't bet on it myself, confident though you say you are, Christine. Now I'm going to surprise you again. Do you know what I've been thinking?"

"Oh Lord—you're a perfect devil for holding things, MacEbbisham. Tell me straight out and have done with it."

"This," replied Anne very deliberately. "'Jenny' might conceivably be substitute for 'Jane'—don't you think? Nothing wildly improbable in the idea, is there? Ever thought of it yourself?"

Christine whistled and the action gave her lips an adorable archness. "Hop away, Anne—hop away! Jane Mordaunt? I can't stand for that—it's incredible. Hand me out something better—do!"

"Idiot," retorted Miss Ebbisham. "I didn't actually accuse Jane Mordaunt, did I? Don't put words into my mouth."

"There's never any need to, Anne darling," put in Christine sweetly, "you're never tongue-tied, are you? But that's what I read into your remark. What else did you mean if you didn't mean that?

"Nothing," came Miss Ebbisham's short reply—"all I meant was that 'Jenny' was short for Jane."

"Really?" returned Christine. "You surprise me—is that so—really *short*?"

Miss Ebbisham's cushion was well and truly thrown. "Well 'long' then, you tantalizing fathead."

CHAPTER XIII

INSPECTOR Baddeley looked carefully at the dead woman's bag as Roper held it out to him, and thought over what had just been said.

"I think I can see what you mean, Roper," he remarked at length. The bag was cream colour in moiré with a gilt catch on each side to open.

Roper pointed to the two catches. "Those stains are undoubtedly blood stains, sir," he announced. "I've seen Doctor Elliott and shown them to him, and he says there's no possible doubt about it. When the bag came from the bottom of the well it was dirty as you know and it was extremely difficult for anybody to say what the marks were. They might have been caused in several ways. But I cleaned it up a bit and scraped some of the dust off and then I could see that these stains here were different. It seems to me, sir," said Roper waxing unusually eloquent and warming to his subject, "that the point is that there are no others like 'em anywhere else on the bag. See what I mean, sir?"

Baddeley looked at him searchingly. "Roper, you'll make a detective yet; you're a credit to your mother and the Force," he declared. "I think I see where you're driving. But go on. Let me hear some more. Let me see if I'm thinking the same way as you are."

Roper flushed with pleasure at his superior's praise, for Inspector Baddeley was not a man who distributed bouquets lavishly or indiscriminately.

"Well, sir," he said, "what struck me then was this. It's a strange thing that the only stains of blood on this handbag should be on the catches that you use to open it. If the poor lady had the bag with her when she was attacked and held it during the sort of struggle that must have taken place when she was murdered you would expect to find blood stains, *if there were any at all, mind you,* splashed on the bag as you might say anywhere and everywhere, sort of all over the place! But these stains are evenly distributed—if you can say that they are distributed at all. They're round about and on *each catch* and nowhere else. Have you got me, sir?"

Baddeley nodded. "Good—and what do you deduce from that, Roper?"

Roper screwed his face up as an indication possibly of methods embracing the policy of Safety First. Habits are hard to break! "Don't know that you can call it deduction, sir. That's putting it a bit too high. Seems to me it's more like ordinary common sense. But what I do think is that somebody—in all probability, Mrs. Mordaunt's murderer—opened the bag by using the two catches and then threw the bag down the well. Seems to me it's much more likely that the murderer had blood on his hands than Mrs. Mordaunt and that it was he who touched the catches—and not she."

"I was too quick to praise you a moment ago. You're still in the goose stage after all. You ought to know well enough, Roper, that Mrs. Mordaunt's hands and fingers have no blood stains on them. That was one of the first things I looked for when we recovered her body from the well. I made sure that you noticed me."

Baddeley cupped his chin in his hands and looked fixedly at the handbag again. Roper, shrugging his shoulders under the implied reproach but by no means discouraged thereby, came back to his original point and the opinion he had put forward with regard to it.

"That means then, sir, when it's all boiled down, that you're inclined to hold in with my theory?"

"Oh yes—come to that, Roper, I am. Not that you've given me anything fresh to think about. As a matter of fact it fits in rather with an idea of my own; an idea that I had already formed about the manner of the lady's death. Have a look at these, will you, Roper?" The Inspector took from his pocket his note-book and from the leaves of his note-book the few pieces of charred paper that he had picked up on the grass near to the well. He held them out to his subordinate in the palm of his hand. "I picked these up close to the scene of the murder. How about the idea that there were papers in this handbag that Mrs. Mordaunt carried? That these were documents affecting or possibly incriminating 'Creeping Jenny' and that she was murdered for possession of them and not for the dud sapphire as was supposed? How does that strike you, Roper?"

Roper nodded. "Shouldn't be surprised if you're right, sir! It certainly would appear to fit the case and the circumstances."

"If that's so, then, Roper," continued Baddeley, waxing enthusiastic as his theory began to assume more definite shape, "the question arises—did Mrs. Mordaunt keep an assignation with somebody? That is to say—purposely—deliberately. The odds are very much in favour—seeing the time, how she was dressed and assuming she carried what we suggest she did. Did she know the identity of 'Creeping Jenny'; did she suddenly find it out, perhaps; or did somebody else, by chance, discover who 'Creeping Jenny'—" Baddeley came to an abrupt stop. Then, as the new idea took hold of his imagination, "By Jove, Roper," he almost whispered, "that's a very different idea—that is—still—all the same—"

"What is, sir?" inquired Roper with dutiful respect and becoming appreciation. The Inspector frowned and then shook his head.

"Wait, Roper; wait. Perhaps I'll tell you in a day or two; that is if things go as I hope they will."

"You're fairly optimistic then, sir?" questioned Roper again. "You're on to something?"

Baddeley smiled enigmatically. "I wouldn't say that, Roper; I wouldn't go as far as to say that at this stage of the case. I've been at the game too long to build castles. But this talk that we've just had together has set me thinking and it's just on the cards that I may have been able to put two and two together." He rubbed the ridge of his jaw with his fingers. "I'm not going to tell you everything I'm thinking, Roper, but there's no reason as far as I can see why I shouldn't tell you some things. For instance, here's a piece of information that's by way of being news to you. I called at this very house—'The Crossways'—days before the murder. You didn't know that, did you? That's a surprise for you, my boy, isn't it?"

Roper's eyes opened in plain incredulity. "You called—"

"Ay, Roper. I interviewed Mr. Mordaunt himself. You weren't aware of that, were you?"

"I don't understand even now, sir," contributed Roper sturdily. "I don't quite see what the idea is that you're trying to—"

Baddeley embarked on an explanation. "As you know, Roper, I was put on to the 'Creeping Jenny' business after the robbery occurred at Sir Gilbert Craddock's place—the people at Lewes hoofed me into it at his request—and certain facts which came to my notice over at Cranwick made me call here. Made me have a chat with Mr. Mordaunt. An interesting little chat it was too. Then, by Moses, there comes another 'Creeping Jenny' business in the very house where I've just called—followed by a murder! A damn funny coincidence, Roper; say what you like about it. Funny if my call fanned the flames, what?"

Roper stared at the Inspector fixedly. The fascination of the idea that Inspector Baddeley had propounded to him was beginning to grow in his brain as well. He licked his lips and was surprised to find how dry they were. An ordinary constable has enormous advantages over a "plain-clothes" unless, of course, he's a member of the local Band of Hope and at that precise moment the arid Roper remembered the fact.

"You mean, sir," he commenced, but Baddeley's eagerness and interest in his theory prevented Roper completing the sentence.

"I mean this, Roper"—Baddeley's hand came down heavily on the table in front of him in emphasis of his statement—"that the key to the 'Creeping Jenny' business lies here in 'The Crossways' and this last affair has brought matters to a climax. I'd lay a guinea to a gooseberry that somebody else discovered the fact and that's why—"

"They murdered Mrs. Mordaunt?" Roper was unable to restrain himself. The words leaped to his lips.

Baddeley eyed him steadily, and the look had a touch of queerness and even of reproach about it.

"I didn't say so, Roper. I wasn't going to say so, even. Other things happened in this house on the fatal night besides the murder of Mrs. Mordaunt. Remember her strange, almost unaccountable apprehension about the safety of this Lorrimer sapphire? Why on earth should she be so anxious about 'Creeping Jenny' *unless she knew something*, or, on the other hand, unless—" He paused, reflecting on the various points of the case as he marshalled them in his mind. "But that's my secret, Roper—for the time being at any rate."

Roper's disappointment at the Inspector's abrupt termination was manifestly acute. But he made one more attempt to fathom Baddeley's opinion.

"Tell me one thing, sir. What's your real idea? Is this 'Creeping Jenny' person a woman as she makes out to be—*or a man*? That's the point I can't make up my own mind over, sir, because one or two features of all the affairs in which she's been concerned don't seem to tally with what I might call my idea of 'femininity'—don't you agree, Inspector? After all a woman's a woman and when she—"

Baddeley shook his head. "I am not satisfied *myself* yet. But 'femininity,' as you call it, Roper, is a darned peculiar thing." The Inspector laughed reminiscently. "I knew a woman who was elected an Alderman on her local Council. She was so full of the triumph of her sex as she called it that she swore she'd eventually live to be Mayor of the Borough and nominate her old man as Mayoress—to teach him his place, so she said."

"Did it come off?" queried Roper.

"No," said Baddeley laconically. "It came unstuck."

"Why?"

"The old man taught her something instead. She resigned her seat in less than six months."

"What made her do that?"

"Twins—although she didn't know there were two of 'em when she resigned."

Roper chuckled at the Inspector's pleasantry.

"All the same," went on Baddeley, "coming back to our little discussion, there's one gentleman in 'The Crossways' giddy throng that puzzles me considerably." He drummed with his fingers on the table. "I can't quite get him or his business and inquiries in his direction don't help me. Quite the reverse, in fact—they tend rather to increase my suspicions."

"Who is the man?"

"Mr. Russell Streatfeild," returned Inspector Baddeley quietly.

Roper nodded slowly. "I'm listening, sir."

"Yes, Roper, Mr. Russell Streatfeild causes me a certain amount of wonderment and—I may as well admit it—uneasiness. In the first place—what is he, Roper?"

"I understood, sir, that he was a solicitor—an old friend of the Guv'nor—Mr. Mordaunt."

"That is the story that is told me, Roper. But here's rather a curious fact. Bennett, the gardener, who expanded wonderfully under the influence of a little flattery regarding his horticultural efficiency, has been in the Mordaunts' service for just on eleven years, so he tells me. But although Streatfeild is represented by Mr. Mordaunt as an old friend—Bennett tells me *that he has never seen him before*! Funny, don't you think, Roper, that this old crony—you've seen how thick they are—Mordaunt and Streatfeild are always together—has never stayed at 'The Crossways' before? What do you think yourself?" Baddeley rubbed his hands and continued. "Now a second point—take the solicitor part of the question. Russell Streatfeild is certainly not old Mordaunt's own solicitor, that is to say in the sense of transacting his legal business. I've made it my business to establish that fact and also to find out incidentally who is. I put an inquiry or two—round Cranwick and district—discreet inquiries of course, Roper—and I have discovered that Henry Mordaunt's solicitor is Reuben Oldershaw of Lewes. You know the man I mean—his place is at the end of the High Street. Oldershaw has been solicitor to the Mordaunt family for two generations. Mrs. Raikes, one of the ladies staying here, happens to have been a Miss Oldershaw; she's the sister of this Reuben Oldershaw."

Roper nodded again. "I'm beginning to see things a bit clearer. It's all of a piece."

"It is, Roper—and I haven't finished yet. There's a third point about Russell Streatfeild still to come. According to Mr. Mordaunt, Streatfeild is a partner in a firm called 'Hyde, Streatfeild and Digby.' I'm certain that they were the names I had given to me. But when I casually inquired where their place of business was, Mordaunt told me 'London'—just that—vaguely—no more. Quite a small place, I believe—London. But I didn't press him for any more information at the time. I decided to wait a bit longer and go into the matter again myself. Well, Roper my boy, I've already done a bit of nosing round and I can tell you this. *There's no such firm as 'Hyde, Streatfeild and Digby' to be found in any London directory.* Therefore, friend Roper, I find myself saying—'what's this gentleman's game?' Also incidentally—what is Mordaunt's game?"

"Not without reason," concurred Roper. "It's certainly a thing that wants a bit of looking into; sifting, so to speak. You can't do too much sifting in cases of this kind. The bloke that I was under up in the North was a fair devil for it. He'd go so far as—"

"That's what I'm going to do; also have a look round the history of the first Mrs. Mordaunt and then the antecedents of the second Mrs. Mordaunt; the one that's been killed. I can't get it out of my head that there's a lot about her that wants explaining." Baddeley walked to the door and opened it to find Mitchell the butler on the point of knocking.

"I beg your pardon, Inspector, but Mr. Mordaunt would like to see you in the library at once. He sent me to tell you so, Inspector."

Baddeley frowned as he considered the message. "Is he alone?"

"No, Inspector. Mr. Streatfeild, Mr. Francis and Captain Lorrimer are with him."

"Any idea what he wants me for?"

"No, Inspector."

"Very well. Take me to your master, will you?" When the Inspector entered the library, Mordaunt was seated with Russell Streatfeild and Captain Lorrimer on either side of him. Francis Mordaunt was standing. Mordaunt's greeting to Baddeley was ready and rapid.

"Something very strange has come to light, Inspector. My son here has just discovered it. Come this way, will you, Baddeley?"

Mordaunt beckoned him out of the room, the others following on his heels. The K. C. led the way up the main staircase.

"Bedrooms," thought Baddeley to himself. "Mrs. Mordaunt's in all probability—that's where we're bound for."

But he was mistaken. On a turn of the staircase Mordaunt stopped and turned dramatically in the direction of the Inspector. "Do you mind looking at this, Inspector Baddeley? For I have no doubt that you will find it extremely interesting."

Inspector Baddeley found himself gazing at the hand of the silently-eloquent Polyhymnia. But his own silence was of the ordinary variety—for the very reason that at the moment words failed him.

CHAPTER XIV

RECOVERY soon came to him. "Where the hell did that come from?" he demanded pointing to the key.

"I wish I could tell you, Baddeley. My own curiosity would like that question answered as much as yours. But what do you make of it?"

Baddeley ignored Mordaunt's question and took the key from the fingers of the statuette. "Who did you say called your attention to it—your son?"

"Yes, Inspector, my son. Would you care to ask him any questions about it? He's here to answer them should you consider it necessary. I told him to come along with us."

The Inspector examined the key with great care. "I suppose you are quite aware what this key is, Mr. Mordaunt?" he asked.

The man addressed eyed his questioner steadily. "I think I know what you mean, Inspector, but I haven't actually tested it yet. But I take it that this key is the key of my wife's bedroom door. Personally I haven't the shadow of a doubt about it."

"Exactly what I think myself, Mr. Mordaunt. And to find it on the fingers of this stone image fairly beats the band. There's somebody in this house here trying to pull the wool over my eyes. Somebody who thinks he's damned smart." He turned to Francis Mordaunt. "Do I understand that you discovered this business, sir?"

Francis nodded rather negligently. "That is so, Inspector. I imagined that my father had made that clear to you. I must say that *I* understood what he said."

"H'm! When did you first discover the key?" Francis Mordaunt consulted his wrist watch with an exaggerated assiduity.

"Approximately a matter of half-an-hour ago, Inspector. A little less, if anything."

"Did you happen to be walking upstairs at the time or coming down?"

The young man looked at Baddeley curiously. "I was going upstairs, Inspector Baddeley, and my birthday's on the seventeenth of October. My favourite flower's the gardenia."

"Thank you for the information, Mr. Mordaunt, and there's no call for a gibe on your part, either. I had a reason for my question—though perhaps your intelligence didn't realize the fact."

A spot of colour burned in each of Baddeley's cheeks while Francis Mordaunt whitened under his usual tan. The latter seemed to be on the point of replying but his father, seeking to pour oil on troubled waters, summarily checked him with raised hand.

"Confine yourself to answering the Inspector's questions as they are put to you, Francis, please! We have many more things to do than to indulge in recriminations or criticism of one another." Francis plunged his hands into the pockets of his trousers and stuck out a determined jaw. But he said nothing.

Baddeley returned to the attack. "I'm perfectly certain that earlier in the morning this key was not where you recently found it. For the very good reason that if it had been I should have seen it myself. I used this staircase on several occasions this morning and I'll go bail this heathen lady—Polly Hymn-Book or whatever her name is—wasn't playing St. Peter *then*. So therefore that key's been placed there since this morning and the person that put it there is very likely still in the house and in all probability Mrs. Mordaunt's murderer." He looked at the group of men to whom he ventured the statement with an odd touch of defiance. "If any one of you gentlemen that's with me now is able to help me in any way—if only by the merest trifle—may I ask you to do so in any circumstances? Any reticence and withholding of vital knowledge will mean me working under a very heavy handicap. I appeal to you, one and all." His eyes rested on Russell Streatfeild as he spoke and he saw at the same time that Captain Lorrimer had noticed it and was watching Streatfeild as intently as he was. But Streatfeild, seemingly unconscious of the two scrutinies, gave no sign and the Mordaunts also maintained silence. Baddeley made a last attempt. "I'm quite aware, gentlemen, that it's unlikely that anybody among us here knows anything about this key business. At the same time it's very evident that there's somebody in the house that does, and it's possible that one of you may suspect that somebody. I know quite well you gentlemen's ideas of what you call 'playing the game.' You're all a bit tight-lipped when it comes to a question of what you consider is 'telling tales.' I took the *Boys' Own Paper* for years when I was a boy and revelled in Talbot Baines Reed, so I think I can honestly say that I know what I'm talking about and I understand how you feel. Granted all that, however—there's another side to the question if you'll allow me to say so."

Mordaunt answered him immediately. "Rest assured, Inspector, that each one of us here is only too anxious to help you all he knows how. I can assure you, too, that Captain Lorrimer intends to leave no stone unturned to recover his jewel and I will avenge the murder of my wife if it takes me years to do it. So rely on each one of us, Baddeley."

"Very good, sir. I'll work on that understanding." Baddeley turned away from Mordaunt. "Oh, while I think of it, sir, could you give me your address in town, sir? I fancy Mr. Mordaunt did give it to me a day or two ago but I've been careless and mislaid it?" Baddeley made a pretence of searching through his pockets. His request was addressed to Russell Streatfeild.

"In town?" queried the solicitor casually.

"Yes, sir. The address of the firm of which you're a partner, what we'll term your professional address. Did Mr. Mordaunt tell me it was in Ely Place or was it—?"

Streatfeild interrupted him. "I'm afraid you're running past yourself a bit, Baddeley. I have nothing whatever to do with Ely Place. Mr. Mordaunt could never have told you that. Hyde, Streatfeild and Digby went out of business some years ago. For excellent reasons, too. Both Hyde—er, and—er—Digby are dead. I am the sole survivor."

"Sorry to hear that, sir, but I seem to have some recollection of a solicitor named Digby dying now you mention the fact—about four years ago—wasn't it? Would that be about the time or am I a trifle—"

"You haven't any recollection of it at all, Inspector Baddeley. I am quite certain on the point. You are entirely under a misapprehension. Mr. Digby's death was unreported and aroused no comment worth mentioning."

Baddeley bit his lip at his discomfiture. There was a note in Streatfeild's voice that seemed to hold a hint of warning. What the devil was this man playing at; what was his little game? The Inspector decided for the moment to steer a middle course;

danger always seemed to lie near extremes. He therefore retreated a little.

"Suppose my memory must be playing me false then, sir, and I'm mistaken. How long ago was it?"

"What, Mr. Digby's death?"

"Yes."

"I really couldn't give you the exact year, Inspector. Is it dreadfully important?"

Baddeley laughed but there was a strong suggestion of effort about the performance. "Not a bit, sir. At my game I suppose questioning other people becomes a sort of second nature and we lose ourselves sometimes. Did Digby die before Hyde?"

"They died together, Inspector. In one another's arms, which was the end that each of them would have chosen had he been asked. Quite touching, I assure you, Baddeley. They were kicked to death by wild butterflies."

He turned on his heel and left the speechless Baddeley almost purple with volcanic indignation. The other saw the back of Streatfeild's shoulders moving convulsively.

Coincidentally with the seeds of wonderment being sown in Inspector Baddeley's mind concerning the puzzling behaviour of Mr. Russell Streatfeild, the man with two dead partners, Peter Daventry was deciding upon taking a certain step. He had been considering this particular action for some little time and at last he had determined to take the bull by the horns and move in the matter. Taking fountain pen and a sheet of note-paper he ventured upon the writing of a letter. For a period he wrote easily and smoothly but after a time the task would have appeared to a careful observer to have become a matter of much greater difficulty. Eventually, however, he completed his letter to his satisfaction and read it through carefully. Thus took an appreciate time for the letter was a lengthy one. Had the same careful observer before-mentioned been present and looking over Peter Daventry's shoulder at the completed effort this is what he would have read in Peter's small but distinctive handwriting.

"'The Crossways'
"Near Cranwick,
"Sussex.
"October 11th.

"MY DEAR BATHURST,

"Salaam, Sahib and many of 'em! If this letter is in the nature of a surprising incident to you cast your weather-eye upon the address. When you have digested the valuable information therein contained—say unto yourself 'whose image and superscription is this?' For I, Peter, of the ilk Daventry, erstwhile companion of your noble self in much dirty work at the crossroads and other unsavoury resorts, am once again involved in a sinister piece of business. You have doubtless had full Press information re 'The Crime At "The Crossways"'—the looting of the Lorrimer sapphire and the murder of the poor lady who was my hostess. I know what a glutton you are for the columns that crawl with crime. But it has penetrated to my dull brain that if I provide you with the data right from the gee-gee's mouth as it were,' (from the 'os' of the 'oss—not bad that) you will help me more than anybody—knowing you as I do—'O my Hornby and my Barlow—long ago'! Therefore, open thine ears to hear the law, O my Bathurst, and incline them to the voice of little Peter. For in choirs and places where they *can't* sing here followeth the anthem. I blew down here last week—for the weekend! Joy! But short-lived! 'It melted like a cloud on the silent summer Heaven.' Personnel—varied—but distinctly select. I got my invitation, of course, through being an old friend of the Mordaunt family—the Guv'nor and Henry Mordaunt were very thick for years, used to divide doughnuts in the Tuck when they were boys and when the occasion of Molly Mordaunt's 'twenty-first' rolled along they honoured yours truly with the alluring old R.S.V.P. Now for the names of the gallant band that sat down to dinner on the night when the trouble began to warm up. Men first. Adrian Challoner—*the* Adrian Challoner—no need to describe him (remember his 'Aubrey Tanqueray' that we saw together?); a man named Raikes—his son Jack Raikes—dippy on Jane Mordaunt, and who had been at Winchester with Francis Mordaunt. He'll talk for hours if you'll let him on Rockley Wilson and how there never was his like—or ever will be. But not to me! I choked him of after a bit and thought of you. Uppingham for ever! Captain Cyril Lorrimer, M.P.—Molly's fiancé—seems a very decent sort although perhaps inclined to put on a bit of roll—properly taken the count though over what's been happening down here these last few days; Russell Streatfeild, a tall, grey-haired, clean-shaven solicitor, friend of old Mordaunt's—they follow one another about—he and H.M.—like the lamb and Mary, proper Damon and Pythias sort of business—and lastly the two male Mordaunts—Henry, the famous, and Francis his only son. The women are mixed—as usually happens at this sort of crush—but taking everything into consideration, distinctly above the average in qualities of attraction. We have the two daughters of the house who floated about (prior to the murder of course) with their twain swains, Lorrimer and Raikes, Mary Considine (a peach of a girl this)—any relation to your Considines by the way, of Considine Manor—I intended to ask her as a matter of fact, but the idea skidded somewhere; a Miss Anne Ebbisham who strikes P.D. (that's me) as being extremely efficient and equally charming (unusual combination); Christine Massingham, the actress, played in 'Purple Depths'—remember—and a winner all over from a looks' standpoint; Mrs. Lorrimer—Lorrimer's mother, and Mrs. Raikes, mother of the 'Manners Makyth Man' merchant who reveres Rockley. I think that little catalogue covers the whole menagerie. Now for doings up to the fall of the last wicket. Bowlers' names and full analysis. Everything went swimmingly till Papa Mordaunt poked the breeze up us at dinner. 'Creeping Jenny' entered the arena via the Post! Quite openly, she advertised herself as positively appearing at 'The Crossways' that night; her objective being Lorrimer's sapphire which seems to have been pinched by the way by a strange coincidence many moons since from the jolly old Mordaunt clan. '"Convey" the wise it call.' Well, Lorrimer turned pasty-white— real floured Albino—when he heard the news and swore that Jenny would toil all night and catch nothing—or words to that effect. You know the old stunt—'what I have I hold, by Gad—and my dripping sword for the scurvy knave that comes a-pilfering'! Well, anyhow, old Challoner rose to the spirit of the occasion and offered to bet that the 'Jenny' girl pulled it off—a hundred Jimmy O'Goblins I fancy was his offer. To my utter surprise the Ebbisham girl snapped it like a shot; licked it up like a Tortoise-shell Tom well away with his daily dose of Alderney cream. 'Done,' she gurgles, 'and I'll have the money in the morning.' Most of us opened our eyes, I can tell you—the Ebbisham girl seemed so sure of her ground. Why? That's the point that's got me guessing. It had when she made the bet and it still has. Who had been telling tales to little Anne? A hundred of the best—mind you—not a box of chocolates with hard centres. Well, we all slid off to Uncle Ned and personally I slept like the proverbial old peg, whip or humming, whichever you like to put your shirt on. But the news quickly buzzed round in the morning that something was vitally wrong; that Mrs. Mordaunt's bed hadn't been slept in and that Mrs. Mordaunt herself was missing. You've doubtless read how she was found—in the old well down at the end of 'The Crossways' grounds—stabbed through the heart. Wearing her evening cloak and with her 'pochette' affair found lying near her.

"Now for some additional startling details that have reached me down here but which aren't reported in the Press as far as I have been able to see. (a) Lorrimer had *two* sapphires—one a 'dud.' Mrs. Mordaunt had some strange premonition or something the night before she was murdered that the gallant would lose his ring if he didn't keep his eyes skinned and 'watch out.' She begged him to let her mind the family keepsake during the night. Lorrimer compromised on her suggestion by giving her the imitation. This imitation has been found down the well by Baddeley and close, I believe, to Mrs. Mordaunt's dead body. So much for the sapphire! (b) Adrian Challoner has had a dagger stolen from the dressing-table in his bedroom. Just such a weapon as indicated by the wounds on the dead lady. So Francis Mordaunt tells me. Moreover there is no sign of this dagger anywhere about. At least so report has it. (c) What has happened to the 'pukka' Lorrimer sapphire? This question is influenced by the fact that it has been stolen from a very cunning hiding-place in Captain Lorrimer's bedroom. One devised by Lorrimer himself! It was concealed in a stick of shaving-soap but the thief apparently knew this little bit of news and profited thereby—no doubt it was child's play for 'Creeping Jenny.' Or perhaps there are two of 'em and they hunt in 'Pears.' (Damned good that.) Anyhow—she left her usual card and joyous greeting—but that's by the way. The whole thing's got me whacked to a frazzle—although I've been trying to use your methods in order to freeze on to something. Not a hope! Not an earthly! I haven't the foggiest! Can you suggest anything? As a matter of fact Lorrimer's rather keen on you butting into the case but Papa Mordaunt isn't having any and properly choked him off when he coughed up the idea. Of course it was mine in the first place as you may guess. Still, as I said, Papa M. won't hear of the idea so there's an end of it. It was like a carmine cloth to an Andalusian. If you can possibly spare the time, drop me a comforting line and if it's not asking too much of you, let me know what you think about the whole bag of tricks. If you can suggest any line of action that I can conveniently take up, with reasonable hope of success, don't hesitate, old man. In the meantime bags of apologies for having troubled you. Au 'voir, old son!

"Chin Chin and likewise Tinketty-Tonk,

"PETER DAVENTRY.

"P.S. The Ebbisham girl's eyes are wonderful. They make me all 'swimmy.' So are Christine Massingham's if you catch 'em in the right light. I'm going to try this evening."

* * * * *

Having dropped the epistle in an out-of-the-way pillar box (Peter had resolved to take no risks in the matter but to post it himself) he started to cross the broad expanse of heath and common that lay between him and "The Crossways." He had over three miles to cover as he had purposely come some distance for his postal tryst. For a matter of twenty minutes or so he had swung along jauntily thinking over his letter to Anthony Bathurst and the sinister events of the last few days. It was quite on the cards, he reflected, that Bathurst would see a glimmer of light shining through the haze of the puzzle as he had presented it to him and be able to put him on the road to a solution. It was amazing how old Bathurst could pick out the right strand from the tangled ends of problems like this one and although on this occasion his attack would be as it were from a distance, Peter hoped secretly that his précis of the case would be sufficiently illuminating to counteract this condition and achieve results by correspondence. He was so engrossed in this traffic of thought that he was hardly conscious of the approach across the coarse, tussocky grass of the man who accosted him.

"Pardon me," said the stranger, raising a broad-brimmed hat, "but would you be good enough to tell me if I am going in the right direction for 'The Crossways'? I've come over from Cranwick and I seem to have gone amiss somewhere. I'm not sure that I haven't taken the wrong turning somehow or the other."

Peter looked at him curiously. The man was a gentleman— that is to say in the usually accepted sense of that much-abused word. His speech was cultured and his clothes, although old, "right." He was fair with a fresh complexion and "toothbrush" moustache. Peter put him down as somewhere in the early twenties, a year or so junior to himself.

"Certainly," he replied. "But you need not worry. You can make 'The Crossways' quite easily this way. When you get to the edge of the heath cut across the road that you'll find directly in front of you and then cross the stile and turn sharply to your left. Carry straight on from there, past the church and then on beyond an old cow-byre and you can't miss it."

"Thank you," said the young man. "Thanks awfully. Sorry to have—"

Then Peter said something which, immediately it had been spoken, he regretted and also the impulse that had prompted it.

"As a matter of fact," he said carelessly, "I happen to be going to 'The Crossways' myself. I'm staying there as it happens. If you care to accompany me—delighted."

At once he could have sworn that the young man was taken aback and that a strange look of something very much like annoyance flitted across his face. Simultaneously Peter Daventry began to wonder—that look—that expression—where the devil—

But his period of wonderment was very brief. It was summarily checked by the stranger. "I—I—I'm afraid I've misled you. I suppose I must have spoken as though my personal destination was 'The Crossways.' I'm sorry, although it was quite unintentional on my part. I'm not really going there, you see. I simply wanted to have a squint at the place as I passed through. I'm on a sort of walking tour, I suppose you'd call it—and hearing such a lot and reading so much about 'The Crossways' these last few days set my curiosity going. I thought I'd like to—Put it down to morbid inquisitiveness," he broke off rather lamely and evidently waiting for Peter to say something.

Without appearing to do so Peter looked him over. Save for the ground ash that he carried in his right hand he had nothing at all with him. Of impedimenta he was beautifully free. Travelling light for a walking-tour, concluded Peter Daventry. He had known two fellows up at Oxford with him who had once tramped best part of the way across England with a safety-razor, shaving brush, two tooth-brushes and one suit of silk pyjamas between them. They had joyously explained afterwards to an admiring and interested circle, that had hung upon their words, that one had worn the jacket and the other the trousers when bed had been really essential. Peter Daventry, who had been one of the above-mentioned circle of auditors to which reference has been made, had formed the opinion that these occasions of dormancy must have been extremely rare—the beer had been too good for any time or opportunities to be wasted. But this chap had no signs of "personal props" of any kind!

"That's quite all right," declared Mr. Daventry. "I understand perfectly and it doesn't matter in the least. But you can come along with me just the same as I suggested. When we get there I'll—"

"You're very kind but I couldn't think of it and if you'll excuse me I'll push on at once. I've got to be in Pyfold by this evening, and I've none too much time now." Turning on his heel he waved a valedictory hand and walked rapidly ahead; leaving a rather irritated Mr. Daventry behind him.

Peter followed his figure with a look of sorely-puzzled interest, for the last glance he had had of the man as he turned had only served to strengthen his curiosity and intensify his previous feeling of wonderment. "Now where the devil"—he said to himself as he stared after the stranger—"have I seen your face before?"

CHAPTER XV

THE NEXT twenty-four hours yielded nothing to Inspector Baddeley—nothing that is to say that he considered of any importance. It is true that the key that had been discovered on the fingers of the Muse of Eloquence fitted the lock of Mrs. Mordaunt's bedroom door but he had felt certain of that before he tried it. Just as he was beginning to get a trifle despondent, for several lines of inquiry that he had followed up had proved barren and profitless, something unexpected turned up. And as is very often the case in affairs of the kind that he was investigating, it came from near at hand quite spontaneously and not as the result of any direct piece of investigation on his own part. On the Thursday morning following upon the murder he had called at "The Crossways" with reference to the inquest on the body of Mrs. Mordaunt which had been fixed to take place on the following day. Henry Mordaunt received him in his study and from his manner it was quickly apparent to the Inspector that Mordaunt had news for him. The K.C. came to the point almost immediately. "Something's turned up, Baddeley, and from a most unexpected quarter too. I heard of it last night first of all but as I knew you intended coming along this morning I thought it would keep till you came. Very likely there's nothing in it, so many of the stories that are brought to one's notice peter out into nothing directly they're looked into, that I've grown chary of accepting anything at its face value. But you never know; the unlooked for is always happening, and you'd better hear this yarn for yourself. I think you'll be able to assess it better if you do than if I give it to you second-hand." He touched the bell on his desk for Mitchell to appear.

The butler looked even more pale and cadaverous than usual. "Tell Bennett to make himself presentable—if it's necessary, that is—and bring him in here to me, Mitchell."

"Yes, sir." Mitchell bowed stiffly and withdrew.

"Bennett's my gardener," added Mordaunt to Baddeley, by way of an explanation that was unnecessary. "He was with my son and me when we found my wife's body. A story has been brought to him which he felt forced to bring in turn to me. You shall hear it yourself when he comes."

"Reliable man?" queried the Inspector.

"Absolutely, as far as I know. I've no complaints against him, if that's what you mean; always found him efficient and trustworthy."

"Been with you a long time, hasn't he?"

"Several years. Recommended strongly by Sir John Harrison, the banker over at Pyfold. As I said, he's suited me."

"H'm," muttered Baddeley, "all right as far as it goes."

Mordaunt came to what was almost an expostulation in defence of his servant. "Bennett's a man far above the average and right away from the ordinary gardener. He's more of an all-round man than most of them. For instance I'll give you an example of what I mean. I run my gardens as far as practicable upon what I try to make business lines. It interests me to work that way. Especially the kitchen garden. Bennett prepares a statement in the nature of an inventory for me at the end of every year. All vegetables grown and er—produced, are priced as they are gathered and used in the kitchens at the market price reigning at the time, Such things as potatoes and onions and all vegetables that are husbanded for the winter, are also priced before they are stored. So far he has produced eminently satisfactory results and I am more than pleased with him and his work. There's not much leakage, I can tell you."

Bennett upon arrival wasted no time and came to what he had to say very quickly. "What I'm going to tell you, Inspector, is not my own story. I'd like you to understand that at once. If it had been you wouldn't have had to wait so long for it. I'll tell it you as it was told to me—then you can decide for yourself what you'll do about it." His face grew more serious. "What I've got to say," he proceeded, "goes back to the night of Miss Margaret's engagement and the dinner that you, sir, gave in honour of the event." He gestured towards his employer. "Which is, I suppose, the night that the mistress was murdered or at any rate just before. Cook hadn't been feeling too well for two or three days—had a touch of gastric 'flu I believe—and Mrs. Mordaunt had arranged for her to have extra help in the kitchen. I didn't know of this at the time, I've simply heard of it since. The result was that Perkins, one of the kitchen-maids that comes from the village, offered to bring her mother along to give a helping hand if one was required. Mrs. Mordaunt was quite willing and Perkins' offer was fixed up as you might say. Well, to cut a long story short, the old girl came along and gave a hand generally, helped during the evening and then helped afterwards with the washing-up and so forth. After that they had a bit of jollification in the kitchen, opened a bottle of something and drank Miss Margaret's health and future happiness. You can guess the style."

Mordaunt cut in with a corroboration. "That is quite true, Inspector. I know all about that. It was all in order. I gave orders that a couple of bottles of port were to go along to the kitchen, just for celebration, you know. Go on, Bennett."

"Well, sir, as you may guess one glass meant another and I fancy with old Mrs. Perkins it became a case of 'we won't go home till morning'—begging your pardon, sir, of course, for putting it that way. Now I'm coming to what she's told her daughter who's told me. Her home's in the village—about half-an-hour's walk from 'The Crossways' and when she left here it was close on one o'clock. She was going out, she says, by the small gate behind my storehouse, the gate that opens on to the big meadow, and she swears that she saw a woman a few paces ahead of her going in the direction of the old well."

Baddeley whistled. "She does, does she? This is getting interesting, Bennett. Go on."

Bennett shook his head somewhat despondently. "There isn't much more to tell you, Inspector. I wish that there was. All that Ada—that's the maid Perks, her daughter—can get out of her is that the woman she saw was wearing a yellow dress. That is how the old girl describes it, anyhow. She says she just managed to get a glimpse of the colour once, before she turned off through the gate. The old lady never remembered this till yesterday, so Ada says. I should think she guzzled too much port and got a bit fuddled. You can't tell me, that if that had happened—"

"One minute"—Baddeley interjected almost fiercely—"did she see this woman's face at all? Do you know? Could she recognize her if—"

"Can't help you there, Inspector," answered the gardener almost lugubriously. "I've told you all I know. If you want to know any more you'll have to talk to the old girl herself. Ada says she can't get any more out her, so if she can't, I'm darned sure there's not much more to be got. If you're thinking of going down to the house, I'll be pleased to direct you."

Here Mordaunt put a question to the gardener. "There's one thing I don't quite understand, Bennett. There may be nothing in it, I admit—but why did this girl Perkins confide in you? Why didn't she come up here directly she had heard her mother's story and put the whole thing into the proper hands? I'm not suggesting it's any fault of yours, Bennett, but I think that's what the girl should have done. It was the right procedure for her to adopt."

Bennett coloured under the inquiry. "Well, sir, if you'll pardon me saying so, Perkins thinks a rare lot of me. She's an intelligent girl, sir, that's had a decent education—night school and the wireless not to mention a good grounding in cross-word puzzles—and she'd as lief be Mrs. Bennett as Mrs. Anybody. She's always had a strong fancy for me and when I took her to see 'The Admirable Crichton' on the pictures last August Bank Holiday—that was what you might call the crowning touch, sir. It put a sort of seal on her affections as you might say. She relies on me and brings me all her troubles—that's the reason she told me about this."

"H'm, I see. I accept your explanation. Well, what do you say, Baddeley, are you going down to see this woman or has Bennett here told you enough?"

The Inspector shook his head at the latter part of the question. "Shall have to see the woman first hand, I'm afraid, Mr. Mordaunt. Perhaps I shall be able to pick up a bit more. You can take me down now, if you like, Bennett. Is it convenient?"

Bennett nodded. "Quite, sir, if Mr. Mordaunt will give me leave now. I'll take you down there straight away. I shouldn't be surprised if you're expected, in a manner of speaking."

Baddeley raised his eyebrows. "Expected?"

The gardener explained. "I told Ada I should have to tell the master and I expect she's passed on the news to her mother. That's what I meant by you being expected. Nothing more! They won't kill no fatted calf for you. Is it O.K., sir?" He referred his last question to Henry Mordaunt.

"Certainly, Bennett. Take the Inspector down to Mrs. Perkins whenever he wants you. Dulverbury, isn't it?"

"Yes, sir. About half-an-hour's walk, sir, on the straight road to Pyfold."

"Very well then. Bennett," clinched Baddeley, "I'm ready now and we'll waste no time. Take me along at once, will you?"

The lady who had assisted at the eleventh hour to celebrate Molly Mordaunt's betrothal was short and stout. Her heaviness was not only physical. Her face was lined and creased and she was obviously not a joyful mother of children. She wiped her hands on her coarse apron upon the arrival of Inspector Baddeley and "Mr. Bennett from the big house," and then used the same article to dust two chairs in the "best room" in order that her two visitors should be seated, albeit not too comfortably. Her story of the incident that she had witnessed in the grounds of "The Crossways" was virtually as the Inspector had had it from Bennett. All the same he determined to put one or two additional questions to her now that he had the woman herself in front of him.

"Was this woman you say you saw a stranger to you, Mrs. Perkins? Could you state that with certainty?"

"Oh, yes, sir! It was nobody I knew, sir, and nobody I'd ever seen before." Mrs. Perkins wiped her expansive mouth in an attempt to emphasize her statement.

"This was about ten minutes to one, you say?"

"Yes, sir."

"What sort of a woman was it? Could you describe her at all, do you think? Was she tall, short, fair, dark, thin—"

Mrs. Perkins, the mother of the romantic Ada, shook her head. "I couldn't answer any of them questions, Mr. Inspector. I was walkin' behind her, you see. But she 'ad on a lovely dress. Kind of a yaller dress it was. The sort of dress that you see when you're going—"

Baddeley interrupted her. "What about her face? Did you catch a glimpse of her face at all? I know what you said just now, but could it have been Mrs. Mordaunt herself? That's a point I'd like cleared up."

The fat face of Mrs. Perkins grimaced as she pondered over the question. Finally, after some consideration, she ventured on a decision.

"It wasn't Mrs. Mordaunt, I'm dead sure of that. It was a white face—or whitish—you know what I mean—*pale*. It was a lady right enough, I could see enough of her to be able to tell that. But more than that I couldn't say, Mr. Inspector, not if I was promised a sackful of money, so it's not a bit o' use you askin' of me." Mrs. Perkins rubbed her nose with the back of her hand to the accompaniment of a very audible sniff. With this expression of opinion Baddeley had perforce to be content. But he was not done with yet. On his way back from the cottage at Dulverbury to "The Crossways" he thought of a plan, simple in operation, but which nevertheless might prove very effective. Upon his arrival he outlined it and Mr. Mordaunt listened to it gravely.

"Have you any objection, sir?" inquired the Inspector, when he had finished.

"I don't like it, Baddeley, I won't pretend that I do. This old woman may be imagining things for all we know. The idea doesn't appeal to me at all."

"What harm could it do, sir; and the good it might do would be incalculable."

Mordaunt hesitated. Baddeley saw it and the advantage he had gained, and hastened to follow up his point. "It's only fair to everybody here, sir. After all we ought to make use of the chance. It's our duty lying straight and plain in front of us. Think of your late wife, sir; think of your daughters; think—"

Suddenly Mordaunt threw up his head and yielded to the Inspector's persuasion. "Very well then, Baddeley. I'm agreeable, have it your way." The mention of his daughters by the Inspector had been sufficient to sway his judgment and to turn the scale in Baddeley's favour.

"Any objection to the method I adopt?" Baddeley put the question bluntly as was his habit when dominated by an idea.

"Depends what it is, naturally. You must let me have your proposals more fully. Then I can let you know whether I'm favourably disposed towards them. I can't say unless I know the exact line you suggest taking."

Baddeley thought hard for a moment. "I want Mrs. Perkins to see every one of the ladies that's in this house. I don't want her to see photographs of them for instance. I want her to see each one of them walking in front of her, in the same position, that is, as she says she saw this figure in front of her in the grounds on the night of the tragedy. That's my test, nothing else. Nothing alarming about it; nothing likely to prove disturbing. The essence of simplicity. Do you mind coming outside for a moment, sir?"

Mordaunt showed signs of surprise but obeyed the Inspector's suggestion. Standing at the study door Baddeley pointed across the wide hall. "I take it that all your guests are still here? I asked that they should be, you know."

"Yes, Inspector. In accordance with your desires none has left. I intimated to all of them what you said you wanted."

Baddeley nodded. "Good. There will be some sort of dinner this evening, I suppose. In that room?"

"Yes. We shall dine very quietly in there."

"And the ladies, I take it, will adjourn after a time to these other rooms as usual?" He indicated the rooms to which he referred.

Again Mordaunt signified agreement. As he did so, Baddeley pointed to the statuette of Polyhymnia showing at the bend of the stairs. "That turn of the staircase where the statue is, very conveniently commands the exit from the dining-room and also the entrance to the other rooms." Baddeley stopped and looked at Mordaunt. The latter, however, did not speak. "Get my idea, sir?"

Mordaunt frowned. "Go on. No half-measures. Let's have it in full."

"I want this Perkins woman to be up there. I suggest that she can be dressed as a servant of the house. If you like her daughter can be with her. If she's there when the ladies go across from one room to the other after dinner and sees them from her position up there she may be able to identify the one we want."

Mordaunt's frown deepened. "Supposing one of the ladies ascends the stairs and sees her there? What will she think?"

"That won't matter. Look at it for yourself. There's no reason that I can see why some of the servants shouldn't have had duties to perform upstairs and be coming down again, if that should happen. She would be taken for one of the servants."

"I don't like it, Baddeley, as I told you just now and I'll only consent to your proposal on one condition."

"Which is, sir?"

"That if Mrs. Perkins picks out any lady as the person she saw in the grounds, you take no action in the matter without first consulting me. I must insist on those conditions being observed absolutely. After all, I've a right to—"

"All right! That's agreed, sir," conceded Baddeley. "I'm willing to stand by that. I'll be in here, sir, so the report can come in to me at once. I'll leave that part of the business in your hands, sir." He gestured towards the room they had just vacated.

"That's settled then. I'll be along this evening." Baddeley waved a good-bye and departed.

* * * * *

It was with an exceedingly grave face that Henry Mordaunt some hours later reported the result of the Inspector's experiment. Baddeley, sampling one of "The Crossways" best cigars in one of its best chairs answered the light tap on the study door when it came with unconcealed eagerness. He was about to speak directly Mordaunt entered the room but the look on the K.C.'s face checked him. Although Mordaunt looked so concerned he showed no hesitation about reporting what had transpired.

"Mrs. Perkins has identified one of my guests, Baddeley. And it would be idle for me to pretend that I am not very much disturbed thereby. I simply can't believe what she says, but in justice to the woman and the story that she tells I must admit that she appears absolutely certain with regard to it."

"Who is it?"

"Mrs. Lorrimer! This Perkins woman picked her out at once, without the slightest hesitation."

"By her dress?"

"No, Baddeley. Not by her dress! Mrs. Lorrimer is wearing black this evening. By her *face*! And also she says by the way she walked."

Baddeley's eyes glinted. His face grew hard as he pondered over this latest aspect of the affair.

"What action do you intend to take, Inspector?" Mordaunt's tone betrayed his anxiety.

"For the moment, sir, *none*. I'm going to watch points and make a few inquiries." He took his hat from the table. Mrs. Lorrimer again! She it was who had known of Challoner's dagger and the secret of the shaving-soap. Why had she been in the grounds that night? What had she to do with "Creeping Jenny"?

CHAPTER XVI

ANTHONY BATHURST read Peter Daventry's letter with great interest. The morning he had received it saw him take a stroll into the country, find a convenient five-barred gate, seat himself on the top thereof, fill his pipe and light it, take Peter's letter from the pocket of the tweed jacket he was wearing and read it again—more times than once. He smiled at several of the Daventry whimsicalities and noted the more important points of the letter with accompanying movements of his head. Truth to tell the "Crime at 'The Crossways'" as the more sensational Press had it had engaged no little of his attention—there were many features of it that he considered of more than ordinary mystery—which is tantamount to saying that it exercised for him the usual fascination. Taking note-paper from his pocket-book and with pencil in hand he replied to this letter that he had received. For quite an appreciable time the pencil travelled smoothly and swiftly over the paper. This is the form in which it reached Peter Daventry at "The Crossways" near Cranwick, Sussex.

"October 14.

"MY DEAR DAVENTRY,

"Very many thanks for your letter of yesterday's date which I have found intensely interesting. As you no doubt surmised I have studied the affair at 'The Crossways' very keenly—having no idea, of course, that you were going to write to me about it. As a matter of fact most recent newspapers would have been exceedingly dull without it. Duller, I think, than usual. Your apologies, therefore, my dear chap, for worrying me, were totally unnecessary. Indeed I must thank you for a very clear exposition of several points in the case of undoubtedly grave importance. Which alas have not been made too clear in the daily Press. The affair has an additional fascination for me since my old friend Inspector Baddeley from Lewes has, I understand, been placed in charge and Mary Considine who figured with him in the very first affair that I ever investigated, also appears to have been a guest in the house when the murder took place. Please remember me to each of them if you get a favourable opportunity. I may even get you to whisper something in Baddeley's ear for me. But more of that later.

"You ask me if I can give you a line upon which to work with a view to solving the mystery. Rather a tall order, my dear and ingenuous Daventry, seeing how much I don't know, but here's trying. It seems to me from what you tell me in your letter that the three most significant features that sort themselves out from all the others are the adventures of the *two* sapphires, the stealing of Adrian Challoner's dagger and the rather extraordinary bet made by Miss Ebbisham. Made *with* Challoner—note. I have considered this last item very, very carefully, for I confess that I find it eminently instructive and intriguing. It seems to me to be a whole course of instruction in itself. Remember, my dear fellow, what you may perhaps have been inclined to forget! Namely— that Miss Ebbisham wagered *against* 'Creeping Jenny.' At least that is what I gather from the terms of your letter. Take my advice and concentrate on the *conditions* of the wager. How for instance has the lady appeared since the murder? Remember, laddie—'the turn of a phrase,' 'the slightest gesture' and 'the most thrilling occurrence.' These are the hinges upon which the solution of a case so often swings. Think of the immortal Holmes and the curious incident of the dog in the night time. 'But the dog did nothing in the night time.' 'Exactly, my dear Watson. That was the curious incident.' But happily you are on the spot; you can study the various personal 'psychologies'; you have the 'human' factors right in front of you and they help one so much to assess accurately. They are almost the *sine qua non* in a case of this kind. I tell you candidly, my dear chap, that I have sifted as well as I can from the information at my disposal the various members of 'The Crossways' circle as described by you—ignoring, of course, such irrelevant details as the eyes of either Miss Ebbisham or Miss Massingham (no matter what the light may be) because I cannot see that they can have any bearing upon the case. What about the Mordaunt ménage itself? How do the two girls strike you, for example? Is Molly (the younger, I believe) in love with her gallant cavalier? If so, does he return it? Is Jane's nose (or rather 'was') diverted at all by her father's second marriage? All these conditions suggest possibilities. See how I consider the humanities! *Humanum est errare*, my dear Peter, and human frailties are many and complex. Then—what is Francis like? With whom is he in love? With any of the girls down there? Surely you aren't the only victim of the eyes of Miss Ebbisham? Then there are Raikes and his wife and son, Challoner and this Russell Streatfeild whom you mention. Why is he so thick with Mordaunt? What is their connection or common interest? With *Mordaunt*—mark you—who scouted the idea you say of me being called in to have a look at things. A nice little problem, Peter, my boy, full of strange twists that may lead you anywhere but down the right path. I must say, however, that this Russell Streatfeild of whom you speak, interests me considerably. I constantly find myself wondering about him. Is he all he pretends to be? What does Baddeley think about him—any idea? It might eventuality prove a profitable stunt to attempt to find out. On second thoughts I fling this forward as a highly reasonable suggestion. In fact, you might do as I hinted previously in my letter. Whisper in his ear an inquiry about Mr. Russell Streatfeild. Just in general terms. It would be interesting to hear what he has to say. Then there's another point it would certainly be as well for you to watch. Pieces of evidence in an affair of this sort are bound to come to people from time to time. The question is, are they recognized as such when they *do* appear? I might recognize them—you might do likewise—but there are others! See what I mean? Now just *pour encourager les autres*, if anybody came to you with any evidence—or hint of evidence—detrimental to this man Russell Streatfeild let me have it at *once* as it's possible I may be able to make something of it for you. Or, of course, with regard to anybody else—come to that—but just at present I'm thinking about him particularly. Lastly we come to the servants of the house. How do they shape when tested in the crucible of inquiry? Is there anything at all suspicious about any one of them? For instance, according to the newspaper report in the *Daily Bugle*, Bennett the gardener assisted the two Mordaunts in the discovery of the body. Is he comparable with Calpurnia, the spouse of Julius? But you will no doubt form your own conclusions. Turning to other matters, I have had two very interesting problems since I saw you last—I was called to the cottage at Cutnall Warren where a clay-pipe broken in three pieces served to hang a very sordid and disgusting murderer and I also figured at Sir Austin Kemble's express request in the Hucclecote poisoning drama. In the latter instance I am proud to say that my intervention had a great deal to do with the saving of an innocent man—all through a rice-pudding having got thoroughly cold before being eaten. A little matter of vanilla flavouring! So you see you get compensations sometimes in my game after all. Don't forget about Miss Considine. Although, of course, she may very well have forgotten

"ANTHONY L. BATHURST.

"P.S. I've just thought of something. Have you seen the latest thing in coatees—the real *dernier cri*! Do any of the girls down there wear one? I like them immensely."

* * * * *

Peter Daventry grinned more than once as he followed the lines of Mr. Bathurst's letter. The grin developed into a laugh when he reached the postscript. Since when had old Bathurst been a connoisseur of the feminine sartorial? His enthusiasm usually dissipated itself in other direction. Peter turned his attention to the letter again and re-read it—this time with much more attention to detail. He noted the three incidents that Bathurst considered the most important. "Concentrate on the *conditions* of the wager." He repeated the phrase aloud in an attempt to imprint it on his brain. What on earth did Bathurst mean by that? The bet was simple enough—surely! What complications were there in it? What complications could there be? He retraced his steps and started again. Challoner wagered that the sapphire would be stolen and Anne Ebbisham that it wouldn't. Stay though—on second thoughts that wasn't strictly accurate. After all, Peter concluded, "Creeping Jenny" was a factor in the bet. More than an ordinary factor, too—a vital factor. Peter whistled softly to himself. The light was filtering through. He began to see now very much more clearly where Bathurst was heading; it all hinged on "Creeping Jenny" then. He went through in his mind the various members of the house party as Bathurst had described them and as he knew them himself. It seemed to him that he couldn't do better than to try a little process of elimination again and see where the results of it landed him. Elimination was a moderately safe principle upon which to work because it meant the discarding of certain obvious people, the segregation of whom in this way would undoubtedly help him when it came to the time for considering others. Unnecessary burdens were always best flung off whether in crime investigation or in anything else. He would begin with the Mordaunts. Assuming that the murder of Mrs. Mordaunt were committed for the sake of possession of the Lorrimer sapphire, which assumption Peter considered was a distinctly reasonable one, surely he could eliminate Henry Mordaunt. If Henry Mordaunt by any strange chance had desired—"oh, curse it," muttered Peter, "I'm snookered from the 'pistol'—right from the very word 'Go.' If I only knew who this blessed 'Creeping Jenny' was I might hope to make some progress—as it is I'm properly up a 'gum-tree.'" He looked up disconsolately to see Russell Streatfeild making his way past Bennett's store-hut towards him. Funny he should happen to be going by at that particular moment. The very man on to whom old Bathurst seemed to be shedding the "spot" light.

Evidently the inquest was over, for within a few moments Challoner, Lorrimer and Francis Mordaunt joined him.

"All over?" queried Streatfeild.

"Adjourned," replied Lorrimer.

"The police followed their usual plea," added Challoner. "Baddeley did as I expected he would do. The Coroner took formal evidence of identification and immediately after that the Inspector asked for the usual adjournment. Which tells the time of day pretty conclusively."

"Baddeley's got something or other up his sleeve," contributed Francis. "He's been to the Governor with evidence of some sort that he regards as confoundedly important. I'm fairly certain of that because of my father's change of attitude for the last couple of days. There's something unpleasant happened. Other things than the inquest and its cause have worried him."

"Talk of the devil," said Challoner, "here's Baddeley himself."

"Good afternoon, gentlemen," said the Inspector, as he came up—rather curtly, Peter thought. The others nodded to the greeting.

"Didn't see you at the inquest, Mr. Daventry, or even you, Mr. Streatfeild." The Inspector looked hard at Peter as he uttered the statement.

Daventry shook his head. Streatfeild disregarded the Inspector's remark. "I had no particular reason to go, Inspector," said Peter. "Did you expect me to be there?"

"Don't know that I thought about it beforehand. I simply noticed that you weren't there, that was all. I saw these other three gentlemen."

"Any news turned up of importance, Baddeley?" demanded Captain Lorrimer.

"Concerning what, sir?"

"Either of the two problems."

Baddeley's reply was evasive. "There's no news of your sapphire, sir, if that's what you're thinking about. I can tell you that without any fear of all the likeliest places where it might be expected to pop up, but so far it hasn't broken cover as you might say. Still time's young yet and there's no knowing what the morrow or the next day may bring forth. I'm going up to the house now to have a word with Mr. Mordaunt."

"I'll come with you, Inspector, if I may. I'd like to walk up with you. No objection, have you?" Peter spoke lightly but Baddeley detected a vein of seriousness behind the levity.

"Very good, sir. Come along then. I'm going up now."

Peter fell into stride beside him and after a moment or two's walking in silence ventured to break the ice.

"I expect you guessed, Inspector, that I had something to say to you, didn't you? Probably I made it pretty obvious."

Baddeley acquiesced with a smile. "I won't say that I didn't, Mr. Daventry."

"Well," continued Peter, thriving on this semi-encouragement from an official source, "I'd better lead off by announcing that I've nothing to *tell* you. I've got no new information for you if that's what you're thinking. So don't get bucked too quickly. As a matter of fact the boot's on the other foot. I walked along with you because I wanted to ask you something. Regrets and all that if I'm a disappointment."

Baddeley frowned and he took no pains to conceal the frown. "Ask on then, although I'll give you no guarantee that I'll answer your question. Or questions," he added with a touch of pessimism and remembrance.

"Only one," replied Peter brightly and hopefully, "and quite a simple one at that." He bent down and whispered something in Baddeley's ear. It was the text that Mr. Bathurst had dictated in his letter. "What's your private opinion of Mr. Russell Streatfeild?"

Baddeley immediately became eagerly alive. "And what in thunder do you mean exactly by that question, Mr. Daventry? *What do you know?*"

"Nothing!" replied Peter ecstatically. "'Pon my honour, Inspector! All I've got is a lingering doubt or two. Do you agree with me that the gentleman's worth watching?"

Baddeley looked at him very steadily. "Since you've asked me, I'll be quite candid with you. I'm not at all satisfied in that direction, Mr. Daventry. His behaviour puzzles me. And when anything like that happens, I sit up and take notice. You can put your shirt on that every time."

Peter rubbed his hands. Bathurst had put his finger on the old spot, it seemed! At any rate it was plain to a blind man that he and the Inspector saw eye to eye concerning Mr. Russell Streatfeild. Somehow Mr. Daventry felt conscious of a greater measure of contentment.

CHAPTER XVII

As BADDELEY came away from his interview with Henry Mordaunt he was determined upon a certain course of action. No sooner had he come to the decision than he resolved to carry it out at once. He wanted to see the gate through which Mrs. Perkins had stated that she had gone and its exact geographical position in relation to the gardener's store-hut and to the path which led down to the old well. According to Mrs. Perkins' statement the women that she had seen on the night of the murder had been in front of her as she herself had turned off through the gate into the meadow on the way to the Pyford road. He was resolved now to test all the conditions that the statement had implied. As he turned the corner of the gravelled path that would bring him to Bennett's store he saw the tall form of Russell Streatfeild a few yards in front of him. A sudden idea took possession of the Inspector and he resolved to translate it into practice. He quickened his pace and caught up with the man in front. Streatfeild turned at the sound of Baddeley's approaching footsteps. The Inspector nodded affably.

"Having a look round, Mr. Streatfeild?"

"I wouldn't say that, Inspector," returned the other in his unusually high-pitched voice. "Walking along quietly, slowly, and steadily in the garden can hardly be described accurately as having a look round, can it?"

Baddeley laughed easily at the reply.

"You're a stickler for accuracy then, Mr. Streatfeild? Ah, well, I can't blame you. A man who has lost his business partners as unfortunately as you tell me you have done no doubt has to strain a point in most cases. It means that he has such a responsibility thrown on his own shoulders." He changed his tone. "It was seeing you along here that induced me to say what I did. A question of association of ideas. It struck me as a coincidence, you see."

Streatfeild wrinkled his brows as though attempting to fathom the inner meaning of Baddeley's statement. Then he shook his head slowly. "Once again I'm afraid you have the advantage of me. Candidly I fail to follow you."

"Really? Is that so now? I thought perhaps the news might have travelled to you. Apparently it hasn't. As it hasn't, treat what I am going to tell you as a confidence. One or two people here have evidently learned the trick of keeping their mouths shut—you can make another one." He looked round. Then he shot the remainder of his speech directly at Streatfield. "A woman was seen here—just here where we are now—on the night of the murder. Not Mrs. Mordaunt. *Somebody else.*"

"Really," rejoined Streatfeild. "Well, I can't say that I'm surprised. After all, Baddeley, you know, there's the old imperative *cherchez la femme.* It's as true to-day as it was when it was first coined."

Baddeley watched him as a cat watches a mouse. Was it a surprise to him? Or had he been aware of the fact before the Inspector had told him? "Whose evidence is this? From whom has it come?" interrogated Streatfield.

"That question I'd rather not answer for the time being, if you don't mind, sir. But you can take it from me that it's reliable—absolutely."

"Was the er—lady that walked abroad at so late an hour, identified by the person who saw her? Pardon me, who *claims* to have seen her. Let us be strictly accurate, Baddeley, as you pointed out just now—there is always my reputation to—"

"No, Mr. Streatfeild, she was not." Baddeley ignored the sally and confined his reply to the question that mattered. He considered that he had told Mr. Streatfield enough in that direction. "She was pale, my informant tells me, and wore a yellowish-coloured frock. That's about all there is to it." He was fully determined now to make no mention of the experiment with Mrs. Perkins upon the staircase.

"Yellowish," repeated his companion. "I don't think I remember any of our ladies here wearing a frock of that colour during that evening, though, of course, there may be nothing in that. A change could have been rapidly effected. Ladies, I believe, have been known to change their clothes as well as their minds. I'm going in here, Baddeley, if you don't mind." Streatfeild pointed to the door of Bennett's store-hut which they had just reached.

The gardener himself stood in the entrance, pipe in mouth. Although the October afternoon was chilly he wore no coat or waistcoat, just a cardigan jacket over a heavy grey, woollen shirt. His hands with their shirt sleeves rolled over the elbows were thrust deep into the pockets of his trousers as he leaned against the lintel of the door-frame and puffed at his pipe.

Baddeley came to another quick decision, the second of that afternoon. "You are, Mr. Streatfeild? So am I! You're properly down my street this afternoon, blessed if you're not."

Bennett touched his forehead to Russell Streatfeild as he crossed the threshold. Baddeley's entrance seemed to occasion him less pleasure. He returned the Inspector's greeting some-what sourly. Immediately he found himself inside, Baddeley became acutely aware of the strategy of Mr. Streatfeild, for the tables were now turned upon him very adroitly.

"Inspector Baddeley wants a word with you, Bennett," opened the solicitor, turning towards the Inspector.

The gardener and he awaited Baddeley's first move. But this was the reverse of what the Inspector had intended. For it had been his intention to listen to Russell Streatfeild's overtures to Bennett, and unhappily for him that gentleman had very defin-itely resigned to him the offensive. He sought refuge therefore in subterfuge, but with only moderate success.

"Seen no suspicious characters knocking about in the village, I suppose, Bennett?"

"No," replied the gardener; "have you?"

The smiling Streatfeild meanwhile had commenced to wander round the building. Baddeley watched him from the corner of his eye. Backwards and forwards he travelled. On a board at one end of the hut onions had been laid. Streatfeild picked one up and examined it.

"James's Keeping?" he inquired of the gardener.

Bennett nodded. "Yes, sir. I don't know a better. You can't beat it."

Streatfeild passed on to a heap of parsnips. "These should be good, Bennett. They're showing the first touch of frost, too, which means so much to the flavour of a parsnip. 'The Student,' I fancy. Am I right?"

"Quite right again, sir. I dug those first thing this morning. Mr. Mordaunt's very fond of them."

"Ever make parsnip wine?"

"No, sir. Very tasty though I believe, sir. I've heard my grandmother talk about it."

"Excellent for gall-stones, Bennett. I knew a very bad case that was completely cured by it, when everything else had been tried and had failed."

Baddeley began to chafe with the irritability of impatience. This man was playing with him, with all this horticultural "punk"; making a toy of him. And what annoyed him all the more was the undeniable fact that he himself had asked for it. He had deliberately placed himself in the position. Waked into it with his eyes open!

Streatfeild had now come to a halt, in front of a shelf. On the shelf lay a number of brown paper parcels. Bennett saw what he was doing and ventured upon an explanation.

"They're my pricing sheets, sir. A kind of inventory that I take for Mr. Mordaunt at the end of each year. I've done it ever since I've been here. It's a little fad of his and he insists on it being done, between Boxing Day and the thirty-first of December. All other work has to be put on one side for it. Everything produced by the gardens at 'The Crossways' is priced at current market price on the sheets here so that the Guv'nor's able to get some idea of what the gardens really bring him in. Takes three or four days to work it all out."

Streatfeild nodded. "I see! You keep a record of course of all the stuff you actually use during the year?"

"In a book, sir. What the Guv'nor calls a Daily Issues Book. I make my price-sheets out from the entries in this book adding on the value of the stock I've got on hand. It's a kind of stock-taking as well, you can see that."

Baddeley coughed rather loudly. It was an attempt to call attention to his presence there. But Streatfeild was unheeding. He paid no attention to the cough whatever. He prowled round the hut again, almost aimlessly it seemed to the Inspector, especially as he came back to stop again in front of the shelf on which were the parcels.

"Let me see," said Streatfeild. "How long have you been here, Bennett?"

The gardener grinned. "That's funny! The answer's on that shelf, sir—if you only knew it. I complete eleven years' service for Mr. Mordaunt on the sixth of next January. Every one of them ten parcels on that shelf in front of you counts a year."

"Do you know that's very interesting, Bennett? As a matter of fact something of that was in my mind when I asked you." Mr. Streatfeild paused, rubbed his chin, and flicked the ash from his cigarette as he looked into the gardener's eyes. "Especially as there happen to be eleven parcels on the shelf and not ten."

Bennett looked incredulous. "Eleven?" he muttered.

"Eleven, Bennett," reiterated Streatfeild. "What shall we call it—the Leap Year parcel—this one that has no business there?"

The realization came home to Inspector Baddeley that it was high time that he took a hand. He accordingly ranged himself alongside the solicitor. He thought that he was beginning to see through that gentleman's little plan. The gardener still looked blankly at the pile of parcels on the shelf.

"I can't understand it, sir," he muttered. "I've never put any other parcel on this shelf, sir. Somebody else must have been in here and—"

"Suppose we investigate, Bennett," suggested Mr. Streatfeild hopefully. "It may teach us something."

Bennett stretched up and took down the parcel on the top of the pile. He knocked the dust from it and held it out for the two men's inspection. "There you are, sir," he said in an attempt at explanation. "I stick a label on each one as you see has been done in this case and then write the year on the label in blue pencil. Look here for yourselves, gentlemen."

They looked and saw the big "1927" figures in the blue lead pencil Bennett had mentioned.

"The obvious course, Bennett," pursued Mr. Streatfeild, "is for you to find the parcel without the label of a particular year—the er—redundant parcel, shall we say? The extra turn. I fancy it may prove to be an ugly duckling among packages."

Bennett took down the parcels one by one, blowing the accumulation of dust from those that carried it. When he came to the fifth in the pile he announced success.

"Here you are, sir! Here's the one you want. I can't understand it, but there's no label at all on this one so I'll go bail it's not one that *I've* shoved up there. Somebody else has had a finger in the pie."

Inspector Baddeley stepped forward quickly and took the parcel from him.

"The zealous Inspector has it, Bennett," declared Mr. Streatfeild silkily. "He has forestalled me. Open it, will you, Inspector? Satisfy an overmastering curiosity of mine to which I will cheerfully admit."

Baddeley frowned. He didn't at all relish Streatfeild's tone but he untied the string that fastened the parcel and unwrapped its brown paper covering. He disclosed a number of papers and read out the writing on the top one. "Stock of Potatoes (Main Crop) at 31st December, 1923." Baddeley uttered an exclamation of dismay.

"You've struck a mare's nest this time, Mr. Streatfeild, and no mistake. This is one of Bennett's own parcels, one of those he's just been telling us about. The label's come off it, that's all."

Streatfeild rubbed his chin with his fingers as he considered Baddeley's remark. There was a curious look in his eyes which as the Inspector looked up he was quick to notice. "May I see the papers, Inspector?" he asked with a cold quietness.

Baddeley handed them over without comment. Streatfeild looked carefully at each sheet from Potatoes to Jerusalem Artichokes and passed them back to the Inspector.

"Hand me the brown paper that was outside this parcel, will you, Inspector? The paper that you took off. I'd like to have a look at it for a moment."

"Certainly—want the string as well?"

"No, Inspector! If I did I should have asked for it. Thank you."

They saw him examine the brown paper and rub the surface with the tips of his fingers.

"How do you stick these labels on, Bennett? Do you use gum of some kind?"

"Yes, sir. There's a bottle on the shelf there. It's not half-an-hour ago since I used it. Shall I get it for you?"

"Not for the moment, Bennett. I don't fancy I shall require the gum. You will get me something more important, if you don't mind. Give me the parcel with the label '1923' on the outside, will you?"

Bennett looked a trifle puzzled at Streatfeild's request. He expressed his doubt in words, evidently at a temporary loss what to do. "1923, sir? I don't quite—haven't you got the 1923 lot?"

"Think of what I said. I haven't the parcel that is now bearing the '1923' label, Bennett, which is surely a very big difference. Don't you see now what I mean?"

The gardener scratched his head and began to turn over the brown paper packages that remained on the shelf.

"Here you are, sir," he announced eventually. "Right at the bottom, last one of all."

"This, Baddeley," declared Mr. Streatfeild, "will, I fancy, contain a certain interest for us all. Will you open it, Inspector, or shall I? Just as you please!"

Baddeley took it with an ill grace and ripped off the covering string. As he did so he gave a quick gasp of astonishment. The parcel contained a woman's apricot-coloured evening frock and Bennett the gardener failed to repress a shudder at the sinister red stains that showed plainly upon the front. Notwithstanding what Baddeley thought about it there was no doubt that the inquisitive Russell Streatfeild had scored this time.

CHAPTER XVIII

FIRST THE key of Mrs. Mordaunt's bedroom turns up and now this frock!

"There's one thing, gentlemen," continued the Inspector, with flashing eyes, "I'll kill two birds with one stone when I do finish with this case. I'll not only solve the mystery of Mrs. Mordaunt's murder but I'll lay 'Creeping Jenny' by the heels. Because that's what this means." He pointed to the frock that he had uncovered. "Blood stains on a woman's frock! The owner of this frock murdered Mrs. Mordaunt. I'll lay a million to a mouse-trap on it and 'Creeping Jenny' has broken another commandment this time. She's gone back two places in the Sinai table." He paused and looked at Streatfeild who ventured no immediate reply. Instead he picked up the frock and carefully examined it. "Woman or no woman," continued Baddeley, "she's clicked for the nine o'clock walk this journey, for I swear I'll have her before I'm finished." At this moment the Inspector decided that Streatfeild's silence worried him. When he spoke again he spoke very quietly. "Wonderful intuition of yours, Mr. Streatfeild! Come to think of it you couldn't have done better if you had *known* there was this evidence in here. No offence, sir, but there's an old saying: 'those that hide can find.' Of course there's no suggestion on my part of anything like that in your case, but what put you wise? I'm dying to know."

Streatfeild shrugged his shoulders. "I make a point of thinking things out for myself, Inspector. Let me commend it to you as a diverting and invariably instructive practice. In my case it's been forced upon me. I lost my two partners, you see, some years ago and it threw me on to my own resources. Did I ever tell you about it? It was a sad business." Mr. Streatfeild, having delivered himself of the shot, turned on his heel and made his exit.

Baddeley glared at his retreating figure.

"He's a rum 'un," remarked Bennett, "and I'd like to know what he's up to. Old friend of the Guv'nor's!" He spoke contemptuously. "I don't think! He's never stopped at 'The Crossways' before in his life. Leastways, not since I've been here. What do you think he asked me this morning?"

"What?" demanded Baddeley.

"What kind of collar-stud I wore!"

The Inspector grew curious again. "Tell me about it," he ordered.

"Oh, he rolled in here this morning with a special kind of back collar-stud in the palm of his hand. Did I wear one like it? Was it mine? He seemed quite pleased when I told him it wasn't."

"Damned funny how he put his hooks into this frock," declared Baddeley. "That's got me guessing, I don't mind admitting it. I'll take this parcel with me, Bennett. Good afternoon. If you hear any more of Mr. Russell Streatfeild at any time, let me know, will you?"

Having declared himself of this parting remark, Baddeley tucked the tragic parcel under his arm and walked rapidly away towards the house. He determined to strike while the iron was hot and to go at once to what he himself termed "the fountain head."

He was shown immediately into Henry Mordaunt's study. The latter was sitting at the table and showed signs of the strain of the recent ordeal connected with the inquest.

"Well, Baddeley," he said, "what is it you want now? And I do hope you won't keep on adjourning this inquest business. The affair's got on my nerves too much as it is. I can't stand much more. I don't know what I shall be like if I've got to endure this suspense indefinitely with a succession of adjournments."

"I don't think you need worry over that, sir. The next fortnight may teach us a lot, should, in fact, enable us to clear up the entire affair. Actually speaking things are moving pretty quickly." He laid his parcel on the table in front of Mordaunt and nodded towards it. "Have a look at that, Mr. Mordaunt, if you don't mind, and be prepared for a bit of a shock."

Mordaunt jerked his head back, startled and surprised. "Why? What do you mean, Baddeley? Is it anything that I shall—"

"Look here, sir," Baddeley lifted the parcel and slipped off the string. Unwrapping the brown paper he took out the frock with its tell-tale blood stains and spread it out on the dark table.

"Good God, Baddeley!" exclaimed Mordaunt, "where in heaven's name did you find this?"

Baddeley related the story of Streatfeild's discovery in Bennett's hut with little attention to detail. "Wonderful man, your *old* friend Streatfeild," he stressed. He proceeded at the same time to jog Mordaunt's memory. "Remember Mrs. Perkins' story and her definite evidence afterwards? 'A yellowish dress' and 'that's the woman that just crossed the corridor'—Mrs. Lorrimer. The evidence now is damning against her, and yet I'm not satisfied." He moved his shoulders to express his dissatisfaction. "No, I'm not satisfied, no good saying I am. It's the 'Creeping Jenny' part of the business that gets me down because I'm certain in my own mind that there's a connection somewhere. But where? I can't find the answer, Mr. Mordaunt, and that's a fact. Do you know what I've a good mind to do?" He paused and looked at Mordaunt as though he were inviting the latter's answer.

"What?" asked the K.C. curtly.

"Show this to Mrs. Lorrimer and ask her if she can identify it as her property. We needn't say anything of the story about her having been seen in the grounds on the night of the murder and we needn't tell her anything of the circumstances in which this frock was found. Merely show it to her and then ask her the question."

"What's the idea?" demanded Mordaunt.

"Wouldn't it be better if we kept this to ourselves? Surely we shall then—"

Baddeley considered for a moment or two but in the end stuck to his guns. "I don't think so, sir, and I'll tell you why. Circumstances alter cases, you know. Sometimes in our game it pays us to let certain information leak out. It forces the criminal sometimes to take a certain action and in doing so to show his hand. In this instance something may happen out of this that will give me a line to work on."

Mordaunt raised his eyebrows. "When do you propose doing this?"

"Now, if convenient to you. There's no time like the present, sir. That's a motto that applies with equal force to most things. Suppose you send for Mrs. Lorrimer this minute? Ask her to come down here to see you. You needn't let her know I'm here. Let her think you're alone. I promised you when I tried that other experiment with Mrs. Perkins that I wouldn't move any more in the matter without consulting you and I've kept that promise—I haven't moved. Quite frankly, Mr. Mordaunt, I'm still not sure of my ground and I'm hoping the interview I suggest with this lady will help me a good deal."

"All right," conceded Mordaunt, although somewhat reluctantly, "as long as you stick to what you say and don't go any farther, I'll do it. I'll send for Mitchell and tell him to ask her to come along here." He walked across the room and rang the bell.

Mitchell obeyed the summons and accepted the instructions. He did know where the lady was. "I will inform Mrs. Lorrimer of your wishes immediately, sirs. She is in a deck-chair in the garden in conversation with Mr. Francis and Miss Jane, sir. I happen to know that because she asked me some time ago where Miss Jane was and I directed her accordingly."

The Inspector replaced the stained frock within the parcel. Mordaunt sat back in his chair and quietly awaited Mrs. Lorrimer's coming.

When she entered the study after a few minutes' interval her habitual self-possession did not desert her. Surprised as she undoubtedly was to a certain extent to find Inspector Baddeley there, she nevertheless betrayed no sign of the fact.

"You want me, Mr. Mordaunt? What is it, please?" By now she was decidedly more at ease than Mordaunt himself, for by this time he wished heartily that he had not embarked upon Baddeley's venture. In his mind he called it a damned delicate position. He gestured towards the Inspector.

"I'm sorry to trouble you, Mrs. Lorrimer, and I hope I haven't seriously disturbed you. But you must blame the Inspector here rather than me. He wishes to ask you a question."

Mrs. Lorrimer raised her head ever so slightly, but the movement was significant for it contained the essence of combat. She sensed that Baddeley was antagonistic.

"Yes, Inspector," she said coldly, "what is it that you have to ask me?"

Baddeley coughed. "Firstly, madam, a very simple question, indeed. I admit at the same time that it's rather a personal one. But you must forgive me that and remember that I'm conducting an inquiry into a case of murder. A case that, as a proposition, is far from simple. Do you possess an evening frock of what I should call an 'apricot-ish' colour?"

Mrs. Lorrimer's surprise at the Inspector's question was very obvious. She took no pains to conceal it. Her answer was prompt and frank. "I thought my wardrobe was my own concern, but I do, Inspector. And I'm at a loss—"

Baddeley held up his hand. "All in good time, madam,—we'll come to the whys and wherefores a little later. Did you bring the particular frock with you to 'The Crossways'?"

Mrs. Lorrimer nodded. "I did, Inspector. It was one of several frocks that I brought with me. I'm rather extravagant in that direction, I'm afraid, like most members of my sex. And this was a rather special occasion. But in the case of that particular frock it has been waste of time for I have never put it on. It clashed, you see, with one of Miss Ebbisham's and it's a habit of mine to avoid that sort of thing if it's possible. So it had its journey for nothing." She held the edge of the table tightly with her right hand and Baddeley noticed how white her knuckles were.

"You never wore it?" he queried. "Where is it now, then?"

"In my wardrobe, I presume, where I hung it when I unpacked my case. Where else should—"

"Have you actually seen it in your wardrobe lately?"

Mrs. Lorrimer shook her head blankly. "I don't know that I could answer that question. I don't think I *could* say that I had actually seen that particular frock. It's difficult—you see. It is hanging up with at least half-a-dozen others of mine. That's the point. Does one notice—"

Baddeley made no answer. Instead he picked up the brown paper parcel and took out the frock.

"Is that your frock, madam?" he asked quietly as he held it up to her.

The lady addressed gave a low murmur of astonishment. Then she slowly nodded her head. "It is, Inspector. But how does it come to be here?" But even as she spoke her eyes caught the tell-tale stains and the words froze on her lips. Mordaunt could see that her eyes were fixed on and never left the gruesome marks. What did Baddeley intend to do now? he wondered. It seemed to him that Mrs. Lorrimer's natural curiosity would take a deal of satisfying and he didn't see for the moment how the Inspector would be able to carry out his original intention and avoid saying any more. Before Mrs. Lorrimer could find more words to express her feelings Baddeley spoke again.

"There must be no mistake about this, madam, for there are more frocks than one in the world. Please go up to your room, look in your wardrobe, and see if your frock is there. Let there be no doubt whatever that this is your frock."

There was an ominous gravity in Mrs. Lorrimer's tone as she replied, "I will do what you say, Inspector. But there is no doubt about it being my frock and it must have been stolen from my wardrobe. I wish there was a doubt, but there isn't." She closed the door quietly behind her.

"You heard what she said, Baddeley," exclaimed Mordaunt, as soon as they were left alone. "She hasn't worn that frock since she's been down here. What do you make of that?"

Baddeley twirled his smart little moustache. "Mrs. Perkins says differently, Mr. Mordaunt. She was right about the frock, remember! Why shouldn't she be as right about the woman that wore it? Seems to me she ought to be—other things being equal."

The door opened softly for Mrs. Lorrimer's return. Her face was white and drawn. "It is as I said," she declared quietly—"that frock is mine. It has been taken from my wardrobe by some-body—but for what purpose?" She pointed to the garment as it lay on the table—itself a silent accusation. "Tell me, Inspector," she said, "are those marks I can see on it—*blood stains*?"

"They are, madam," returned Baddeley with heavy dignity, "although I hadn't intended to tell you as much. This frock was worn by the woman that stabbed Mrs. Mordaunt, and it's my job to find her."

Tangible accusation almost had crept into his words. This Mrs. Lorrimer sensed, as her reply showed.

"Then I, at least, am innocent, Inspector, for as I told you, I have never worn the frock at 'The Crossways.' And I know of no reason whatever why I should have murdered Mrs. Mordaunt. Can you think of one?"

Baddeley found the question disconcerting. He made no reply.

CHAPTER XIX

JUST ABOUT the time that Inspector Baddeley was interviewing Mrs. Lorrimer in Henry Mordaunt's study over the matter of a blood-stained frock, Peter Daventry received something in the nature of a shock. Coming round by the tennis courts he ran fall tilt into Miss Ebbisham who was obviously in a hurry. Before Peter could formulate an adequate apology for what he described as his abominate clumsiness, Anne Ebbisham had waved his attempt on one side and asked him a question.

"Mr. Daventry," she said, "please tell me, did you go to the inquest to-day?" She looked at him engagingly and as she did so Peter definitely came to the conclusion that his adjective "wonderful" did her eyes considerably less than justice. He jerked himself from the idyllic to the ordinary.

"Er, no, Miss Ebbisham, as a matter of fact I didn't. It's rather a beastly, sordid business, you know, and I managed to give it a miss. Why do you ask?"

"Oh, nothing," she replied, rather unconvincingly. "I just wondered how things had gone, that was all. Just feminine curiosity on my part. Of course I had no particular reason for asking."

Peter proceeded to explain. "But I can tell you how things went if that's all you want to know. I've seen two or three of the chaps that did roll along to it and they told me. Nothing much happened actually! It was adjourned."

"Adjourned?" she repeated after him. "Why, do you know?"

"Oh, for no real reason, I believe. It's quite a usual procedure in cases of this kind. The police arrange it that way and the Coroner falls in with their desires. Baddeley isn't ready for a verdict yet a while so he adopted the ordinary course and asked the Coroner for an adjournment."

"I see," she murmured. "Till when, do you know?"

"No. I didn't hear that, Miss Ebbisham. But for about a fortnight, I expect. That's about the usual."

His eyes travelled over her slim form with undisguised admiration. How topping she always looked—fit, trim—clean as a whistle—"steel true and blade straight"! Not only was she always perfectly turned out but she possessed at the same time the far less common knack of knowing how to put her clothes on. At this particular moment he couldn't fault her. He ran his eye over her again appraisingly. Her shoes, her stockings, her— Peter's process of cataloguing came to an abrupt standstill. The words of Anthony Bathurst's postscript swam through his brain and brought a summary closure to his appreciation. *Miss Ebbisham was wearing one of the latest things in "coatees"!* He rubbed his eyes—mentally. Trimmed with biscuit-coloured lace it matched her sleeveless frock most admirably.

The afternoon was warm and sunny, well in keeping with the reputation of St. Luke, who had made many "former treatises" similarly and Miss Ebbisham was taking full advantage of the Saint's kindliness. She caught the look in Peter's eyes and wondered what he was thinking. Simultaneously he in his turn sensed what she was doing.

"What do you think of the affair now, Miss Ebbisham?" he questioned.

"You heard what I told Mr. Challoner the other day, Mr. Daventry. I haven't shifted my position since then one little bit, I assure you. How could I? Nothing has happened as far as I know to cause me to change my opinions."

Peter determined to take a chance. "Don't think it too utterly low-down of me to ask you, Miss Ebbisham. It was a private matter really, I know, although there was a certain amount of publicity attached to it, but have you paid up yet?"

Anne wrinkled her nose. "Paid up? To what do you—?"

"Your sporting bet with Mr. Challoner about 'Creeping Jenny.'" Peter felt his cheeks redden as he made his meaning clear. The actual sound of the words seemed to stamp them with an even more colossal cheek than they inherently possessed. But Miss Ebbisham appeared to harbour no resentment. If she did she hid it successfully. She laughed a little nervously. But there was no trace of this nervousness in her reply when it came.

"No, Mr. Daventry." Her mouth set firmly in lines that her companion hadn't seen before. She went on in an attempted vindication of the position that she had taken up. "You were there that night, you heard the terms of my bet with Mr. Challoner. When I am convinced that it was 'Creeping Jenny' who stole Captain Lorrimer's sapphire then I'll pay Mr. Challoner what I've lost. Till that's proved, I'm not paying. And I consider that I'm perfectly justified and quite sporting over it. In other words I'll pay when I hear the 'all right' called." The colour flooded her cheeks and Peter became an irretrievably lost soul and additionally Miss Anne Ebbisham's most humble and obedient servant.

"Every time," he supported warmly. "I'm with you all the way with regard to that, Miss Ebbisham. Anybody with the slightest sense of decency must be. This 'Creeping Jenny' business may be somebody throwing dust in the eyes of the police for all we know. You wait before you settle—and don't pay till *everything's* settled."

She nodded and hurried off. As he watched her making her way in the distance he thought of the coatee again. Old Bathurst was absolutely on the old spot again with regard to them—they undoubtedly were the goods. "Chic" to the extreme. He felt sorry that he hadn't spoken to her about Russell Streatfeild while he had had the chance. He'd like to know what she felt in that direction and her opinion was worth something, too—he felt sure. Miss Ebbisham was a very capable young lady.

While he was thus communing with himself he was approached by Captain Lorrimer and Adrian Challoner.

"I say, Daventry—can you give us a minute?" opened the latter. "Lorrimer and I want a word with you for a moment or two if it's convenient. We've had by way of a chat together, he and I, and we've decided to come along to see you."

"Right-o!" returned Peter. "What's the trouble?"

"Only the ever-present one," interposed Lorrimer, "which is quite enough with which to be getting on. But the point is this—Challoner here isn't satisfied with the way things are going. He doesn't think Baddeley's making much progress and as he very accurately points out each one of us here in the house must perforce remain under a certain amount of suspicion until the affair's cleared up. That's so—you can't get away from it. See what I mean, Daventry?"

Peter nodded. "Quite. I'm feeling much the same myself about it all. But what do you suggest that any of us can do in the matter? How can we move? Aren't our hands pretty well tied?"

Adrian Challoner took up the tale. "Well—I've come along to Lorrimer since the inquest with a suggestion with which he's fallen into agreement. And we've come to this arrangement. We're going to do a bit of investigating on our own account. We've talked it over and I think the best man with whom we can join forces is Streatfeild. We must obviously leave out Mordaunt himself and also Francis Mordaunt mightn't cotton on to the idea—very naturally—and if that were so Francis would probably find it somewhat awkward and embarrassing to work with us and at the same time row in along with his father. So we're going to omit them both from our counsels. Streatfeild, on the other hand, impresses me quite a lot; he seems to me to be a distinctly able man. Now what do you say, Daventry, to making a fourth? If you don't care about it—say so—and we'll blow along to Jack Raikes."

Peter hesitated before committing himself. "What does Lorrimer think about it? Concerning Streatfeild, I mean," he at length asked Challoner. "You didn't tell me."

Captain Lorrimer answered upon his own behalf. "It's rather strange that you should have popped up with that question, Daventry. For the very good reason that I do not share Challoner's feelings with regard to Streatfeild. I may as well be quite frank about it. Personally, I'm inclined to distrust the man. Several things about him that I've noticed force me to make that statement. But inasmuch as linking up with him will enable me to watch him pretty closely I've consented to fall into line with Challoner's proposal. They're my sentiments in a nut-shell."

Peter pricked up his ears. What did this mean? What did Lorrimer know—he must have a definite reason for talking as he did? He agreed with him entirely. Perhaps by questioning Lorrimer he could discover something that would strengthen his own feelings in respect to this man Streatfeild. He put the idea into active shape. "I take it you've a good and valid reason for speaking as you have done? Something definite has occurred that has caused you to hold such views?"

Lorrimer jerked his head emphatically. "You can take it for granted that that is so although I'm not going to make any direct statement. I don't go about with my eyes shut any more than you do, Daventry, and as I said just now I've noticed more than one thing about Streatfeild that I regard as extremely suspicious to say the least of it. Something always seems to turn up where Streatfeild's been kicking around. Things happen! Maybe mere coincidences, of course—all the same I for one am not satisfied."

Once again Peter harked back mentally to the letter that he had had from Anthony Bathurst. How right he had been all round as things had subsequently worked out. Peter resolved to stand firm.

"Well, gentlemen," he declared with steady composure, "you asked me for an opinion and I'll give it to you. I think you're making a mistake. In fact, I'll go farther even than that—I'm sure you're making a mistake."

"Mistake? How do you mean?" The question came from Adrian Challoner.

"In working *with* Streatfeild. If you do that you may be forced to give something away to him that may eventually prove disastrous to your plan of campaign. It seems to me to be essential that Streatfeild should be in the opposite camp to that of the investigators."

Challoner bit his lip. "I certainly see your point, Daventry, but I don't know that I altogether share your views there. Still, I asked for your opinion and you're perfectly entitled to give it. We can't then count on your er—co-operation?"

"Not with the man under discussion, Challoner," replied Peter promptly. "Under other conditions I might be disposed to offer my services if you still wanted them. Shouldn't care two hoots."

"Very well, Daventry. That's all I wanted to know. Come along, Lorrimer. We'll see what Jack Raikes has to say on the suggestion."

He spoke somewhat curtly and turned on his heel. Lorrimer followed him.

"I seem to have disturbed the serenity of the *consommé*," murmured Mr. Daventry to his irrepressible self. "Ah well, we shall see who's right in the long run. I may be able to give Mr. Streatfeild a little attention from the front row of the pit; we'll leave the dress circle to the Challoner combination. Sometimes you see a bit better when you aren't too close; don't see the 'three-and-a-half' so clearly."

An hour later saw him engaged upon his second epistle to Anthony Bathurst. In it he found time to satisfy that gentleman's somewhat strange curiosity concerning the coatee and also to mention what he had heard regarding Mr. Russell Streatfeild.

Mr. Bathurst, as always with correspondence, reread the letter more than once before he essayed the art of reply. When this latter reached "The Crossways," Peter Daventry confessed to a certain amount of disappointment.

Bathurst told him this time was not to watch Russell Streatfeild as he had expected would be the case, but on the other hand, to watch Inspector Baddeley. To Mr. Daventry's way of thinking this was a most unattractive proposition. What on earth had happened to make Bathurst change his mind?

CHAPTER XX

"ROPER," said Baddeley, two days later, "come over here and look at something, will you?"

Roper finished sharpening his pencil and obeyed. He saw in front of the Inspector a number of typewritten slips. Five or six he thought at first glance. Looking at them more closely he saw that each contained a list of people's names.

"These lists," explained Baddeley, tapping the table with some show of enthusiasm, "are full of interest and are decidedly instructive. They contain the names of guests who have attended certain country-house parties that have recently been held in different parts of the country. Look at the heading that I have had typed above each list and you will see at once what I mean. Recognize the names?"

Roper looked at the name and address that headed each list. He read them off silently. They were (A) Lady Grantham, Cumberlege Court, Dringe; (B) Mrs. Stanley Medlicott, Critchley Lodge, Lullingham; (C) Mrs. Arthur Midwinter, Skene House near Crawley; (D) Mrs. Annesley Topham-Garnett, Wychwood near Rustington; (E) Lady Craddock, Cranwick Towers, Cranwick and (F) Mrs. Henry Mordaunt, "The Crossways," near Cranwick. Having done so he nodded to the Inspector with complete understanding.

"I get you, sir. These are all the 'Creeping Jenny' episodes. You've lettered them, I fancy, in the order of their occurrence."

"Quite so, Roper. That's just what they are and what I have done. Now listen to me." Baddeley shifted his position, threw one leg over the other, lit his pipe and settled down more comfortably. "Do you remember the conversation I had with you the other day, Roper? I told you some of the facts then but not all of them. But among the things that I did tell you was the fact that I had thought fit to call at 'The Crossways' re the 'Creeping Jenny' business—*before the murder* of Mrs. Mordaunt. Remember?"

"I do, sir."

"I didn't, however, tell you why I came, Roper. But I'm going to now. Getting it off my chest may help me a bit. Listen." Baddeley leaned forward and told Roper the details of the motor car and the tracks that he had discovered down Hangman's Hollow. Roper whistled softly as he took in the meaning of the information. "Now, Roper, let's cast our minds back to the Bournemouth murder or, to be more accurate, the Iford murder, and also to the shooting of Police-Constable Gutteridge that night near Stapleford Abbotts in Essex. What did our people do in each of those cases as soon as they knew something?"

Roper wagged his head in his wisdom. "I think I see your drift, sir," he declared. "You mean that an arrest was made in each instance that wasn't actually for the—"

Baddeley interrupted him with a movement of approval. "In the first case the murderer was arrested on a comparatively trumpery charge relating, I believe, to an insurance matter and in the second case one of the murderers was arrested on an ordinary charge of 'drunk and disorderly.' But great events from little causes spring, Roper, and each of the birds was carefully kept in cold storage. Preserved till the time came for the big attack to be launched on him."

Baddeley's sharp eyes twinkled. "Caught the 'bus, Roper?" he queried.

"I think so, sir. Though I don't yet know the particular route."

"Don't worry about that; you will in a minute, because you'll be seeing the destination-indicator. That's where these lists come in." The Inspector tapped the pieces of paper that lay in front of him. "I've made it my business," he continued almost at once, "to collect this information. Goodness knows why it wasn't done systematically before by Bell because the evidence that made three of the 'jobs' look like 'outside' business may have been so easily faked. That was evident to me right from the first. Now, Roper, here comes the crux of the question. There are no less than four names that occur in every one of these lists. How does that strike you? Damned peculiar, isn't it?"

"Four?" murmured Roper, questioningly. "That seems rather—"

"Yes, it does, doesn't it? Nevertheless there are *four* and talking won't alter it."

Roper moistened his lips, his interest by now most thoroughly aroused. "Whose are they, sir?"

"Look for yourself." Baddeley pushed over the six slips of paper. Roper made the necessary examination.

"Mr. Francis Mordaunt," he said slowly, "Miss Jane Mordaunt—Miss Margaret Mordaunt—and Miss Anne Ebbisham. That correct, sir?"

"You've hit them, Roper. Now, what do you say about it, eh?"

Roper shook his head doubtfully. "I'd rather listen to you for a bit, sir. I never was much good at 'finding the lady,' not to mention the fact that there's one too many here to pick from."

Baddeley smiled a smile of intense self-satisfaction. "Four names, Roper! Think of them again in case any one of 'em should elude you. Seriously though, doesn't anything suggest itself to you in a great hurry?"

"Do you mean the three Mordaunts all being there?"

"I do, Roper. I said the other day that 'The Crossways' contained the key to the 'Creeping Jenny' mystery and to-day I'm more certain of it than ever. Everything points to it! Supposing, for argument's sake, Mrs. Mordaunt discovered the real secret of the burglaries some time before she was murdered and the criminal took this very effective means of closing her mouth? Dead women, Roper, are just as uncommunicative as dead men." Baddeley sat and studied Roper's face as the full significance of the Inspector's remarks gradually came home to him.

"Quite right. What are you going to do, then, sir?" eventually questioned Roper.

"What do you think, Roper? What would you do if you were in my place? If you made any move at all what would it be?"

"I don't know, Inspector, now that you've asked me, and that's a fact. It's difficult to say. For instance, taking the story that you told me just now at your own valuation and accepting that the Mordaunt car was used in the Cranwick Towers affair—what's the motive? That's where I'm stumped. Surely, none of—"

Baddeley turned over the leaves of his note-book in rapid search.

"Francis Mordaunt has been gambling for some months now and according to my information has only had two winning weeks since Ascot. That's four months ago, Roper. I won't say that he's lost large sums but his total losses must have caused him a serious amount of financial embarrassment. His father's not a rich man by any means. Also—don't forget the name of his elder sister—'Jane'—short for 'Jenny,' my lad, and it doesn't take a Holmes to cotton on to that." He snapped the elastic of his note-book as he closed it in emphasis of his next remark. "Roper, I'll confide in you, I'm going to take a chance. I'm going to apply for a warrant for the arrest of Francis Mordaunt." He rose and paced the room.

Roper screwed up his face in surprise. "On what charge, sir?"

"On the charge of being primarily responsible for the various 'Creeping Jenny' robberies, of course. I shall charge him with being 'Creeping Jenny' himself, or herself if you prefer it. Then the fat will be in the fire. Then the fur will fly. I guarantee that that will loosen the tongues of more than one of 'The Crossways' crowd. I'll call the tune and some of them will dance."

Roper started to shake his head but rubbed the lobe of his ear instead. "Yes—I see what you mean, sir—although I can't say that I'm as confident as you are over it. Still—that's neither here nor there."

"You see, Roper," continued Baddeley in evident extenuation of his contemplated move, "where am I in the murder case proper? I've set inquiries going in at least a dozen different directions. There's somebody inside that house that knows a great deal more than is healthy; that's plain to anybody with half an eye. Take the key incident alone. That key was deliberately hung on that blooming statue while I was actually on the premises. Then take the frock business. Mrs. Perkins is prepared to swear that Mrs. Lorrimer was in the garden that night. Mrs. Lorrimer swears that she has never worn the frock that Mrs. Perkins says she was wearing. Where's the weapon that was snaffled from the theatrical chap's bedroom? Not a sign of it anywhere up to the moment.

I'm like the old farmer, Roper, who kept on drinking claret at the Harvest-home—'I don't get no forrarder.' But if I arrest Francis Mordaunt I'll go bail I *do*. I'll bet you things will move—*somehow*." Baddeley spoke with an immense amount of confidence.

Roper thought of something. "When did you get on to the Craddock burglary, Inspector?"

"What do you mean by 'when'?"

"How long after the actual theft?"

"Two or three days—not more."

"There were mud-stains on a rug in Lady Craddock's bedroom, weren't there, and some glass broken?"

"Quite correct, Roper."

"Did you actually see the broken glass, sir?"

"No, I heard about it from Inspector Bell."

"You don't know then for certain where the broken glass was? On the floor of the room *inside* or on the ground beneath the window—*outside*?"

"Yes, I do. It was inside on the floor of the bedroom."

"Well then, sir, that looks to me pretty conclusive—that proves—"

"That proves nothing, Roper, absolutely nothing whatever. And I'll tell you why. The thief could easily have leaned through the window next to the broken one—they're casements as it happens—from the *inside* and given it a blow from the *outside*. And that was what he did do; I'm pretty certain of it."

"Still, pity you didn't see the broken glass yourself." Roper spoke slowly.

"Why?"

"It might have made you more sure of your ground. There's nothing like seeing things for yourself—first-hand."

Baddeley laughed at Roper's evident misgivings and the laugh was intended by him to brush them aside. "Trust me! I know what I'm talking about, Roper, and those that live longest will see the most."

Within two days the projected blow fell. Baddeley armed with his warrant arrested Francis Mordaunt as he had foretold that he would. To say that his action created consternation through the County generally and at "The Crossways" in particular is to put the matter very mildly. Henry Mordaunt—the boy's father—was stupefied. Francis himself openly laughed at the Inspector's action and hurled bitter sarcasm at the head of Baddeley. The recently-devised combination of investigators comprising Challoner, Lorrimer and the younger Raikes, suspended the operation of its inquiries *sine die*. Peter Daventry found himself—almost against his will—obeying the injunctions of Anthony Bathurst—namely—watching Inspector Baddeley. Was this last surprising stroke the action that Bathurst had anticipated? In Russell Streatfeild's eyes there seemed to lurk a glimmer of amused satisfaction. If he said nothing there was no doubt that he thought a lot. Among the ladies the consternation reigned in an even more marked condition. Anne Ebbisham appeared to be more puzzled by the march of events than ever and Christine Massingham was not slow, once again, to observe her friend's state of mind. The Mordaunt girls blended indignation at their brother's arrest with a kind of questioning wonderment and accepted the sympathetic ministrations of Mrs. Lorrimer very gladly. This state of affairs reigned very generally for some appreciable time, until Henry Mordaunt threw aside his condition of numbed shock and aroused himself to something approaching action. His first deliberations were with Streatfeild who listened to his impassioned outburst very patiently, very courteous, and very sympathetically. Streatfeild's reply, logical but critical, had the effect of brightening his host considerably. "You really think that?" he asked.

"I do," had been Streatfeild's answer. "You have nothing to worry about. I've covered my tracks as far as Baddeley's concerned, all the way through the piece. Take the matter of the key, for instance. What would have happened if he had traced that to my possession? There's no knowing where it would have landed me."

Mordaunt looked straight at him. "Have you been able to—?"

Streatfeild inclined his head. "Yes. Yesterday, I think it was! And I am not surprised."

Mordaunt's eyes held a tremendous query but his companion—seeing it—refused him satisfaction.

"Wait till the time comes. To move now might end in disaster. Besides there's the sapphire. We must wait for news of that."

The glance that Mordaunt gave him was full of curiosity. But he asked no more questions.

Although he had been the instigator of the plot between himself and this other man, he had since discovered that Streatfeild was the stronger character of the two and would carry his opinion if it ever came to a conflict of wills between them. The experience was relatively new to Mordaunt—he usually got his own way it may be said—and therefore by reason of its novelty he found the situation somewhat refreshing. He watched his companion as he strode up and down the room, hands clasped behind his back and thinking deeply. Eventually Streatfeild turned and spoke to Mordaunt again.

"At the same time Baddeley's last move has positively surprised me. I don't mind admitting it. I had prepared myself for more than one emergency but certainly not for this particular one. Quite frankly it's rather taken the wind from my sails. And the worst of it is, it complicates matters somewhat."

Mordaunt acquiesced gloomily. "I can see now what the trend of his mind was when he called here before—just after the Cranwick Towers robbery. I confess it was an eye-opener to me at the time. Evidently he's been concentrating on the idea for some while."

"Very likely."

"More than that I should say. It's almost a certainty. The question that must agitate us now is what's going to happen next? It's the complicated nature of the affair that prevents one proceeding to a clean-cut issue. I'm positive when I think of it that Baddeley suspects me in some ways, but how I can't say. To a great extent therefore, on that account, my movements are necessarily hampered. What is more I fancy that Daventry also is keeping his weather eye on me so you see between the pair of 'em—" He broke off and shrugged his shoulders.

"Is Daventry the man you think put—?" Mordaunt's sentence was unfinished but Russell Streatfeild knew exactly all that he had intended to convey.

He laughed lightly in reply. "Oh no—not for a moment. You need have no fears on that score. If I only knew what to do with—" Suddenly a light came into his eyes and he bent over and whispered to Henry Mordaunt.

CHAPTER XXI

THE FIRST results of Inspector Baddeley's unexpected thrust were to say the least somewhat surprising. The second results were much more than surprising—they were staggering. It has been said already that the two Mordaunt girls were very naturally the victims of fierce indignation. This was the predominant feeling that they harboured. Francis and they had always been tremendous pals, particularly so in the case of Molly the younger. Jane, as befitted an elder sister among children who possessed no mother, had always been stronger-minded and as a natural sequence more self-reliant. It would have been strange had circumstances not made her so. She sympathized intensely with her sister's anger at this latest development of the situation but she was perhaps less fierce and certainly much less vindictive. Whereas Molly Mordaunt would have prescribed for Baddeley either the nethermost dungeon or something with boiling oil in it that she herself would cheerfully have administered, Jane was a firm disciple of more moderate methods. She urged her sister to wait patiently for the inevitable dawn that would follow the darkest hour, and pointed out with a patient submissiveness that Baddeley's position in the matter was very different from their own. Molly, refusing to be comforted, flounced away to her lover. She found him in a contemplative mood.

"Cyril," she commenced impetuously, "can't you do anything?"

He looked at her curiously, wondering to what exactly she was alluding. "I?" he demanded. "How do you mean, sweetheart?"

She stamped an imperious foot.

"About Francis. What's the good of being a Member of Parliament if it doesn't help in cases like this? Can't you tell this utter fool of a policeman how absurdly ridiculous it all is?"

"My dear child—"

"I'm not a child." She stamped again and an earwig, late of a dahlia, entered Valhalla instantaneously. "For goodness sake talk sensibly. If you—"

"My dear girl, please be sane then and tell me *what* I can do. I can't move with nothing to support me. I must have proof to take to a man like Baddeley, *'evidence'* that he's bound to recognize. I can't go to him and demand your brother's release because I'm an M.P., or because I'm engaged to his sister. Now, can I? Surely you don't want me to tell you that."

She twisted and untwisted her handkerchief round her fingers. "It's all your fault," she stormed at him, after the manner of women. "If you hadn't brought your beastly, mouldy, rotten old sapphire down here, none of this would have happened and poor Olive wouldn't have been murdered."

This was too much. Lorrimer lost his temper. "Be quiet," he cried. "If you can't discuss the matter reasonably and sensibly, please don't discuss it at all. Try to be just, too. You are well aware of the reason that I brought it. When I think of that and of what it meant to you—to us—and of what you so unjustly said just now—it makes my blood boil. I'm sorry as much as you are about Francis, even if I don't allow it to turn my head. We are all sorry—but we don't make the exaggerated fuss about it that you do."

She winced at the stroke, but Lorrimer, unheeding, went on. "After all, the fact remains, there's been a murder and I've lost my sapphire. That's a side of the question that you don't seem able to appreciate." He turned away from her moodily as she burst in.

"Your sapphire! It's as much ours as yours when all's said and done. On your own showing! It belonged to our family before one of yours stole it from him—you admitted that yourself, when you told the people its history."

"That isn't true," he cried heatedly. "Why do you twist words? It wasn't stolen at all. It was won from him in a dicing contest."

"Same thing," she interrupted, with more than a tinge of spite. "I haven't your Nonconformist mind for making such nice distinctions. I consider it belonged rightfully to my father much more than it ever did to you."

As she spoke a thought flashed through Lorrimer's mind and he decided there and then to mention it to Challoner and Jack Raikes. When he turned to answer he placed his hand upon her arm.

"Molly," he commenced, "whether you look at it—"

But the younger Miss Mordaunt was in no mood to listen. She flung off the hand of her lover unceremoniously and dashed away from him straight down the walk that ran by the yew-clipped hedge.

Lorrimer watched her with a twitch of the shoulders. On the point of turning his eyes caught sight of Anne Ebbisham coming towards him in company with Christine. Molly dashed by them with an impulsive wave of her handkerchief.

"What have we here?" remarked Miss Ebbisham to her companion. "A lover's tiff? Tut-tut!" She half-turned and looked after the hurriedly-escaping Molly. "Trip it gently, pretty sweeting," she murmured, "even though your journey doesn't look like ending in the generally approved fashion."

Christine laughed deliciously. "My dear Anne," she murmured sweetly, "don't jump to conclusions. It's always an unsafe proposition. There's more than one man in the world."

Anne eyed her quizzically. "For Molly Mordaunt, do you think?"

Christine smiled as she considered the question. "Perhaps not," she conceded. Then the imp of roguishness entered her soul and overcame her. "Any more than there is for Anne Ebbisham."

Dark lightning flashed from the Ebbisham eyes. "Explain yourself, Christine, please," she countered. "Who and where is this Adonis? I confess I'd like to meet him."

Christine laughed lightly. "At the moment I know not, Anne darling. But I shall be pleased to tell you his name. I was thinking of Inspector Baddeley. Although I admit he fills the bill in another way."

A little pink flush tinged the Ebbisham cheeks as Miss Massingham's delicate shaft winged home. *"Touchée,"* she grimaced. "With things as they are—one has to be—"

By this time Captain Lorrimer had come up to them and Anne's sentence went unfinished. Whether his recent interview with his fiancée lent enchantment to the present view or whether the events of the past few days had tended to disturb the accuracy of his previous judgments in the Courts of Love, Lorrimer for the first time found himself in the same gallery as Peter Daventry and supremely conscious of Miss Ebbisham's attractions. He formed the opinion that to linger for a little while would be far from a waste of time. After all, there was much about which he could legitimately talk. Anne seemed to divine what was passing through his mind as she rallied him.

"What have you been saying to Molly, Captain Lorrimer?" she demanded half-reprovingly, and with a shake of an accusing forefinger. "I know that you must have been saying something. The poor lamb scuttled past us just now as though the mint sauce was only a matter of a few minutes behind and its dainty aroma already in her nostrils. Christine here fairly blinked at her. The pace was so alarming."

Lorrimer was frankness itself. He laughed brightly and outlined what had transpired between Miss Mordaunt and him. "What could I do?" he asked, suppliantly. "I can guess of course how Molly feels and I suppose it's only natural that she should, but surely she must see that I am as helpless in the matter as she herself is. There's no doubt Francis will be cleared in time, but—"

Anne Ebbisham regarded him shrewdly. "You feel certain that Francis is innocent, then?" she asked of him.

Lorrimer raised his eyebrows in unaffected astonishment. "Why, Miss Ebbisham, what do you mean? Aren't you certain of it yourself?"

The lady moved her hands in silent eloquence. "In a way I am, I suppose, but you see I can't forget that I have a certain amount of respect for this Inspector's ability. He doesn't strike me as a man that would take any step without very good reason. Therefore I find myself asking the question over and over again, 'Why has he arrested Francis Mordaunt?'"

"Without getting an answer, I suppose," returned Lorrimer.

"No," flashed back Anne, "that's the poisonous part about it. I do get an answer and when I do I see the Baddeley mind working which only makes matters worse."

Lorrimer looked puzzled. "Why? I don't know that I—"

Christine came to his assistance.

"Haven't you guessed, Captain Lorrimer," she said deliberately, "the reason for Baddeley's action? It is not unfathomable surely. Francis Mordaunt appears every time with 'Creeping Jenny.' Where she is, he is. Where he's been, she's been."

His look showed his failure to understand. "It is so," she nodded. "Look at it for yourself. Francis has been stopping in the house on the occasion of every one of the 'Creeping Jenny' stunts. Didn't you know that?"

Lorrimer shook his head. "I certainly didn't. I've never even troubled to think it out, come to that. But is that true? Are you absolutely sure of your facts?"

Anne confirmed Miss Massingham's statement. "Absolutely."

Lorrimer whistled.

Miss Ebbisham continued, "And there's no doubt that that's why the indefatigable Baddeley has snared his bird. That's the particular card upon which he's banking. But in justice to Francis there is something else to be said. The same set of circumstances applies to others. With him—in these various county mansions where Jenny has operated—have been his sisters two, Jane and Molly—whose love is true—also one other—last but not least—the grinning skeleton at the feast." She dropped him a mocking curtsey. "There you are, rhymes at random while you wait."

Lorrimer stared, again at a loss for comprehension.

"One other?" he queried eventually. "Whom do you mean?"

Miss Ebbisham spread out her hands in self-introduction. "I," she exclaimed dramatically, "I—Anne Ebbisham! The girl who has often stood at the cross-roads and—" She paused.

"And what?" asked Lorrimer, eagerly curious.

"Powdered her nose," replied Anne solemnly. "What did you imagine I'd done? Out Turpinned Turpin? Good gracious no."

Lorrimer's admiration was now very evident. "Yet you could steal with success, Miss Ebbisham. That is, of course, if you seriously set out to try."

"I don't think I understand you, Captain Lorrimer," replied the lady.

Lorrimer laughed with gay gallantry and shrugged his shoulders. "Perhaps I expressed myself crudely," he ventured. "I will endeavour to explain my meaning more dearly. Let me put it like this. While 'Creeping Jenny' is stealing—shall we say—diamonds—you could be stealing—shall we say—hearts? Do you understand me now?" His glance now was quite frankly admiring.

Anne crowed with delight. "How bee-yutifully expressed! All the same though, you misjudge me and I think perhaps you are inclined to underrate my humble intelligence. Do you know how?" Her eyes brimmed with undisciplined mischief as she put the question to him. Had he seen it and them, Peter Daventry would have feverishly ransacked the etymological store to find more adequate adjectives with which to frame further eulogy. Either to Anthony Bathurst or any other.

Lorrimer shook his head. "I'm afraid I don't," he answered.

"No? Then I'll tell you. Because I've never yet found a heart worth the stealing. My version is 'who steals hearts, steals trash.' Unfortunate perhaps, but nevertheless true. And for Truth I have invariably been a stickler. Isn't that so, Christilinda? Support me, my child, or I am undone."

Lorrimer smiled and cut in before Miss Massingham could reply to Anne's question and request. "I believe you, Miss Ebbisham. There is no need for Miss Massingham's corroboration. Your word shall be unchallenged always, as far as I am concerned. Still I'd like to say this: if you were not the truth-teller that you claim to be and whom I have accepted as such—but exactly the opposite—one would be quite within one's rights in calling you a 'lovely' fib-teller, wouldn't one? For that description would fearlessly defy contradiction."

Anne tossed her head in indignation. "Don't be personal, Captain Lorrimer. That isn't what we were discussing. Please keep to the point. And you, Christine, please stop that idiotic giggling."

But Christine finished her laugh, an effort in which Lorrimer joined heartily. He was evidently unabashed at Miss Ebbisham's intended censure. About to reply again he was arrested by the sight of Mitchell, the butler at "The Crossways," coming slowly towards them. Mitchell never hurried and would have accepted the Crack of Doom with philosophical calm. The two girls caught the look in Lorrimer's eyes and turned to see what had attracted his attention. Mitchell came on slowly but surely and the three people who awaited him were by this time able to see that he carried something in his hand. When he reached them they observed in more detail that he carried in his right hand a small square box-shaped brown paper package, tightly tied with string and with a red daub of sealing-wax showing on the centre of the crossed string. Mitchell spoke to Captain Lorrimer.

"I beg your pardon, sir. But Mr. Mordaunt suggested that I should bring this out here to you, sir. It has just come by parcel post. If you look you will see that the package is marked 'urgent' in the top left hand corner above where your name and address have been printed."

The butler handed over the small package which Lorrimer took and eyed with some curiosity. Then he frowned in uncertainty. "What's this that's important enough to be marked 'urgent'?" Taking out his pocket-knife he quickly cut the string and removed the outer covering of brown paper. It revealed a small square cardboard box, the kind of box usually used by jewellers for the transport of their trinkets. Lorrimer removed the lid somewhat gingerly and almost simultaneously uttered a cry of profound astonishment. The two girls watched him, interested in what they saw, and Anne, at least, was surprised at the effect that the apparently trifling incident had caused upon their companion. Lorrimer turned to them, his hands shaking with emotion and his eyes shining with exultation.

"Miss Ebbisham," he cried, "Miss Massingham, wonders will never cease; look here at nothing less than a miracle of miracles. It's too good to be true. Here's the Lorrimer sapphire, come back to me from God knows where." He lifted the ring with its wonderful stone from the bed of soft cotton-wool upon which it lay.

Anne held out her hand for it.

"Sure it isn't the 'dud' that Francis told us about?" she inquired. "It's quite possible, you know."

Lorrimer laughed her suggestion away almost contemptuously. "Think I don't know the real thing when I see it? This is the Lorrimer sapphire—I, of all people, could never mistake it. I know it too well, Miss Ebbisham. What I can't understand is why on earth—" He broke off and examined the inside of the square box again.

"There's a little card in there," cried Christine. "Look, it's slipped down to the side there by the cotton-wool. Perhaps that will tell you something more about it."

Lorrimer moved the wool and took out the card. It was exactly similar in shape and size to the card that had been left in his bedroom when the sapphire had been stolen. He turned it over carefully and read its message. A different message from that of the previous one. "With 'Creeping Jenny's' compliments. She returns what she took. Why? Well, here's a reason that will serve. She's twenty-five come Christmas Day, on Christmas Day in the morning."

Anne Ebbisham's eyes glinted keenly as she saw it. "This makes me more certain of my opinion than ever!" she exclaimed triumphantly. "The sapphire itself may be authentic but this 'Jenny's' a fake. Did you ever read such piffle? I'll guarantee this robbery was not pulled off by the 'pukka' 'Creeping Jenny' at all." As she spoke the colour flooded her cheeks and Lorrimer looked at her in flagrant approbation. Inspector Baddeley's move had set things humming in many more directions than one, and

Christine Massingham closely observing her two companions of the moment formed certain rather fascinating conclusions.

CHAPTER XXII

SOME HOURS after the sensational return of the Lorrimer sapphire to its owner, Challoner, Jack Raikes, Peter Daventry and Captain Lorrimer himself were still arguing about this latest surprising turn of events. As may be well understood, it had provided a never-ending topic for discussion. The entry of Russell Streatfeild into the room caused the conversation to dry up a little for a brief period, only to break out again even more heatedly ten minutes or so later. In this conversation Streatfeild himself took little part. It seemed that he preferred to listen to the opinions of others than project his own. He had heard from Henry Mordaunt what Lorrimer had told the latter with regard to the act of restitution performed by "Creeping Jenny" and found the views of the various members of the party on that particular point distinctly interesting. Inspector Baddeley had expressed the wish that "The Crossways" visitors should stay on for a few days more and Mordaunt had asked them to fall in with the request.

"There's one thing," remarked Rakes, "it's an ill-wind and so on—this latest business clears old Francis—that's one comfort we can extract from it."

Challoner regarded him seriously for a moment before replying to his statement. "Speaking quite impersonally and leaving Francis out of the argument, purely as Francis—you see what I mean, don't you—may I ask why you say that?"

"Well, doesn't it?" asked Raikes with a stare of wonderment. "If Francis is in 'jug' it couldn't have been he who sent the sapphire back to Lorrimer, could it? And if he couldn't have sent it back it's equally pretty obvious that he couldn't have—"

Challoner stopped him with a quick gesture. "Just a minute, Jack! That's all very well, as far as it goes. Which isn't too far to my way of thinking. Let's examine all the circumstances for a moment. How about the possibility of an accomplice?"

Raikes rubbed his chin. "I admit that I hadn't thought of that."

"Let me explain myself again," added Challoner, "for I don't desire to be misunderstood. The idea of Francis being guilty of these thefts seems absurd to me. For several reasons. For instance how does Baddeley explain the murder? And that's only one thing that I could mention. But letting x = the person under arrest, my accomplice theory re the restitution of the ring still holds good, it seems to me."

Lorrimer nodded. "I quite agree with you. I happened to be talking to Miss Ebbisham when Mitchell brought out the package to me containing the sapphire. She seemed to think that the return of the ring was quite on all fours with her own theory."

"And that is?" Streatfeild asked.

"That the real 'Creeping Jenny' has had no hand in 'The Crossways' affair at all. She's always been as keen as mustard on that."

Streatfeild nodded. "I see. So that's her idea, is it? Confirmed, of course, now as far as she is concerned, by the fact of the sapphire having been returned—eh?"

"I presume so," replied Lorrimer stiffly—"I know of no other reason. What other reason could there be? The lady didn't confide in me, certainly."

Streatfeild nodded again. "She didn't? Well, after all, I can't say that I'm surprised at her more than anybody, entertaining the views that she does. Time will tell if she's right, of course."

Adrian Challoner flung a quick glance in his direction. "I realize that the fullness of Time solves most problems, Streatfeild, but I fancy that I read into your remark rather more than a mere generalization. May I inquire what it is?"

Streatfeild smiled at him. "Nothing remarkably mysterious, my dear Challoner. Suppose 'Creeping Jenny' did steal the Lorrimer sapphire, contrary to Miss Ebbisham's expressed opinion, and has turned away from her wickedness that she hath committed and done that which is lawful and right—shall she not save her soul alive?"

Puzzled looks met him all round.

"I have evidently mystified you," went on Streatfeild. "Let me clear the air. This suggested attitude can be proved more conclusively by wholesale repentance, can it not?"

"You mean—"

"I mean this! If 'Creeping Jenny' should happen by any chance to make restitution all round, well then it seems to me that this theory that you ascribe to Miss Ebbisham vanishes into thin air."

Two or three of his hearers shook their heads doubtfully before Lorrimer spoke again. He translated his scepticism vigorously. "What you say is possible, of course, but the more I think things over, I'm inclined to row in with Miss Ebbisham's theory. Because I'm pretty certain that I'd never have seen my sapphire again if the real 'Creeping Jenny' had taken it. Any more than any of the other people who have been robbed will get their property back. And say what you like about it—there's soundness in that argument."

"Possibly," rejoined Streatfeild, "and yet there may also be soundness in mine. I commend it to your attention. As I said before—time will tell. Then we shall see who's right."

There was a dead silence in the room as he rose and walked to the door. Turning as he reached it, he asked a question. "When is Baddeley's ban about getting away from here to be lifted? Does anyone know?"

"The day after to-morrow," replied Lorrimer curtly. "I inquired of Mr. Mordaunt only this morning."

"Thank you," replied Mr. Streatfeild as he closed the door behind him.

"Seems anxious to get away, doesn't he?" asked Raikes of Peter Daventry.

Peter shook his head but whether in dissent or assent Raikes was unable to say. Peter was passing, to his own surprise, through an unusual mental emotion. During the morning of that day he had been reminded by something which by the coming of the afternoon he was unable to remember, of the man he had met on the heath last week and of the resemblance which he had so far failed to identify. As Streatfeild had stood at the door and asked that last question another haunting, fugitive idea passed through his brain and strive for its capture how he would, it nevertheless persistently eluded him. He thought over and over again of the stranger who had accosted him and asked the way to "The Crossways" and then he turned his attention to thoughts of this other man, Streatfeild. At last he threw the problem aside and gave it up. He had just reached this decision when he was brought back to contemplation of the present by the sudden entrance of Henry Mordaunt and Inspector Baddeley. It was the first occasion that the former had seen the Inspector since the arrest of his son and, as may be readily guessed, the atmosphere was far from congenial.

"Lorrimer," exclaimed Mordaunt testily, "Inspector Baddeley is the bearer of more astounding news. In fact I find it difficult these days to dissociate him from the sensational. But it will interest you, Lorrimer, to know that you are not alone, as I believe you are imagining you are. I understand that the fact is that 'Creeping Jenny' is going the whole hog and has served all her clients alike."

"What?" cried Challoner. "Are you serious?"

"I was never more serious in my life," retorted Baddeley, taking up the challenge. "What has happened to Captain Lorrimer here has also happened in all the other cases in which this 'Jenny' person has figured." He took a list from his pocket and referred to it. "Sir Graeme Grantham, Mrs. Midwinter, Lady Craddock, Mrs. Stanley Medlicott and Mrs. Topham-Garnett have all had similar communications. In each case the article stolen has been returned with a card bearing precisely the same message as Captain Lorrimer's." The Inspector stopped, wiped his forehead with his handkerchief and looked round. "Moving, aren't we?" he suggested caustically. "We know when 'Jenny's' birthday is—or when she says it is—which is very different."

"Meanwhile, what about my son, Inspector?" demanded Mordaunt. "Surely this has made a difference. How long is the outrage of his imprisonment to continue?"

Baddeley's jaw set. "He will stand his trial. Outrage or not, Mr. Mordaunt, his arrest set the ball rolling and you can't deny it. Which was precisely my intention that it should. And you ought to thank rather than censure me if it eventually is the means of him being proved innocent."

But Mordaunt was far from being mollified by the picture Baddeley had painted. His reply was coldness itself. "There was never any necessity of proving that as far as I can see, Inspector. So your statement, I regret to say, leaves me unmoved."

Challoner seized this moment to ask Baddeley a question. "I understand, Inspector," he said, "that you have no objection now to any of us leaving here the day after to-morrow. May I take that as official?"

Baddeley considered it for a second. "I did say that, it's true, but anyhow I shall be over here again on that day and will settle the question then." He turned to Mordaunt. "Where is Mr. Streatfeild? I would like a few words with him."

Mordaunt rang for Mitchell. "Oh Mitchell," he said on the latter's arrival, "find Mr. Streatfeild, will you, and tell him that Inspector Baddeley wants him down here. He can't be far away; I passed him on my way here about twenty minutes ago."

Mitchell departed on his errand. Five minutes passed. Ten minutes passed. Challoner, Lorrimer and the others secretly wondered what it was that caused Baddeley to want Streatfeild at this juncture. They also began to notice the Inspector's growing impatience, a condition that he took no pains to conceal. At length the butler returned. He addressed Mordaunt.

"I am very sorry, sir," he announced gravely, "but Mr. Streatfeild is nowhere to be found. I have looked for him everywhere and at last I—er repaired to his bedroom. Besides the fact that the room is empty the gentleman's bag is gone, together with his personal belongings. I should say, sir, from all appearances that Mr. Streatfeild has left 'The Crossways.'"

CHAPTER XXIII

MR. HORACE Hutchings, night porter and attendant of that somewhat notorious block of flats known to the world at large as Radway Mansions, Virga Vale, sipped his cup of Bovril with becoming carefulness and entered upon an arithmetical calculation in the blank portion of his evening newspaper's column headed *Stop Press*. His eyes gleamed with delightful anticipation as he did so for Mr. Hutchings was now engaged upon what was very nearly his favourite occupation, he was working out the precise financial gain to himself of an "each way treble" that in his own description had "clicked." He had three-quarters of an hour to spare before the time came for him to go on duty. "'Robin Adair' of the good old *Bugle* hadn't half had a day," so Mr. Hutchings reflected to himself. Four winners, a second and a non-runner. "Seven times half a dollar," he muttered radiantly to himself, "is seventeen and a tanner plus a third— seven runners only and thank God for it—is another five and tenpence making twenty-three and fourpence plus my stake is—" He sucked the top of his pencil in his endeavour to locate the precise market value of Eldorado and at that moment there came a somewhat aggressive rat-tat-tat upon the front door of the Hutchings' abode. Mr. Hutchings looked at the clock on the mantelpiece and frowned. He received no inspiration from the effort. Who was this that knocked at this time of the evening?

"See 'oo it is, Clarice," he sang out to the wife of his bosom— "and if it's the Salvation Army come a-begging for something tell 'em I'm a strict R.C. and a little critical of some of their doctrine." He cocked his ear attentively as he heard his wife's tones in conversation at the front door. Then she called him.

"'Orace! You're wanted. Here's a gentleman to see you. Shall I take him in to the front room or will you be coming to the door?"

Mr. Hutchings drained his Bovril and rose with deliberation solemnly to his feet.

"Blasted fool," he muttered under his breath—"where's 'er tact, conversin' with sanguinary strangers—when will women learn to 'andle situations—'tain't as though I ain't taught her neither. She ought to know better."

He straightened himself and called along to her, "All right! I'm coming. Who is it? His Majesty or The Harga Karn?" He made his way up the passage.

"Good evening, Mr. Hutchings," said the visitor, "but I should be extremely obliged if you could spare me just a few moments of your valuable time. As I was explaining to this lady when you came up, I shall be very pleased to recognize your services suitably should you be able to assist me in the direction I require."

"Suitably." Mr. Hutchings pondered over the word. It seemed to have a pleasant ring about it. Taken on the whole and reflecting on the extraordinary success that had attended the morning efforts of "Robin Adair" he looked like having a "good day." He peered up at his visitor's face. "I go on duty at nine, sir," he remarked, "depends what it is you want. You see I ain't got a lot of time. If it lays in my power—"

"'Adn't you better arst the gentleman in?" suggested Clarice Hutchings. "You can't very well talk business on the mat, can you now? Where's your ettykwet?"

Her husband, seeing the social quality of his evening caller, accepted the justice of the suggestion and Russell Streatfeild followed him into the little living-room. Mrs. Hutchings herself was just in time to slip through the door of the said room before the privacy-seeking Horace could close it in her face. A matter of a short head, no more. There was just the possibility, she considered, that she might be "in" this. Streatfeild took a note from his wallet and held it up to Hutchings between his fingers.

"This pound, Hutchings," he said, wheedlingly, "is yours, provided you can give me the information I desire. First of all how long have you been night-porter over at Radway Mansions?"

"Ever since a little argument I took part in with a few ruby 'Uns. I was demobbed the latter end of 1919 and got this job in the February of 1920. That's your first question answered, sir."

Clarice nodded vigorous corroboration; perhaps Horace had already qualified for a part of the pound.

"Good," exclaimed Streatfeild, "that fact suits my purpose admirably. For I've no doubt now that you are in a position to give me the particular information for which I have come.

Listen to me and we'll soon see. Do you remember a lady who resided, I believe, at No. 5 Radway Mansions, Virga Vale, some three years ago under the name of Mrs. Galloway?" He watched the night-porter keenly. Hutchings nodded sagaciously.

"I do, sir. Very well indeed. Funny thing, she was only passin' through my mind a day or two ago. And a very nice young lady she was too. Open-'anded and generous. Many a time she's said to me, 'Hutchings, you're a treasure. Get yourself something with this.'"

"Good again," declared Streatfeild. "Just to make certain that there's no mistake about the lady being the one I mean have a look at that, will you?"

Hutchings took the photograph that Streatfeild held out to him and passed it over to his wife. "That's 'er, Clarice, isn't it? No mistaking that for Mrs. Galloway, is there, my gal?"

Clarice made curious clucking sounds indicative of agreement. "Looks a bit older as you might expect," she added, "but there, none of us gets younger, do we? Barring, of course, monkey-gland." She returned the photograph. "Where is she now?" she inquired. "Gone abroad to join her 'usband? Went tea-plantin' in Burma, didn't he, with her brother? She was waitin' to hear from 'im."

"The lady has not gone abroad," replied Mr. Streatfeild. He had caught her last words. The interview looked like ending more profitably to him that he had expected even. He followed up immediately.

"So there was a husband, was there—and a brother? What was the brother like?"

"Never clapped eyes on 'im," replied Clarice, brightly. "If you arst me he was nothing to write 'ome about. That was the opinion formed. He kept out of the way, 'e did. Call 'im a proper bad hegg and you won't be far out." She folded her arms after the manner of her class pronouncing unfavourable judgment.

"The missus is quite right," affirmed Hutchings. "I never saw Mrs. Galloway's brother—we only 'eard about 'im."

"And the husband?" inquired Mr. Streatfeild. "Did you ever see him?"

"Bless your 'eart, sir. Of course," replied the porter, "he often came to Radway Mansions, half a dozen times a year or so—and stayed for a time! Mr. Barrington Galloway 'e called himself, fellow wot 'eld his nose in the air, so to speak. Often couldn't see my 'and 'eld out in front of 'im, or wouldn't perhaps 'ud be nearer the mark. He 'ad the best of his marriage bargain. There's no two opinions about that."

Streatfeild felt in his breast pocket again. "Is that gentleman on the right there anything like the Mr. Galloway whom you knew?" He pointed to a group-photo cut from an illustrated paper.

"That's 'im," declared Hutchings. "That's my lord the Dook. The one 'olding 'is arms out. So 'e's back from Burma, is 'e, planted all the tea there is to be planted, eh?"

Streatfeild handed over the promised price of the information. "I hope to turn what you have told me, Mr. Hutchings, to very satisfactory account," he declared. "Good evening."

On his way back from the home of the night-porter he reflected with extreme pleasure upon the fact that he had slipped away from "The Crossways" (and Inspector Baddeley) just in time. But he shivered a little as he thought of the key of the murdered woman's bedroom door. That might have turned out to be a very nasty business!

CHAPTER XXIV

NOVEMBER had already reigned for nearly a week. One by one the various members of the house party had followed the example of Russell Streatfeild and found their respective ways back to the normal routine. Francis Mordaunt awaited trial for the "Creeping Jenny" robberies and Inspector Baddeley became less and less confident of the result thereof as the days went by. The case that he had prepared to bring against the accused man was a strong one from many points of view, but he was perfectly well aware that he had taken a distinct chance when he applied for his warrant and made his arrest. It was idle for him to pretend that the results for which he had hoped had materialized and he was quite unable to assess accurately the meaning of the sensational restitution that "Creeping Jenny" had so surprisingly made. In every instance there was no doubt whatever that the article she had returned was the very same article that had been stolen, and in no case did it appear any the worse for the theft. Truth to tell Baddeley found himself growing more and more uneasy. Whatever his arrest of Francis Mordaunt had brought about with regard to the burglaries there was another very plain fact to be faced—it had achieved absolutely nothing in respect of the murder. Here Baddeley was forced to admit reluctantly that he had reached the very end of his tether. Nothing that he had followed up had been productive. He contemplated the situation as it now appeared to him, very ruefully. However, had he known, succour was at hand and from (to him) a most unexpected quarter. On the fifth day of November that was ushered in with a mixture of rain and fog, Peter Daventry, throwing aside all consideration of Guido Fawkes and his "Gunpowder, Treason and Plot," decided to take a morning off from his not too exacting duties in Cornhill and run along to have a palaver with Anthony Bathurst. He had not seen him at all since their interchange of correspondence, although he had called at his flat on one occasion when Mr. Bathurst had been out. This time he happened to be more fortunate as the man he very much wanted to see was in. Cheered at the news, Peter ascended the stairs like an elated eland. Bathurst greeted him in his own inimitable manner and waved him to the recesses of the big armchair by the fireside.

"Curl up in that, Daventry, and make yourself comfortable. There are cigarettes and tobacco at your elbow. Also what will you drink? I think there's plenty of Scotch. Sir Austin Kemble hasn't dropped in to see me for some little time."

Peter named his poison and settled down luxuriously. Anthony looked at him quizzically.

"Well, laddie, come to settle the 'Crossways' puzzle? I can conceive no other reason for a visit at this time on such an absolutely filthy morning."

Peter Daventry laughed.

"My dear old Bathurst, why should I do the old dissemble? I *have* come to ask you a question or two and I might just as well admit it. Because the fact is the damned business is becoming a nuisance to me—a perpetual source of worry—a jolly old Man of the Sea weaving his tibiae and fibulae round the highly-respected old collar-bone." Peter stopped and flicked the ash from the end of his cigarette. "It's giving me an 'acking corf, 'orrible pains in the lumbar region and fiery spots before the peepers. So here I am for you to rumble me. How are you posted now in connection with it?"

Mr. Bathurst thought it over for a moment. "I've followed it pretty closely, I think, on the whole—but anything you consider I may not know—any of the more intimate details, for instance—let me have them—because they're more helpful very often than those that are made so public." Peter drained his glass, recited all that he knew and eventually reached the point of the return of the stolen articles by "Creeping Jenny." He repeated the message that purported to have come from that elusive lady and explained fully to Anthony how her restitution operations had been comprehensive and complete. Anthony rubbed his chin.

"And meanwhile I see from the papers that Baddeley has arrested Francis Mordaunt, eh? That's the position, isn't it?"

"That's what the purblind idiot has done—and for the life of me I can't see why. Can you?"

"It depends," replied Mr. Bathurst guardedly.

"Baddeley may know something that you don't know. There's always that possibility, remember. Help yourself. Your glass is empty." He nodded in the direction of the decanter.

"I suppose so," conceded Peter. "All the same I'm of the opinion with others that the old Baddeley bean has struck a snag this journey. Don't you think so yourself? Lorrimer thinks so. So does Challoner, so does Jack Raikes. Lorrimer has written to me telling me so. Here's his letter. If you agree with us over it I'll know we're right."

Anthony took the proffered letter from the envelope, read it and smiled at Peter's eagerness.

"You want my opinion, do you? Well, from what I know of the case, perhaps I do agree with you. Does that satisfy you?"

Peter grinned in appreciation. "It gives me a warmer feeling round the old aorta, that's certain, but I can't say that it leaves me very satisfied. Nothing short of clearing the whole beastly mess up will do that." He drained his glass and refilled it for the second time. "To tell the truth, old man, I've been muzzy all through the innings. You know—thick in the head—properly addle-pated! When you wrote to me in reply to my first 'chit' to you and gave me several noggins of advice—something was always turning up to send me into little Alice's own country. And without the old White Bunny to guide me either. One afternoon I met a young feller-me-lad inquiring for 'The Crossways.' When I told him I'd take him along to the ancient pile he refrigerated. Such an idea as going there was apparently farthest from his thoughts. Do you know, Bathurst, I'd swear I'd seen his dial before somewhere. But do you imagine I can think *where*? Not I. Not to save myself from the Ling-Chee. Then take that other Johnny that you warned me against, Comrade Streatfeild. He floated about everywhere—L.U.E., R.C. and L.C. to say nothing of 'Noises off.' Don't forget, too, that others felt like you about him, as I wrote to you, when you asked me. What's his business with Henry Mordaunt, anyway?"

Mr. Bathurst nodded. "Yes. I remember what you wrote and told me about Streatfeild. But, tell me more of this other person who inquired the way to the Mordaunts' house. How old would you say that he was?"

"Two or three and twenty," replied Mr. Daventry—"not more."

"H'm," said Anthony. "That sets me wondering. It's strange how a chance remark will do that upon occasion." He rose and paced the room. Suddenly he turned and went to a pigeonhole of his desk. Taking several miscellaneous papers therefrom he selected one and placed it in front of Peter Daventry. It was a small picture of a young man in costume seated upon the trunk of a tree. "Is that anything like the young fellow you met? I have a strong idea that it may be."

Peter gazed at the picture spellbound. He saw the young man arrayed in doublet and hose but the face was the face of the man who had met him and asked him the way.

"Great snakes, Bathurst," cried Mr. Daventry in the throes of excitement, "who's this supposed to be? Because this is the man I met on the heath that afternoon. I haven't a doubt about it."

"No it isn't," replied Mr. Bathurst; "you're quite wrong. You'd be a lot of good as a witness, wouldn't you? It merely happens to be like him, that is all." He stopped, smiled at Peter and rubbed his cheek with his forefinger. "And when I think of the message that 'Creeping Jenny' sent with her parcel of 'returns' I'm not denying that it betrayed a touch of whimsicality that I find distinctly arresting." Anthony chuckled. "The touch of the master," he added.

"Or mistress," mumbled Peter.

"Yes," returned Mr. Bathurst, "or mistress."

CHAPTER XXV

"MURILLO'S," murmured Captain Lorrimer to his fair companion as he gracefully gestured her to a seat, "is unequalled for a little dinner such as we want to-night and such as I am fortunate enough to have quite constantly when I am staying in London. Although of course this evening's meal will be the 'finest Elphberg of them all.'" He looked into the dancing eyes of the lady to whom he spoke.

"Why?" asked Anne Ebbisham artlessly of her escort.

"Need you ask?" replied Lorrimer as charmingly as he could. "There is a mirror facing you. The mere inclination of your head will surely satisfy—"

Anne tapped him on the arm with her theatre-programme. "That's very nice of you but—"

Miss Ebbisham paused as a waiter seemed to materialize from nowhere and present himself at Captain Lorrimer's side.

Lorrimer frowned as he looked at the man. "You're not my usual waiter—where's Benito?" he asked.

"I do not know, sir," replied the waiter in a tone that bordered upon the apologetic. "I 'ave not seen 'im. Perhaps 'e is not 'ere this evening. But if you wish it, sir, I will ask the *maître d'hôtel*."

"Thank you, if you would." Lorrimer turned to Anne at his side. "I must have Benito if I can possibly get him. It's more than a mere whim on my part. He's incomparably the finest waiter I ever struck and I want this evening's dinner to be perfect in every way." He smiled at her meaningly. "Do you mind me wanting that?"

"I hope he isn't old and withered, been with the firm since the Flood, so to speak. These hardy fixtures and faithful retainers bore me stiff." Anne Ebbisham laughed merrily.

"On the contrary," replied Lorrimer, "he's—but here comes the *maître d'hôtel*."

"Benito will be here in one minute, sir. He was engaged elsewhere when you came in, otherwise he would have attended to you as usual. Because he knows Monsieur is particular over the dishes what he chooses. But I will give him orders." He turned to depart.

"Good," said Lorrimer, "tell him to bring a Bronx and a Martini directly he comes."

When the much-heralded and belauded Benito did arrive bearing the two cocktails Miss Ebbisham began to understand why her escort favoured him so markedly. Tall, for an Italian, his touch was faultless. Perfect in suggestion, assiduous in advice, Benito was as anxiously-fastidious to please his patron as his patron was fastidiously-anxious to be pleased.

"I was in the seventh heaven of delight to get your letter," Lorrimer remarked. "I think it's most sporting of you to have written and to have come. I read it twice and then pinched myself to make sure that I wasn't dreaming. But there—I oughtn't to have told you that."

Anne grimaced. "I felt that I must talk to somebody; somebody who would be sympathetic." Lorrimer nodded, found her hand and gave the fingers a surreptitious but assuring squeeze. "How did you get my address?"

"From your mother."

"I was actually at Cannes when your letter came. I went there after the tragedy,"—he patted her hand in appreciation. "I came away at once, got back the night before last and wrote to you from my Club."

Anne nodded and replied, "You see I'm worried over Francis Mordaunt." She stopped for a second but then went on again. "His trial's due to commence next week." She crumbled a piece of bread into small pieces upon the white cloth. "Tell me," she continued and Lorrimer could easily read the distress in her eyes as she spoke, "do you think he's guilty, Captain Lorrimer? Do you think there's the slightest chance of it?"

Lorrimer shook his head. "Candidly, Anne—on the evidence as I see it—I don't! But I suppose we must concede that there is such a thing as a chance that he may be. It's just on the cards— let us say—that another society 'Raffles' has arisen. But as to its necessarily being Francis—" he broke off and shrugged his shoulders.

Miss Ebbisham threw out another question. "You're not too helpful, are you? Do you think he'll be acquitted? That's even more important, isn't it?"

"It's more easily answered, Anne, because I most certainly do. I don't think Baddeley can pull enough out against him to bring off a verdict. If the trial were in Scotland, I should expect a verdict of 'Not Proven.'"

Anne sighed and looked considerably relieved. "I'm pleased to hear you say that. I can't tell you how pleased. If you hadn't said that I might have felt inclined to—" She paused.

Lorrimer regarded her curiously. "To what?" he asked. "Confide in me?"

She laughed, but the effort was almost mirthless. "Hardly that. 'Confide' isn't the word which would properly express my feelings. Almost to confess something to you." Her mood changed suddenly. "But I won't on second considerations. Not this evening, at least." She changed the subject adroitly. "What did you think of Adrian Challoner this evening?"

"Excessively clever, as always. But it's nearing the end of the run of 'Broken Threads' and he's got two eyes on his next show.

He's always like that. Lionel Ambler tells me—and nobody should know better than he—that the new show's going to be his finest for years."

Anne nodded. "He's very confident, I know. When's the *première*? I ought to know but—"

"Friday of next week—and young Mordaunt's affair comes off on Tuesday." He teased her mockingly. "So you'll know the worst before Adrian Challoner's first night."

She flashed a quick glance at him. But Lorrimer had turned in his chair and she was unable, from her position, to determine exactly what his remark had been intended to mean.

"By the way," she said, "my godfather's giving a big dinner party here after the *première*. He's done so before under similar conditions. I heard from him yesterday—he told me all about it in his letter of invitation. All 'The Crossways' crowd are to be asked to come. Your Molly and her sister, Francis himself if all goes well on Tuesday—all the lot. But I expect you'll be hearing yourself. Do you think Henry Mordaunt will come?"

"Hardly likely," considered Lorrimer, "in the circumstances. Challoner can hardly expect him to, can he? Still he might if the trial ends satisfactorily; it's over two months since the murder and a man can't bury himself for ever. But if he does you can bet his shadow Streatfeild will be close behind him." He turned and beckoned to his impeccable waiter.

"Benito."

"Your pleasure, sir."

"This lady and I desire a liqueur."

Benito bent over and became eulogistically voluble as he portrayed the outstanding merits of a certain brandy—a brandy (so he said) that had inspired Caesar to cross the Rubicon—a brandy that had resigned Napoleon to the burning of the Kremlin, a brandy that the Guise had supped on the Eve of St. Bartholomew—a brandy that had induced Marie Antoinette to—Captain Lorrimer indicated that he and Miss Ebbisham would attach themselves to the distinguished company that had preceded them. That is, of course, according to Benito.

CHAPTER XXVI

LORRIMER'S prognostications proved to be accurate. The case against Francis Mordaunt collapsed and several observant visitors to the white-washed Court formed the opinion that Inspector Baddeley deliberately allowed it to take this course. Certainly he took no especially violent steps to prevent it. Peter Daventry had travelled down for the trial and much to his delight had succeeded in enlisting as his companion Anthony Bathurst of all people. Most of "The Crossways" house party attended—in various capacities—with the exception of Jack Raikes and Russell Streatfeild.

Henry Mordaunt heard the result with unalloyed delight and gave the impression to those around him that a great weight had been removed from his shoulders. The four girls, Anne, Christine, Jane and Molly Mordaunt were just as frankly over-joyed—a condition which seemed almost universal around the countryside. Challoner motored bank to town in his Daimler, and dropped Henry Mordaunt at "The Crossways" on the way. He had been particularly anxious that Mordaunt should accompany him and had prevailed on Jane to drive her brother home in Mordaunt's car while her father travelled with him. As he alighted from the Daimler Mordaunt was seen to shake his head.

"It's very good of you, Challoner," he said—"and I know you mean it with the best intentions, but don't expect me on Friday, although I may change my mind. Francis and the girls can pop along if they choose. But while this horrible mystery hangs over this house, over me, and over the lives of so many of us I feel that everything has become more or less futile. Thank God—one cloud has lifted to-day. Perhaps the other will soon follow suit. I will take to-day as a favourable omen and trust that the Fates will be kind." He waved his hand to Adrian Challoner and walked sharply up the drive leading to the house as the car sped towards London.

* * * * *

The premiere of "Sin and a Woman" was a triumphant success. It was a far finer play than "Broken Threads" which had preceded it. Its reception by pit, gallery and stalls was overwhelmingly enthusiastic and there was early evidence to the initiated that it was destined for an unusually long run. The dialogue was crisp and clever, the characterization clearly-definite and the big scenes built up with intense power. The well-advertised assassination scene outside the House at Westminster was a personal triumph for Adrian Challoner himself. The critics praised it with one exception—Shannon Skoffer of the *Daily Bugle*. He said that Challoner's performance would have been wonderful if he had only been assassinated directly the curtain went up. He added that the play as presented was appalling, but if the maid had moved the wineglass in the second act to the side-table instead of placing it on the tea-table (centre), the play would have taken rank as the greatest drama since the days of Garrick. But Brodribb St. Clair in the *Morning Message* wrote—"Adrian Challoner in plays of this nature is incomparable. He exalts us to the heights and he drags us to the depths by sheer projection of personality—in his case a flaming trinity of consciousness, power and will. 'Sin and a Woman' should play to capacity for a very long time." At the close of the performance there were the usual cries from a packed house for the "Author." For a long time these met with no response. At last so long-repeated did they become and so impatient the audience, that Challoner came before the curtain and thanked the audience courteously for the wonderful reception. He informed them that as far as he knew the lady who was responsible for the play was not in the house. But he assured his hearers that he would convey the opinion of the audience to her at the first possible moment. Eventually the audience dispersed. Half-an-hour later Challoner motored to Murillo's in his big car. He had previously arranged that Anne should come into his dressing-room immediately after the show and accompany him and Christine Massingham down to the restaurant. As he entered, a girl on either side, the *maître d'hôtel* came forward obsequiously to meet him.

He favoured Challoner with a low bow.

"But it is that I have arranged your tables with the greatest effort of diplomacy, M. Challoner. You are in the 'Diadem' room as was your wish and everything will be truly magnificent for you."

"Good," said Challoner, "that's as it should be." He wiped the perspiration from his brow with a silk handkerchief. "By Jove, Anne, I worked like a horse to-night to get it over, and I suppose you did much the same, Christine. It's fairly taken the steam out of me. Anyhow—we're here. Cut along, you girls—you know where to come—the 'Diadem.'"

As Challoner entered the room reserved for his party, there came to him a feeling of intense pleasure and satisfaction. The bronze-coloured chrysanthemums that had been used for decoration lent the room a touch that seemed to him as he took it in for the first time almost barbaric in its appeal. One by one his guests entered and he greeted them. Then he referred them to the cards upon the tables bearing their names.

"One thing I'm thankful for," muttered Anne to Miss Massingham behind her, "there's no band to assassinate my conversation. Cheers!"

Just as the company moved towards the two tables, the eyes of Adrian Challoner were seen to light up. Henry Mordaunt and his son Francis came through the curtained space that separated the "Diadem" room from its neighbouring apartment. In their wake came the tall figure of Russell Streatfeild. Captain Lorrimer whispered in Molly Mordaunt's ear and then turned to her sister Jane and his mother. The two ladies listened to what he had to say and nodded, evidently in approval. Looking up quickly he caught Anne Ebbisham's eye upon him and he flashed her a glance that invited approbation from her of his prophecy of the previous week concerning Streatfeild. The lady evidently understood the significance of the glance for she replied with her eyes to that effect.

Murillo's is famous for the quality and assortment of its *hors-d'oeuvres* and it was easy to understand on this particular evening how this reputation had been achieved and how more-over it was entirely justified.

Peter Daventry made himself the recipient of self-congratu-lation. He was seated, he discovered, between Anne Ebbisham and Christine, than which at the moment he desired nothing better. Both he and Anne were in their best form, they suited each other admirably and each brought out the best from each.

"What mood are you in to-night, Miss Ebbisham," he rallied her, "after a show such as we've seen?"

"The imperative," she riposted, "so I warn you to beware, Mr. Daventry."

"If thou lov'st me—then beware," he retorted, turning to his other neighbour; "and you, Miss Massingham?"

"Mood?" she queried.

"Yes," he repeated.

"Don't classify me in a mood," returned Christine. "I don't think I altogether like it—put me down as just 'tense.'"

Peter lowered his voice. "I've been collecting 'news,' girls. Don't be surprised at anything that may happen in the near future, about 'The Crossways' business, I mean."

Anne looked at him curiously. "In what way?" she asked.

"About the murder," almost whispered Peter, to a bent head on either side of him.

"Tell me all," fluttered Miss Ebbisham. "I'm simply dying of curiosity! Do you really mean tonight?"

Christine held out a hand to restrain her.

Peter shook his head oracularly. "Good lord, no! What made you think that? I didn't mean to convey anything like that. But I can tell you this, I blew along to old Bathurst quite recently—that's my sleuth-pal, you know—and something I said froze him on to an idea. We were having a pow-wow on the old affair very generally and all that—and Bathurst's a Bright Young Person—take it from P.D.—P.D.Q."

Christine screwed up her pretty face. "But what can your friend do in the matter? I don't see how—"

"What's to prevent him passing the idea, whatever it may be, on to jolly old Baddeley?" Peter had raised his voice by now and the sound of the Inspector's surname travelled down the table.

"Funny you mentioning Baddeley, Daventry," called out Jack Raikes. "I saw him in the 'Ramillies' and again in the Lounge downstairs."

"Quite true," said Adrian Challoner in a voice that seemed to hold a tinge of something like defiance. "I am responsible for that. I invited him to the theatre. At our first meeting the Inspector happened to tell me in the course of conversation that he had never seen me on the boards. So you see, I remedied that at my first available opportunity. I think I owed it to Baddeley to do so. Although as a matter of fact I fancy it was Anne here who prompted my memory in the matter." As Baddeley's name cropped up for discussion after he had so unconsciously set the ball rolling, Peter Daventry's eyes happened to stray across to the other table where Henry Mordaunt and Russell Streatfeild were sitting. At the mention of Baddeley's name by Jack Raikes he saw a peculiar look come into the latter's face. Henry Mordaunt himself looked preternaturally grave and worried. Peter looked across to Challoner and listened attentively to what the latter was saying relative to Baddeley and the theatre. Then his eyes shifted back almost spontaneously to Mordaunt's table. To his utter surprise he saw Russell Streatfeild rise from the table very quietly—almost stealthily in fact, turn and then disappear from the room through the curtained space. Amazed at this strange occurrence Peter looked round among Challoner's other guests to see if the exit had been observed generally. Evidently it had not—for none remarked upon it and all seemed to proceed with their dinners ignorant of Streatfeild's surprising defection. Mr. Daventry fell to considering the possible meaning of this unusual incident. But a minute later a remark from Miss Ebbisham jerked him back to the immediate need of the moment. Evidently she for one hadn't noticed Streatfeild's furtive movement.

CHAPTER XXVII

CAPTAIN Lorrimer motioned to his infallible waiter, Benito, and the latter seeing the gesture flitted to Lorrimer's side.

"Yes sir."

"1 shall expect you to look after *me*, Benito. Don't forget that I consider I've a prior claim on you. Consider me your regular patron. The waiter whom I've had so far is worse than useless. Let me have the wine list again, will you?"

The admirable Benito smiled in answer to the engaging smile of his patron, bowed and obeyed. Peter Daventry answered his companion's remark almost mechanically. He found, strive how he would, that his eyes repeatedly went back to the empty chair that Russell Streatfeild had so suddenly and silently vacated. It had been an end seat—a seat that had had one neighbour only—Henry Mordaunt. This latter alone seemed to be cognisant of Streatfeild's disappearance. Peter watched him carefully. As he watched he grew more and more certain that Mordaunt was privy to it. Three or four times as counted by Mr. Daventry he noticed Mordaunt cast backward glances over his shoulder in the direction of where Streatfeild had made his exit. Then his eyes would move over to where sat his two girls. They were anxious eyes—more than that even—eyes that seemed to be repeatedly asking a question. Mr. Daventry decided to enlist assistance on the affair that was bothering him. He turned carelessly to his neighbour, Miss Ebbisham.

"Streatfeild seems to have taken fright over something. Did you notice it? Shied at a piece of paper or somebody's shadow."

Amie looked over to the table in question.

"Why?" she asked. "Has Mr. Streatfeild—?"

"Gone," replied Peter tersely. "Hopped it. Skedaddled. Seen a spook or something." He lowered his voice again. "Do you know what I think about it, Miss Ebbisham?"

The lady shook her head and invited his further confidence.

"Well, it may sound to you pretty idiotic, but I've a shrewd idea floating through the old grey matter that I've a very good notion as to what made dear old Streatfeild do his little skipping act."

"What was it, Mr. Daventry? Do tell me, please."

Peter's eyes glinted with the seriousness of set purpose. "The mention of the name of dear old Inspector Baddeley. Neither more nor less. Don't fancy it had a healthy ring to the ears of the gentleman we're discussing. Wasn't a bit Skegness to him."

"Skegness?" Anne looked puzzled.

Peter shrugged explanatory shoulders. "The place on the East Coast that used to be 'so bracing'." He seemed a trifle disappointed at having to supply the information.

Anne laughed at his mock sorrow. "I see. Sorry I let you down. I'm not usually slow. But it can't be as you say. I expect you'll find that there's quite a simple explanation in the end. You're suffering from an excess of the melodramatic. It's because of the show you went to this evening. It's been imposed upon you by Adrian Challoner."

Mr. Daventry wagged his head oracularly. "We shall see. But the relentless fist of dear old Father Time will eventually prove the truth of the words of P. Daventry Esq. The moving Finger will write and having writ—I have spoken. Shall I peel you a straight banana?"

Anne made a rather delightful grimace. "You may not. I loathe the things. They remind me of the taste of scented soap and how I used to be washed with it in my nursery days. The beastly stuff used to get into my mouth and I can never eat or even smell a banana without thinking of those times and feeling downright sick."

"All my suggestions you summarily dismiss. You squash them. You turn them down. I am abject." Peter replied to her with an affected ruefulness. "Unless, of course, there's any other—" His eyes examined the dish of dessert under the brightening influence of Hope.

Anne Ebbisham leaned over and tapped him on the arm. "Bear up," she said. "There is still work for you to do—pare me a pear."

"I begin to live again," murmured Peter. "The burden of my existence has become less intolerable. The wind and the rain are, after all, still my brother and sister." He changed his tone. "I always think that 'William' is an unsatisfying Christian name for the juiciest of the juicy, don't you? Why should we be forced to say a 'William Pear' when we might have said a 'Lancelot' Pear or a 'Marmaduke' Pear?"

As he spoke Benito entered through the curtained space that was on Mr. Daventry's immediate right, the space towards which Henry Mordaunt kept looking, and walked slowly to Adrian Challoner at the head of the table. The waiter's usually vivacious face was so grave and he seemed to walk with such definite purpose that those of the party who watched him temporarily ceased their chatter and conversation and listened through a sense of instinct to the words he addressed to the host of the evening. But the message he had seemingly been charged to deliver, although perhaps surprising, was nevertheless eminently commonplace. Most of the people who heard it were ashamed inwardly that they *had* listened. On the other hand it appeared to annoy Adrian Challoner when he heard it.

"I beg your pardon, sir," said Benito in his curious English accent, "but there are a lady and a gentleman in the foyer below asking for a Mr. Barr-ing-ton Gallo-way." His precise articulation of the names jointed the syllables almost absurdly to English ears. There was no doubt whatever now that Challoner was annoyed. He almost glared at the Italian as he interrupted him.

"Why on earth do you worry *me* over it, man? What has it got to do with me?"

Benito's imperturbability did not desert him. Cyril Lorrimer had not labelled him for nothing.

"I am sorry, sir," he said, "but I was about to explain that when Monsieur interrupted me. The lady and gentleman downstairs insist that this Mr. Barr-ing-ton Gallo-way is a member of your party that is dining here to-night and that they must see him on a matter of the life and death." Benito bowed the end of his sentence. As a bow it bordered on the superb. Anne Ebbisham thrilled to it as she listened and saw. She added yet a further tribute of her own to the excellence of Lorrimer's discrimination. But Challoner by this time was frowning.

"There's a mistake somewhere, waiter. There must be. I'll give you my word for it. There's no doubt that these people you mention have made a mistake." He paused and looked round the tables as though seeking somewhere there confirmation of the statement that he had just made. "There is no one of that name in my party. Also the name is quite unfamiliar to me. Kindly tell these people in the foyer that we have no one here of the name they want."

Once again Benito bowed, turned on his heels and departed upon the errand upon which he was bidden. Peter watched him go out and as he turned again in his chair to whisper a remark to Christine Massingham, caught sight of Jack Raikes and Jane Mordaunt gazing at each other as though startled from a condition of comparative lethargy into an excess of excitement. For the next few minutes that followed the exit of the peerless Benito the proceedings went on under the shadow of what was a most pronounced lull. Peter attempted to recapture the mood that had been his and his companion's before the beginning of the incident.

"A witty remark," he announced gravely to Anne and Christine, "will often revive the soul of a languishing conversation. I will uplift my mental spade and delve for one. For there is no doubt that the waiter Johnny with his message from the realms below was to our genial host as a goblet of foaming castor-oil. As a beaker of halcyon hemlock. Let me ask you a question. What is the plural of Galloway?"

Before Miss Ebbisham could frame the words for a reply, there once again entered the immaculate Benito. "It is sorrow to me, most profound, sir," he extenuated to Adrian Challoner, "but I cannot convince the people in the foyer that the Mr. Galloway they ask for is not here. I have implored them to go away, to depart. I have assured them that they are disturber-ers of Monsieur's party. It is of no use. They swear that he was seen by them to come in—that he has not come out—and that it is a matter of the life and the death for them to see him, immediately, at once. They implore me to listen to them."

Challoner began to show signs of losing his temper and Jack Raikes ventured to enter the breach. "But there's nobody here by that name. You've heard what Mr. Challoner has told you. You can't get beyond that. Can't you make these people understand that, waiter?"

Benito gestured helplessly with his hands—palms upwards.

"Look here," said Lorrimer, after a pause of a minute or so. "I've an idea. Will it help matters at all, do you think, if Benito finds out who these two people are? It seems to me that if he were to go down and do that and find out their names and so on it would tend to clear the air a bit and perhaps give *us* more of an idea what it is they want. They may be mistaking the name for some other name very much like it. After all, it's quite an easy thing to do."

Benito looked at Challoner as though inviting his blessing on the suggestion that Lorrimer put forward. The actor-manager gestured a somewhat unwilling consent.

"Very well, then! I've no objection to that being done although I don't know, I'm sure, why we should be bothered with such a matter at a time like this. I'm for sending them about their business. Go down and find out, Benito, will you?"

For the second time that evening Benito went back to the disturbers of the peace of the Diadem room at Murillo's, and the conversation broke out again.

"What do you make of it now?" whispered Peter, softly. "Who are these blighters that will brook no denial? Why is their long-suit persistence?"

Anne shook her head. "Ask again," she muttered—"and something easier than that. I'm not good at conundrums—" She spoke quite calmly but as Mr. Daventry's eyes fell on her hand as it rested on the white cloth of the table he was very surprised to see that Miss Ebbisham's fingers were trembling violently.

"Why," he exclaimed impetuously, "what's the matter with—?"

Benito entered again and walked straight up to Adrian Challoner. "I have been able to obtain information that was desired, sir. The lady and gentleman who say that they must see this Mr. Barrington Galloway call themselves Mr. and Mrs. Orace Utchings."

"But this is absurd," cried Challoner, pushing back his chair from the table. "I know of no people of that name either and I am sure nobody else here does."

"Is it possible that it's Russell Streatfeild whom they want?" Raikes rose and addressed his remark direct to Challoner. "The idea has just struck me for he seems to have vanished into thin air. Perhaps he's this Galloway person and doesn't desire to meet any old friends. Seems to me it's more than likely." He pointed over to the empty chair next to Henry Mordaunt in emphasis of this remark. "Where is Streatfeild, Mr. Mordaunt, do you know? It certainly appears to me that he's cleared out for some reason or the other."

Mordaunt showed signs of uneasiness at these pointed statements. "He excused himself some minutes ago, it is true. Perhaps he's not feeling too well. But I understood from him that he would be back very shortly."

Lorrimer decided at this moment to take charge of the situation; he evidently thought it was high time somebody did. "I'll tell you what," he announced. "To save any more argument I'll go and see these people. Raikes may be perfectly right in his surmise. Perhaps if they describe the man to me it may fit Streatfeild." He waved to his mother and Molly as he crossed the room. "Don't trouble to come down, Benito. I'll find them all right." Benito stepped back from the curtained exit as Lorrimer slipped quickly out. Then he moved his head irresolutely as though thinking over something, and followed in Lorrimer's wake. When he reached the foyer Lorrimer saw two people standing apart from the volume groups that were either entering or leaving. Even from the distance he guessed from their general appearance that they must be the man and woman whom he had come down to see.

"Are you Mr. and Mrs. Horace Hutchings?" he inquired as he approached them.

Hutchings half-turned at his voice and then jerked his hand above his head. A familiar figure slipped like lightning from the middle of a scattered group of people and caught Lorrimer firmly by the wrists.

"You are arrested, Captain Lorrimer," said Inspector Baddeley quietly, "for the wilful murder of Olive Mordaunt—"

Lorrimer sprang aside, wrenched his wrists from the grip that held them, and sent a flying blow to the point of Baddeley's jaw. The Inspector reeled at the force of it and as the onlookers scattered in all directions his assailant dashed for the doors. As he did so the tall figure of Benito fell upon him like a flash and bore him to the ground. The struggle was sharp but short. Lorrimer kicked and squirmed but Benito's vice-like grip held him in such a manner that after a moment or two he was almost powerless to move. Benito pressed an unfriendly knee into the soft part of Lorrimer's shoulder and called over his shoulder, "Handcuffs, Baddeley—quick man, quick! Get him now!"

"Here they are, Mr. Bathurst," said the Inspector. He bent over the struggling form and suited the action to the words.

"Warm work while it lasted," murmured Anthony Bathurst, dusting his trousers. "But on the whole very satisfying."

CHAPTER XXVIII

Mr. Bathurst poked the fire into a blaze and invited his company of visitors to be seated. The invitation taxed the resources of his flat to the limit but after a little sorting-out of legs and arms, comfortable arrangement became an accomplished fact.

"See to the drinks, Daventry," he said. "You know where to find everything, I think, and you look at your best behind a row of bottles."

Peter grinned, but extricated himself from the rest of the assembly and did the honours.

"I like your flat, Mr. Bathurst," remarked Jane Mordaunt. "You bachelors certainly know how to make yourselves cosy. What do you say, Molly?"

She put her arm around her sister but received no reply. The events of the previous Friday evening and their culminating shock had left a mark on Molly Mordaunt's nature that it would take a good deal of effort on the part of time to efface.

"What time must you be at the theatre to-night, Challoner?" asked Anthony.

"A quarter to eight will do. I can make up in a matter of five minutes. It's quite 'straight.'"

"Good! What about you, Miss Massingham? Will about the same time suit you?"

"Admirably, Mr. Bathurst. I'm not on till the second act."

"That's all right, then." Mr. Bathurst consulted his wrist-watch. "Baddeley should be here at any moment now. It is actually ten minutes past the time that he arranged. When he comes, half-an-hour should see the conclusion of this rather remarkable case. I fear that in many ways most of you here are still comparatively in the dark. But I promise you that that state of affairs shall not remain for long." He walked to the window.

"Is it still as foggy as it was?" asked Francis Mordaunt.

"Lifting a trifle, I think," replied Anthony, "and here I fancy is our man. Your father is with him, Mr. Mordant."

Francis walked to Anthony's side at the window and looked out peeringly as though searching for somebody in the mist.

"For whom are you looking?" asked Mr. Bathurst.

"I thought perhaps Streatfeild might be with my father, that was all," replied Francis, "but apparently he's not. I haven't seen him since the dinner."

"Mr. Streatfeild will appear later. I have made arrangements in respect of that," returned Anthony gravely. "The meeting would be appallingly incomplete without him." He walked to the door of the room and opened it to admit Henry Mordaunt and Inspector Baddeley. "Find yourselves seats as best you can, will you, gentlemen," invited Mr. Bathurst, "and Daventry will mix you a drink."

"Thank you, Mr. Bathurst," responded Baddeley with a twinkling eye. "You haven't changed much since the old days, I notice, and I don't know that I would wish you to have done. But you have some news for me, I believe."

Mr. Bathurst smiled at the Inspector's geniality. "Thank you, Baddeley. But we must get to business, as Mr. Challoner here has to be at the theatre for this evening's performance. We have one very important question to settle. The murderer of poor Mrs. Mordaunt has been discovered and will do no further mischief but there is still the matter of what I may term the 'Creeping Jenny' Mystery. We must solve that before we can turn our backs on the crime at 'The Crossways.' I will attempt to elucidate it for you." He turned in his chair and looked rather deliberately at Anne Ebbisham. That lady returned him look for look before she nonchalantly flicked the ash from her cigarette. Mr. Bathurst smiled and continued. "The first robbery you will remember took place at Sir Graeme Grantham's place at Dringe. After that opening affair came several others in fairly rapid succession. In most of them the procedure was in effect the same. An article was stolen when it would have been a comparatively simple matter to have made a much bigger and more valuable haul. To emphasize this, you remember, that in the case of the affair at Mrs. Medlicott's at Lullingham the famous Medlicott emeralds had been at the mercy of the thief but had not been touched. To the psychologist this fact was both interesting and instructive. And inasmuch as every article stolen has since been restored to its rightful owner, in every way unimpaired, it will be readily seen and understood that this 'Creeping Jenny' person is no ordinary criminal. You, Baddeley, suspected Francis Mordaunt. You arrested him and as a consequence burnt your fingers. But in a way you were not so far distant from the truth as you may imagine."

"I am relieved to hear you say that, Mr. Bathurst. Certain features of the case have worried me considerably, I may tell you."

"I expect they have, Baddeley. However, to resume! I will not weary you with details concerning any of the other cases that preceded the affair at 'The Crossways.' That may be said to fall automatically into two categories (a) the robbery of the

Lorrimer sapphire and (b) the murder of Mrs. Mordaunt. We will deal with the theft of the sapphire first and then we shall put our judicial finger on 'Creeping Jenny.'" Mr. Bathurst permitted himself the luxury of a smile. "Who, Baddeley, we must not forget has made complete and utter restitution. I mention that in case some of us here are inclined to judge sinners too harshly. Let me refresh your minds on one point. The 'Creeping Jenny' activity at 'The Crossways' differed in one vital particular from all the others. Warning was sent to the house beforehand. I commend that to your notice—it is most important. You will see why in a moment. But when Captain Lorrimer went to his bedroom on the night of the tragedy the lady who had designs on the Lorrimer sapphire had secreted herself between the wardrobe and the wall. She hadn't much room to move and she left traces of her presence there, I am informed. A tiny piece of biscuit-coloured lace from her coatee was caught on a thin wooden splinter at the back of the wardrobe. From her hiding-place she was able to see Captain Lorrimer place the sapphire in its cunning hiding-place which of course became at once no hiding-place at all."

In the room now there reigned an almost deathly silence and more than one of the five senses of the people who listened appreciated it. Anthony Bathurst continued.

"I imagine that what happened next is this. Awaiting a favourable opportunity, the lady who had watched from behind the—"

Anne Ebbisham could restrain herself no longer. "You're very clever, Mr. Bathurst, but you're *wrong*. Just as though I should have gone into Captain Lorrimer's bedroom when he was in there. Really, I blush for you, Mr. Bathurst! I watched his door from inside my own bedroom—my door was ajar when I saw him go out of his room and disappear. I saw my chance and slipped into his room. I had no real idea then where the sapphire was. All I had to go on was a remark that I had heard Captain Lorrimer make to Mr. Mordaunt that very evening. Something about 'shaving' or 'a shave.' I had felt convinced when I heard him make it that it had a double meaning and perhaps a bearing on the sapphire's hiding-place about which he had so recently boasted. When I walked to his dressing-table and found *two* sticks of shaving-soap—apparently identical—I had an inspiration. Why two, I asked myself? Most men found one enough to last a month or so. I examined them and found the sapphire! Just as I was preparing to get out I heard steps along the corridor. It was then that I got behind the wardrobe, Mr. Bathurst, although I think you're frightfully clever to know that I was behind there at all."

Anthony smiled. "Thank you, Miss Ebbisham. What happened after that? Shall I reconstruct my opinion? Lorrimer, I presume, came in and after a short time went out again. Am I right?"

"You are," said Anne, "and wasn't I just too glad for words. Anne Ebbisham had a nasty five minutes behind that piece of furniture, I can assure you. Well, I returned to my own room—hid the sapphire—pleased to think I had stung my godfather, Mr. Challoner, for a cool 'hundred' and lo and behold when I woke up in the morning the ring was gone—clean as a whistle."

Challoner's interruption came sharply. "I am amazed at the thought of what you have done, Anne, and of what all this must necessarily mean. I can't think what possessed you to embark upon such a career. You've always had sufficient money as far as I am aware. But I also need enlightenment on one statement that you have just made. How had you won your bet with me? You bet me that 'Creeping Jenny' would *not*—"

Anne looked defiant and was about to launch a reply when Mr. Bathurst raised his hand.

"Allow me to explain, Miss Ebbisham. You stole from Lorrimer as a practical joke, intending to return the sapphire in the morning. The whole thing was an adventurous escapade on your part. You sent the letter of warning and you seized your chance of winning a hundred pounds when the opportunity came to you, because if *you* stole the sapphire it was obvious that 'Jenny' would be unable to. Once again am I right?"

"Yes, Mr. Bathurst. The affair was a pure frolic as far as I was concerned, from beginning to end. Everybody was so windy about 'Creeping Jenny' that the idea came to me to pull all their legs. It came to me before I left Cranwick Towers. I sent the letter, accepted the bet and snaffled the sapphire."

"Exactly! And reckoned without one—"

"Thing?" queried Anne.

"No—*person*," replied Anthony gravely. "'Creeping Jenny' herself. Who was in the house with you all the time. Miss Ebbisham stole from Lorrimer. 'Creeping Jenny' stole from Miss Ebbisham."

"How?" demanded Anne. "And who is 'Creeping Jenny'?"

"Ah," replied Mr. Bathurst, "that is the question. But we have her 'restitution' note at least, upon which to work and base certain conclusions. If you remember, she supplied us with the information that her birthday was 'on Christmas Day in the morning.' Baddeley here was inclined to treat the state-ment as misleading and very possibly as fantastically absurd. But happily I do not agree with him on the point. Now, ladies and gentlemen—let me put it to you like this—a boy who is born on Christmas Day whether in the morning or in the evening is frequently named Noel; a girl is just as often called—" Mr. Bathurst paused dramatically. Then flashed out the finish of his sentence, *"Christine."* Wheeling round suddenly he faced the lady whom he had named. "Many happy returns of next Christ-mas Day, Miss Massingham."

CHAPTER XXIX

A BRIGHT red spot burned in each of the lady's cheeks. But she kept her head and her nerve.

"Thank you for your kind words, Mr. Bathurst," she said with a charming smile. "Also I must congratulate you on your skill. You have discovered the truth. I am 'Creeping Jenny.' Or rather I was, because that notorious lady died nearly six weeks ago. I will tell you the whole history—then you must tell me how you found it all out, for to tell the truth I've no idea how you did it. But let it be clearly understood from the beginning that 'Creep-ing Jenny' was never a thief, although she may have appeared to be such." She stopped and looked round the circle of faces with a proud self-possession. "She was merely a borrower and when you hear the rest of my statement you will realize the truth of what I have just said. In August, my only brother came to me for five hundred pounds. He's not all that I should like him to be—and never has been—from the days when we were in the nursery together. But he's my brother—and my only one." Her voice broke a little here and she faltered. Recovery, however, was rapid. "It was hopeless him going to my father for any more—and he told me I was his last chance. When he first approached me I couldn't look at the amount and told him so. He let me see pretty plainly that he intended taking desperate measures. So in the end I promised that I would help him—though how on earth I was going to was more than I then could say or even imagine. He said that he must have two hundred pounds by the following Monday to stave off disaster. I went to my bankers and asked for a loan. They demanded security. I suggested my jewellery. The Manager was awfully kind and said that he would try to meet me if he considered the security was good enough and I lodged it in the bank's strong-room. When I got home and collected it together my heart sank. I realized that I had small hopes of realizing the amount Frank wanted. I was at my wits' end. Then you came into it, Anne." She turned to Miss Ebbisham. "I determined to come to see you to borrow from you. Although I loathed the idea like poison. You see—I'm different from my brother—although we're very much alike facially."

"Mr. Daventry will be interested to hear you say that, Miss Massingham"—put in Anthony Bathurst—"he even mistook your photograph for your brother. He had run into him near Cranwick." Christine nodded.

"Frank told me he'd met somebody from 'The Crossways' and that it had rather scared him. But to get back. When I went down to see Anne she was staying at Lady Grantham's. I got to the house and felt that I simply couldn't worry her—the idea was positively humiliating to me. I looked at my watch, guessed that they were at dinner and decided to catch the first train back to town. As I passed the front of the house I saw a ladder leaning against one of the front room windows. An idea came to me and try as I would I couldn't dismiss it all the way home that evening. I was resting at the time and had invitations to two country houses before the rehearsals of 'Sin and a Woman' were due to come on. But the first of these invitations was three weeks ahead. And Frank wanted money at once. I resolved to 'borrow' one article of jewellery from Lady Grantham's the next night, follow on with one two evenings later at Critchley Lodge where I knew Anne was going and carry on one at a time until I had sufficient for my purpose. When I could I would return them all. I wasn't going out for big things that I should find difficulty in disposing of and I meant to make the whole thing as 'sporting' as possible. I invented 'Jenny,' got my first card typed in order to mystify people a bit, slipped an old mack on and tootled off that evening to Cumberlege Court. I timed myself to arrive at the same time as I had the previous evening. It really was too easy. The ladder was still there—there were repairs to the roof being done in the daytime. The window was easily negotiated and I was away from the house with a diamond tie-pin in four minutes. At Mrs. Medlicot's two evenings afterwards I had a thrill and a narrow escape. No sooner had I found a ladder and entered the bedroom than I heard somebody coming. I got under the bed, Anne—not behind a wardrobe! But that was the only occasion when I had anything like a narrow squeak. I saw my bank people and they lent me three hundred pounds on my own stuff plus what I had already 'borrowed.' Frank was saved for the time being. Well, I had to look ahead so I told the bank that I hadn't brought along all my stuff but was keeping back some of my jewellery in case I wanted a further loan later on. My next three efforts were sufficient to give me all that Frank wanted. Much easier, too, of accomplishment, because I was actually staying in the houses. I raised the entire sum for which he had asked me. In the case of Lady Craddock's ring I faked the evidence of the window and the rug as Inspector Baddeley suspected. I thought it best to vary my methods somewhat and give the impression that the now notorious 'Creeping Jenny' might after all be somebody working from the outside. It was the line I always took whenever the affairs were discussed."

The man to whom she had referred leaned forward towards her. "Just a minute, Miss. Why did you use young Mr. Mordaunt's car that night?"

"I had arranged to let Frank have his second installment of money that night. He had written from Brighton that it was very urgent and that he would come that night for it. I didn't want him at Cranwick Towers and told him to meet me at the top of Hangman's Hollow. I popped up to town—rehearsal had started so it didn't put me out very much—and went to the bank with what I had taken from Crawley and Rustington. I was late—'Creeping Jenny' had pulled off another job on her return—and it hadn't been as easy, either, as the two just previous. So I borrowed Francis's car from the garage."

Mr. Bathurst smiled. "And that night 'Creeping Jenny' died—eh, Miss Massingham?"

"Yes, Mr. Bathurst! Really speaking! I had no designs on the Lorrimer sapphire. I had 'borrowed' enough. But strangely enough, my best friend had—although I didn't know it. I was awake when she returned with the spoils and as I couldn't possibly allow substitute 'Jennys' to be running wild, I had to relieve her of it when she went off to sleep. I thought it would teach her a lesson."

"You little cat," muttered Anne, "and there was I worrying my pretty head nearly off."

"What put you in the position of being able to return the borrowed articles?" asked Anthony.

"Ask Mr. Challoner," replied Christine demurely.

Adrian Challoner looked rather aggrieved. He had not been "on" in this last act and the position galled him. It made him feel that something was radically wrong. "Miss Massingham is the author of my new play, Mr. Bathurst—'Sin and a Woman.' Although, to be strictly truthful, I only discovered the fact a week or two ago. When I was at 'The Crossways' and also on the first night itself I was unaware of it."

Christine smiled gaily. "When I got my advance royalties (blessed word—like 'Mesopotamia') from Surtees White—they're my agents—'Creeping Jenny' was not only dead but buried with a firing party. I flew up to the bank, reclaimed my guilty hoard and returned all the respective parts of it to the rightful owners—see, Mr. Bathurst?"

Anthony nodded. The lady went on.

"And I couldn't resist as a sporting touch giving the clue to my identity in the information about my birthday. But tell me, Mr. Bathurst—not only how did you discover all that you have—but how you come to appear in the affair at all."

Anthony smiled at Miss Massingham's mystification. "That won't take long. Look at me carefully, all of you, and listen to me at the same time." He addressed Jane Mordaunt in a curiously high-pitched voice. "My dear Miss Mordaunt, if at any time you feel that you are unable to—"

A cry of amazement broke from Jane and Christine simultaneously. The voice was the voice of Russell Streatfeild. Miss Massingham cried the name.

CHAPTER XXX

"YES, I WAS there with you all the time, you see." Mr. Bathurst was almost apologetic. "I went down to 'The Crossways' at Mr. Mordaunt's request because he was strongly afraid that 'Creeping Jenny' would have a cut for the 'Lorrimer' sapphire in which, as you know, he takes an extraordinary interest. He suggested that I should hide my real identity and form one of his house party. But I had to consider you, Daventry, and also Miss Considine. For he had told me that you would both be there. I little guessed that Baddeley here would turn up again. If I had, I might have hesitated. As it was, a wig, a judicious use of 'lights' and 'shadows' on the forehead, cheeks and brows, a little 'No. 5' plus a trifling application of Nose Paste, went a long way towards the birth of Mr. Russell Streatfeild. An altered voice went even farther, for this is the most difficult part of one's physical person to disguise. More than once, Daventry, I was sorely afraid you had spotted me."

Peter slapped his thigh. "By Jove—that reminds me. It was you I saw in Streatfeild on the last occasion that you appeared at 'The Crossways.' When you turned round at the door as you were going out and asked about Baddeley allowing people to clear off, I cudgelled my brains at the time to think who it was of whom he reminded me—but to no purpose. Something happened, I think, to make me forget all about it."

Anthony smiled. "A slice of luck for me. But now I must satisfy the curiosity of all of you and let you into my bag of secrets. I began well. For I immediately dissociated the murder of Mrs. Mordaunt from any connection with 'Creeping Jenny.' I will tell you why. Mrs. Mordaunt gave no signs whatever of having gone out that night in a hurry such as one might expect: had she gone out after a thief whom she suspected or whom she had surprised. Her face still retained the touch of cosmetics and her lips showed signs of the application of lip-stick. Her bedroom told a similar story. In fact the whole affair pointed to something far removed from mere robbery. It was obvious that the last thing she had done before going out to her death had been to attend to her complexion. She had deliberately *prepared* to go out. There was a slight depression on her bed where she had tossed her evening cloak before she sat at her looking-glass 'to freshen up' and the various cosmetic accessories were scattered on the table in front of it." Mr. Bathurst leaned forward to the company who listened to him and put a question—eagerly. A question that he answered himself. "For whom does a woman study her physical appearance to that extent? I told myself—either a lover or an old lover—'old' in the sense of 'previous.' It's a remarkable thing but a woman always has a feverish desire to look her best when she meets a lover of former days! To my delight—this assignation theory when tested—held. I prowled round the country near the well and learned something else. There were one or two pieces of charred paper that you afterwards found, Baddeley. They told me nothing that you could call particular so I left them to you. But I said to myself, 'burned letters'—I'm on the right track. And when I found, some little distance away, the torn corner of an envelope that had in some manner missed the burning, I felt more certain still. Look at it for a moment, will you, people?" Anthony produced from his pocket the piece in question. It bore three half-penny stamps that had been cancelled by the authorities—nothing else. The date and time were indecipherable and the postmark had been obliterated, but it looked like "London." "Not much on which to go there," exclaimed Mr. Bathurst—"but just notice how the three stamps have been affixed. It is unusual to say the least. The first two commencing from the envelope's edge have been stuck on in what I will term the ordinary way— they are what we will describe as 'vertical.' Look, however, at the third one. It is lying down as it were—horizontal. A small thing, ladies and gentlemen, but you will hear later on how it served to put me on the track of a murderer. We will get back now to where we were. Hand those cigars round, Daventry—you'd never do to administer a horn of plenty or even sit on a Board of Guardians. The question now was—who was Mrs. Mordaunt's lover—present or past? In that respect let me call your attention to the evidence of Mr. Francis Mordaunt and also of Peter Daventry. They each agreed that Mrs. Mordaunt had suffered a depression of spirits on the *Monday* before the murder. I asked myself what were the changed conditions that this Monday brought? Personally, Monday is a day for which I have never cared very much. By the way, if ever I'm hanged, Baddeley, turn me off on a wet Monday in January. I discovered that on this particular Monday nothing much had happened at 'The Cross- ways' except that *Captain Lorrimer* had arrived and joined the house party. Another small thing, I agree—but I was looking for a lover, so I made a mental note against that gentleman's name. He was certainly a possibility. At any rate it was something with which to be going on. At this stage of the case an interesting incident occurred. The murderer made a slip. Most of 'em do, Baddeley, as you know, and this one reminded me somewhat of the disposal of the I.O.U. in that other baffling case that you and I looked into—'The Billiard-Room Mystery.' Remember, Baddeley?" Mr. Bathurst paused and waited for the Inspector's nod of affirmation. "When Mrs. Mordaunt went out to keep her assignation with the man who afterwards murdered her she locked her bedroom door on the outside and took the key with her. And after the murder—the murderer made a mistake and retained the key. I think he took it from her bag. Why I can't say—but he may at the time have had certain ideas with regard to its future use."

"May have had," exclaimed Baddeley caustically—"he used it to decorate a heathen statue."

Anthony smiled at the Inspector's description and shook his head. "He didn't, Baddeley—he did something that had much farther-reaching consequences than that. He slipped the key into the pocket of Russell Streatfeild's dressing-gown that hung on the back of that gentleman's bedroom door. There is no doubt in my mind that it was done deliberately to throw suspicion in my direction. He drew on his fund of malice and because of his dislike of poor old Streatfeild did his best to incriminate him. I expect he knew that you, Baddeley, weren't too impressed with 'the man with two dead partners,' and would eagerly lap up any evidence that came your way against him."

"You're quite right with regard to your last remark, Mr. Bathurst. I had Streatfeild on my list of 'suspects' for a long time."

"You weren't alone in that, Baddeley," interposed Challoner—"I can assure you."

Henry Mordaunt smiled wearily. "No—I had quite a difficult task protecting your reputation against a number of attacks, Bathurst."

Anthony took up the point. "Against what sort of attacks, sir?"

"Oh—vague hints—head-noddings—the usual specimens that one meets in—"

"Exactly," intervened Mr. Bathurst. "Your reply will assist me to illustrate my next point. When I found the key and I guessed its identity, there flashed into my mind that it might very well prove to be 'the key' in two senses. If the guilty person had chosen me with deliberation for this purpose of incrimination a little finesse on my part might very well give me his identity for he would be almost certain to follow the move up in some way or other. Do you see my meaning, Mr. Mordaunt?"

"Quite, Bathurst. But let's hear the rest. I am still at a loss to—"

"My opportunity came even more favourably than I anticipated and in a peculiar manner. Daventry wrote to me about the case quite unexpectedly, little knowing I was virtually at his side. In my reply, among other things, I also contrived to throw suspicion on this strange man, Streatfeild, and asked Daventry to let me know the nature of any evidence against him that might turn up with full details—indicating that I should find it extremely valuable. I did—for when it came—lo and behold—it was 'ex' Lorrimer. Lorrimer again—mark you! The evidence was gradually accumulating and I have told some of you before the immense significance of this condition. Meanwhile something else of vital importance had transpired. For the benefit of those of you here who don't know of it, Baddeley will take up the story for a bit and tell you of the evidence given by a Mrs. Perkins, mother of one of the maids at 'The Crossways.' Do you mind, Baddeley?"

The Inspector cleared his throat and took up the running. "It won't take me very long. But on the night of the murder, this Mrs. Perkins, who had been helping in the kitchen, saw a woman in the grounds of 'The Crossways' as she herself was on her way home. She told her daughter, who passed on the information to Bennett, the gardener. He in his turn took it to Mr. Mordaunt. Mr. Mordaunt and I put our heads together and took steps, which I needn't describe now in detail, for Mrs. Perkins to see all the ladies of the house party and attempt to identify the one that she had seen in the grounds, if possible. I posted Mrs. Perkins in the house one evening with the result that she picked out Mrs. Lorrimer. When it came to the question of the dress that she—"

"Thank you, Baddeley," Anthony's voice cut into the Inspector's narrative. "I think that I had better deal with the matter of the lady's frock. When I first heard from Mr. Mordaunt about this woman who had been seen in the grounds, the news puzzled me considerably. When I learned of her definite identification I was puzzled still more. The evidence seemed to clash somewhat with the opinion that I had already formed. But you will observe the Lorrimer atmosphere still remained. Had Mrs. Lorrimer been a party to the crime? I was still chewing the problem over when I had a brain wave. I remembered the strong likeness between the mother and the son. Acting upon this I went over the actual ground again very carefully. If my idea of a masquerade on the son's part were correct (he had easy access to his mother's room, remember), I decided that the actual change of clothes would, in all probability, have been effected *outside* the house. To have changed inside the house would have been to court disaster as the disguise under the more intimate conditions of indoor encounter might not have passed muster. Now Mrs. Perkins had stated that she saw this woman near Bennett's hut. I said to myself, 'Had the change been made in there?' Might the frock be in there still somewhere, from the time when the second change was made back to proper clothes? I came to the conclusion that the idea was worth testing. The hut was empty when I entered but on the floor underneath one of the benches I picked up a collar-stud! When I asked Bennett about it later he stated that it did not belong to him. Then I felt certain that I was right. Lorrimer had worn a frock of his mothers to meet Mrs. Mordaunt. It had been stained from the wound and he had very cleverly hidden it in Bennett's shed when he had changed back again—and dropped his stud which he dared not wait to find. I was convinced that the frock was in there somewhere although there were no signs of it and if I hadn't had the stroke of inspiration that I did have, it might conceivably have lain in there undiscovered and untouched for twenty years or more. The particular parcel that contained it should have been safe and secure from prying eyes or curious hands. However Fate willed otherwise." Anthony paused again, took a cigarette from the silver box on the table and lit it. "We now come to the question of motive. Let me, Mr. Mordaunt, express my sympathy to you in what, after all, must inevitably cause you no small measure of distress. But recent investigations have proved to me that Captain Lorrimer and your wife had, in the years before she met you, lived together as man and wife under the name of Galloway. She knew him as Barrington Galloway. They parted, however, and she had not seen him for a considerable time when he appeared at your house in the capacity of your daughter's fiancé! Imagine the shock that it must have been to her. But she behaved splendidly. She gave Lorrimer her ultimatum. He must give up your daughter, Molly, or she would tell the truth even at the cost of her own happiness. The 'Paula Tanqueray' position over again, Challoner. Also she held the whip-hand. She had kept some of his letters. Whether he knew this or not I can only conjecture. But he feared that she would denounce him and that he would lose, not only Miss Mordaunt, but also his Parliamentary career. Anyway he made the assignation with her at the old well. She probably fixed the rendezvous and she took the letters with her as an instrument to enforce her terms with regard to Molly. As we know now she went to her death. She may never have seen the figure of her murderer approaching her. It was very dark and I suspect that he crept up in his disguise and stabbed his victim with an almost silent rapidity. Then he took her handbag, opened it by the presses, and removed the letters that he wanted. Also the key of her bedroom door. He then threw the body and the bag down the well and burnt the letters."

"Just a minute, Bathurst." Henry Mordaunt's voice showed the distress that he was feeling. "Why did he give my wife the imitation sapphire? What really made her approach him over it?"

"He did nothing of the kind. His story was false. She never mentioned the sapphire to him. It was an entire fabrication on his part. He threw the spurious sapphire down the well so that he could give the murder a 'Creeping Jenny' tint. He had, no doubt, his plan and story all prepared in advance."

"Clever that," contributed Challoner—"decidedly clever."

"I will resume," said Anthony. "In the burning of the letters— some of the charred pieces of which you found, Baddeley—he missed the one envelope-corner bearing the three stamps that I have already shown to you. I salvaged it and profited thereby.

Well—there I was with Lorrimer definitely indicated as the murderer by every law that logic and the science of deduction recognize. But I had to establish motive and what was even more difficult—proof. Inquiries into Mrs. Mordaunt's antecedents—in which Mr. Mordaunt helped me tremendously—soon bore fruit and I traced her to Radway Mansions W. She had occupied a flat there as a Mrs. Galloway. To tell the truth I had only thought of Lorrimer as a previous lover—I had not anticipated that things had been so extreme as, without doubt, they were. I routed out the night-porter and showed him a photo of Mrs. Mordaunt—he and his wife identified it at once as the 'Mrs. Galloway' who had lived at No. 5 some years previous. When they identified Lorrimer in a House of Commons group that I produced to them as the 'husband' in the case—there was only one more thing to be done. But this last wanted careful handling. Through the agency of Sir Austin Kemble, the Commissioner of Police, I obtained employment as a waiter at Murillo's—which I knew was Lorrimer's habitual restaurant. I knew he dined there almost every night and I gave him special attention—so much so that he awarded me high rank, I believe, in the Waiters' Championship Class. Then as luck had it just as I was about to strike, he bolted to the South of France." Anthony leaned back and called out to Peter Daventry. "Pour me out a drink, Daventry, will you—and see to the others. Thanks, old man." Mr. Bathurst raised the glass. "I decided, therefore, to seek assistance. I enlisted the services of one who is here now."

Every eye turned towards Inspector Baddeley. Anthony's mouth twisted into its smile, and he shook his head whimsically. "No—not Baddeley. A fairer one than he! Ladies and gentlemen, Miss Ebbisham, detective!"

Anne blushed delightfully and the blush preceded a grimace. "Shall I tell them, Miss Ebbisham?" Anne nodded. Anthony went on. "I had noticed during my stay at 'The Crossways' that our gentleman was excessively impressionable to feminine society. So I prevailed upon Miss Ebbisham here to titillate his vanity. She played up splendidly—wrote to him a letter that I dictated and brought him back from Cannes post-haste. As I thought, he had risen to the bait and as I also anticipated, he wrote to her in reply and fixed an appointment at Murillo's. The appointment was kept, I may say, and it gave me the opportunity of recommending to him an excellent liqueur. When I tell you that the envelope he used was stamped with three half-penny stamps arranged in the same way as on the one I had found near the well and when I also tell you that an *envelope of a letter he had written to Daventry was similarly decorated with the one horizontal stamp on the left of the two verticals*, I knew I had my man. But how to catch him and hold him? That wanted special consideration and it was then that I at last approached Baddeley. I think I am correct in saying that what I told him came as a great surprise."

Baddeley laughed as he confirmed Mr. Bathurst's statement. "It did that, Mr. Bathurst. But I knew you of old, which was good enough for me. And Mr. Challoner's party gave us our chance."

"Yes—it served its purpose very well. I thought perhaps that if Streatfeild were absent from it that fact might arouse our man's suspicions. Miss Ebbisham, of course, was in our secret. So I arrived and played my part and then later on took over Benito's job. Mr. and Mrs. Hutchings did the rest. I worked it out that if they persisted long enough, the man we wanted, having heard his old alias, would grow impatient and go down to them to persuade them to keep quiet and go away. He would be bound to play for safety. The rest you know."

Miss Massingham heaved a sigh of relief. "Now tell me how you guessed about 'Creeping Jenny,' Mr. Bathurst."

"Well, Miss Massingham—when that first warning came, I suspected somebody was about to wear her mantle. The fact that it had been typed on a different machine from the usual one strengthened my suspicion. By the way, where was your typing done, Miss Ebbisham?"

"I used the secretary's machine at Lady Craddock's just before I left there."

"Ah, I thought it might have been something of that kind when you took up Challoner's bet so eagerly. I marked you down as the probable 'Jenny, the second.' But when in the morning you were so unmistakably worried and puzzled, I, in turn, began to wonder what it was in your plans that had miscarried. Had the murder made you too frightened to return the spoils or had the real 'Jenny' turned up and relieved you of them? If so, she must obviously be somebody very intimate with you to have the knowledge that the sapphire was in your possession. I then found the fragment of lace behind the wardrobe. Frankly, at the time when I found it, I was unable from memory to assign it with certainty to anybody. But was it part of somebody's apparel that I hadn't seen being worn? It struck me it might have come from such a thing as a lace coatee so when I replied to Daventry's letter I threw out a feeler. Four eyes are better than two anywhere. The answer came as I expected but it didn't really matter for when it came I had already seen for myself what I wanted to see. You look very charming in it by the way." Mr. Bathurst bowed his appreciation. "My next step was to obtain lists of the various people present at the houses where the robberies had taken place. The name of your close friend appeared in four of them. I then regarded her as a very definite possibility. But I waited to make sure. When the 'restitution acts' came my suspicions increased tenfold and when I read the message that accompanied them, I realized that Truth is very often unrecognized and that this might be a genuine and sporting gesture on her part. I put some more inquiries round in the lady's direction and learned in the process a number of highly interesting facts. Have I her forgiveness?" He turned to the lady.

"You have," murmured Christine, "and I think everybody else's too. For we are indebted to you for the truth, Mr. Bathurst. It is only right that everything should be cleared up."

"There's just one point, Bathurst," put in Adrian Challoner. "How did he come to use my dagger? How did he know of it?"

"That point has occurred to me. It is mere conjecture, of course, but I imagine his mother may have told him. She was with me at the card-table, remember, when it was first mentioned. It has since been found, by the way, in a drawer at his flat. Is there any other question that anybody wants answered?"

"Yes—one." It was Peter Daventry who had spoken. "What was that picture you showed me that I mistook for the man that met me on the heath? Who was it?"

Anthony motioned towards Christine. "This lady in 'As You Like It.' When you called that day I had just finished those inquiries of which I spoke, and had learned of her brother's existence. It was a longish shot, perhaps, but it came off."

* * * * *

Anne rose from her chair when most of the company had gone and faced Peter Daventry. "Tell me, Mr. Daventry—it's your turn to answer a question now—going back to the night of the dinner—something has been worrying me ever since and made me ever so curious. What *is* the plural of Galloway? What did you mean when you asked me?"

Peter Daventry looked extremely uncomfortable. "Well—er—Miss Ebbisham, I hate to pose as a prophet—one of the jolly old 'I told you so' brigade—and er—all unconscious of it at that—but surely there can be only one possible plural—what?"

Anne wrinkled her nose. Then she shook her head. "Tell me then. I don't—"

"Well—er, Miss Ebbisham, what I meant was 'Gallows-way.' Sorry and all that."

He ducked just in time and the book from Miss Ebbisham's hand sailed gaily but mercilessly into the tray of glasses.

"It's time you two went home," declared Mr. Bathurst.

THE END

CPSIA information can be obtained
at www.ICGtesting.com
Printed in the USA
LVHW111403230919
631940LV00002B/89/P